PERSONNEL FILE

Req #: 2014-PL-10945
File #:

TO BE FILLED IN BY IMMEDIATE SUPERIOR:

Detective
MICHAEL BENNETT

6 FOOT 3 INCHES (191CM)   200 POUNDS (91KG)
IRISH AMERICAN

EMPLOYMENT

Bennett joined the police force to uncover the truth
at all costs. He started his career in the Bronx's
49th Precinct. He then transferred to the NYPD's
Major Case Squad and remained there until he moved
to the Manhattan North Homicide Squad.

EDUCATION

Bennett graduated from Regis High School and studied
philosophy at Manhattan College.

FAMILY HISTORY

Bennett was previously married to Maeve, who worked as a
nurse on the trauma ward at Jacobi Hospital in the Bronx.
However, Maeve died tragically young after losing a battle
with cancer in December 2007, leaving Bennett to raise
their ten adopted children: Chrissy, Shawna, Trent, Eddie,
twins Fiona and Bridget, Ricky, Brian, Jane and Juliana.

Following Maeve's death, over time Bennett grew closer to
the children's nanny, Mary Catherine. After years of on-
off romance, Bennett and Mary Catherine decided to commit
to one another, and now happily raise the family together.
Also in the Bennett household is his Irish grandfather,
Seamus, who is a Catholic priest.

PROFILE:

AMENDED REPORT

BENNETT IS AN EXPERT IN HOSTAGE NEGOTIATION,
TERRORISM, HOMICIDE AND ORGANIZED CRIME. HE WILL STOP
AT NOTHING TO GET THE JOB DONE AND PROTECT THE CITY
AND THE PEOPLE HE LOVES, EVEN IF THIS MEANS DISOBEYING
ORDERS AND IGNORING PROTOCOL. DESPITE THESE UNORTHODOX
METHODS, HE IS A RELENTLESS, DETERMINED AND IN MANY
WAYS INCOMPARABLE DETECTIVE.

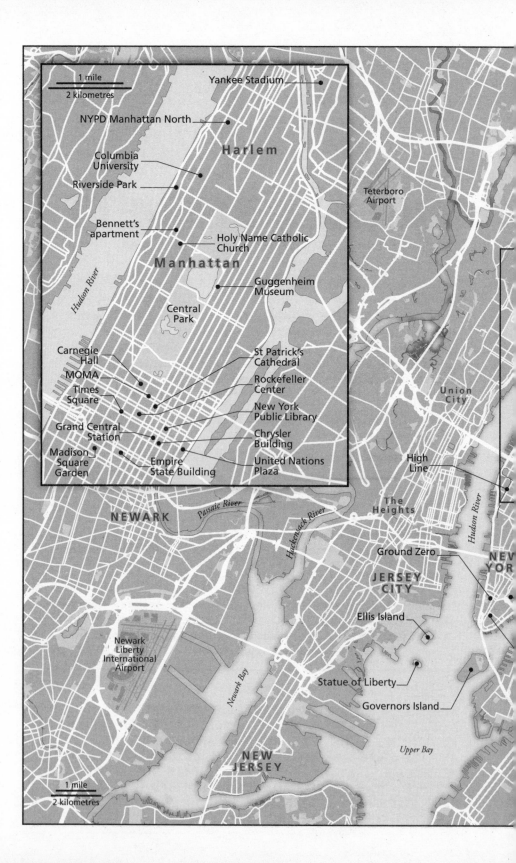

1 mile
2 kilometres

Yankee Stadium

NYPD Manhattan North

Columbia University

Riverside Park

Harlem

Bennett's apartment

Holy Name Catholic Church

Manhattan

Guggenheim Museum

Central Park

Carnegie Hall

St Patrick's Cathedral

MOMA

Rockefeller Center

Times Square

New York Public Library

Grand Central Station

Chrysler Building

Madison Square Garden

Empire State Building

United Nations Plaza

Hudson River

Teterboro Airport

Union City

High Line

Ground Zero

NEW YOR

NEWARK

Passaic River

Hackensack River

The Heights

JERSEY CITY

Ellis Island

Newark Liberty International Airport

Statue of Liberty

Governors Island

Newark Bay

Upper Bay

NEW JERSEY

1 mile
2 kilometres

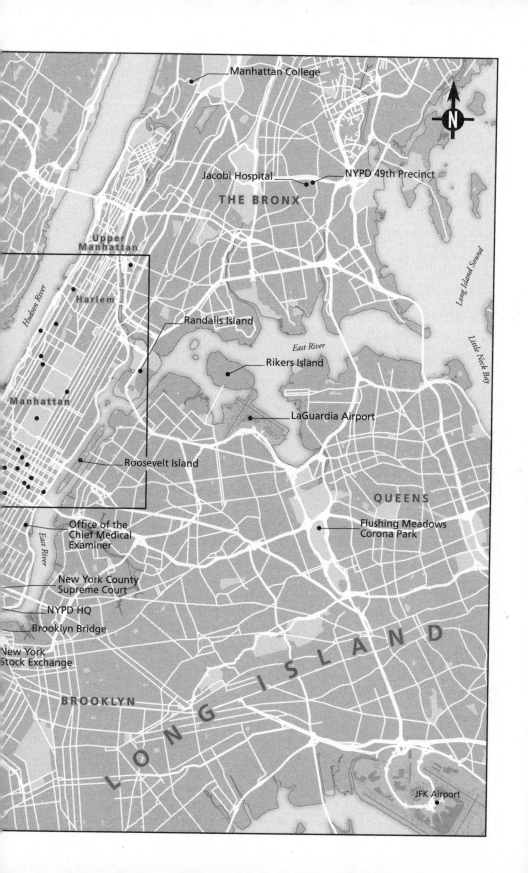

Manhattan College

NYPD 49th Precinct

Jacobi Hospital

THE BRONX

Upper
Manhattan

Harlem

Randalls Island

Hudson River

East River

Rikers Island

LaGuardia Airport

Manhattan

Long Island Sound

Little Neck Bay

Roosevelt Island

QUEENS

Flushing Meadows
Corona Park

Office of the
Chief Medical
Examiner

East River

New York County
Supreme Court

NYPD HQ

Brooklyn Bridge

New York
Stock Exchange

L O N G   I S L A N D

BROOKLYN

JFK Airport

A list of titles by James Patterson
appears at the back of this book

JAMES PATTERSON

& JAMES O. BORN

Cross Hairs

CENTURY

1 3 5 7 9 10 8 6 4 2

Century
20 Vauxhall Bridge Road
London SW1V 2SA

Century is part of the Penguin Random House group of companies
whose addresses can be found at global.penguinrandomhouse.com.

First published by Century in 2024

www.penguin.co.uk

A CIP catalogue record for this book is available from the British Library.

ISBN: 9781529136432
ISBN: 9781529136449 (trade paperback)

Typeset in 12/17 pt Janson MT Std by Jouve (UK), Milton Keynes
Printed and bound in Great Britain by Clays Ltd, Elcograf S.p.A.

The authorised representative in the EEA is Penguin Random House Ireland,
Morrison Chambers, 32 Nassau Street, Dublin D02 YH68

www.greenpenguin.co.uk

John and Emily. Always proud of you.

Cross Hairs

CHAPTER 1

ADAM GLOSSNER HAD to work hard to conceal his smile, sitting on the edge of his three-year-old son's tiny bed. The little boy giggled as he squeezed the doll again. A shaky, recorded voice said, "Oh, geez. C'mon, Rick."

Brooke, Glossner's six-year-old daughter, snickered from the other bed.

Glossner said, "Are you sure you've never watched *Rick and Morty*?"

The little boy kept smiling and shook his head.

"How did Grandpa know you'd like this Morty doll?"

Jeremy shrugged his little shoulders and kept the huge grin on his face. From the other bed, Brooke said, "Grandpa is smart. He said that's why me and Jeremy are smart. It skips a generation."

Glossner couldn't keep from laughing out loud at that. His father often threatened to buy the kids a drum set if he didn't get to see them enough. All Glossner could do now was hug his son and do the little ritual where he tucked the blankets tightly around him. Jeremy was an amazingly still sleeper. Glossner would often find him in the same position in the morning. The boy looked like a tiny mummy.

He stepped over to his daughter's bed and leaned down to give her a kiss.

Brooke said, "Daddy, can we go to the LEGO store soon?"

"Sure. What's my engineer need this time?"

"They have a new Star Wars collection. I just need one more TIE fighter."

"Wow. When did you guys go full science fiction on me?"

Brooke smiled and said, "We're not from the olden days. We grew up this way."

Glossner snorted. "Six whole years of growing up. Nothing like the dark ages I had to live through." He kissed his daughter on the forehead. "Once upon a time, I had to watch the commercials during Giants games. No fast-forwarding and no pausing either."

"Really? All the commercials?"

"Yep."

Glossner slipped out of the bedroom and down the hallway. His wife, Victoria, stepped out of their bedroom suite. She still could walk a runway as a model but looked like she was going out for a jog, in shorts and a T-shirt. She liked to sleep in the same clothes she intended to work out in the next morning.

"I love how Brooke lets Jeremy sleep in her room," Glossner said. "It'll be helpful when more siblings arrive."

His wife said, "You better not expect too many more kids. I'll be too old before you have the volleyball team you want."

He chuckled as he leaned down and kissed her on the cheek. "We've got plenty of time. Want to come out on the balcony with me?"

Victoria shook her head. "I have to give my sister a call, then I'm down for the count." As she turned to walk past him, she gave him a swat on the butt. "Not bad for a guy who doesn't have time to work out."

A couple of minutes later, Adam Glossner stood on his third-floor balcony, gazing out at the park in front of his apartment and the Hudson River beyond it. The air was cool but not uncomfortable. No snow so far this year, but that was always iffy before Thanksgiving. The wind was from the east, so he didn't catch that salty smell that came off the river. He held a snifter of brandy in his left hand. He'd given up smoking cigars in the evening when Brooke told him they smelled gross. He had to admit he felt better for it.

He could see the three closest buildings around a bend in Riverside Drive. Something caught his attention. A movement on one of the lower balconies. Then a boat on the river distracted him. He took a sip of the Rémy Martin Cognac and gazed back out at the river.

His brain didn't have time to process the sound of the bullet before it punched into the side of his head and sent him tumbling through the open French doors onto the Italian tile they'd just paid a fortune to have laid in their living room.

CHAPTER 2

I LAY IN bed, appreciating the dark bedroom. The apartment was quiet. With ten kids, that was rare. My wife, Mary Catherine, had been pushing both of us toward a healthier lifestyle. That included a couple of minutes of focused breathing and meditation every morning. This was my time to breathe and meditate.

I could hear Mary Catherine's light snore. It was cute. Not that I could ever tell her that. She had the belief that she never snored. As Trent once said to her, "You claim you don't burp. But I've seen you burp a couple of times. According to my debate class, that would negate your entire premise. Besides, everyone burps." That had earned my youngest son a stern look and a small portion of roast pork with rice and beans. It also put Trent on notice that Mary Catherine really didn't care for him pointing out her personal habits.

I was mature and experienced enough to know never to make a similar comment. I didn't care if Mary Catherine burped after a pepperoni pizza; I'd act like I didn't hear or smell anything at all. Maybe that was the secret to our very happy marriage. That or the fact that we'd been married less than two months.

Then my cell phone rang. As I picked up the phone, I saw that it was my boss, Harry Grissom, calling me at 6:01 a.m. There was only one thing he'd be calling about this early.

"Hey, Harry," I kept my voice low even though I knew the ring itself would've woken Mary Catherine.

"Sorry for the early call, Mike." Somehow his voice didn't sound quite as gravelly as it did during the day.

"What's up?"

Harry said, "This may shock you, but I'm calling because of a homicide."

"No, really? I thought you might want me to meet for you breakfast or maybe go for a walk."

I sat up in bed, then reached into my nightstand drawer and pulled out the little notebook I always keep there. "Where am I heading before breakfast?"

Harry gave me the address. I said, "Wait. Where?"

"I know. It's close to your apartment," Harry said. "You could probably walk there. We got a problem, though. The body was found a few hours ago, but someone screwed up, patrol got overwhelmed, and no one called us immediately. There's already media on the scene."

"That does make things trickier. I can't believe too many reporters are at the scene of a homicide. Even if it is probably some rich guy based on the address." I stopped and thought about it for a moment. I was careful when I said, "Harry, why is there already media there at this time in the morning?"

Harry said in a flat tone, "It's another victim of the sniper."

CHAPTER 3

THE ONLY KID I encountered during my attempt to escape the apartment quietly was Jane, who often got up early to study. Even by her standards, though, this was a little excessive. I gave her a kiss on the top of her head and headed for the door. A cop's kids know not to ask questions when they see their mom or dad leave early or in a hurry.

Just as I was passing through the door, Jane called out, "Be careful, Dad."

It put a smile on my face.

It took me longer to walk across the street and up to the parking garage where I park my NYPD Chevy Impala than it did for me to drive the few blocks to the crime scene. But the entire trip gave me a little time to think. The media had been playing up the story of two people shot from long range almost a month apart. I think it was the *Brooklyn Democrat* that came up with a catchy name: the Longshot Killer. It was easier to appreciate a good nickname for a killer before you met the victim's family. For now, I respected someone's poetic license.

This was the only victim in Manhattan. The first, Marie Ballard, had been a single grandmother in Queens. The next one was Thomas Bannon, a fireman who lived on Staten Island. I was already racking my brain, trying to find a pattern to the killings.

Every homicide detective tends to note homicides with similar details. You never know when it might reveal a serial killer. I wasn't even sure if I was up for another major investigation after my past few months. But I learned a long time ago that neither the NYPD nor the public cares one bit how tired I am or what kind of mood I'm in.

I pulled up next to a parked patrol car. I recognized the patrol officer but couldn't think of his name as he waved to me. After a dozen steps, I stopped for a moment. I sucked in a deep breath like a free diver attempting a hundred-foot dive. Then I listened to the sounds of the city just waking up. I never know how frantic my life might become as soon as I dive into a homicide investigation. I like to savor my last moments of relative calm.

I noticed half a dozen reporters and three cameramen hovering near the entrance to the building. A young female patrol officer stood by the door, blocking the media people.

One of the reporters stepped right up to the officer, trying to intimidate her. He said in a loud voice, "I live in the building. I demand you let me in."

The young cop let a smile slide across her face. She said, "I'm sure you do. In your mind. But I expect it's more likely you live in a studio somewhere in Queens. I'm just basing that on what reporters at your shitty station are paid."

I let out a laugh.

Before I got any closer, I heard someone call my name. It was Lois Frang from the *Brooklyn Democrat*. She had a decent reputation among the cops for honest reporting and being a straight shooter. I knew she'd worked at one of the big newspapers years ago but left under a cloud of some kind. She seemed to get a charge out of racing around the city, writing about some of the more lurid crimes. She also seemed to love working for the small Brooklyn newspaper. Even if the little paper had more ads than articles.

Lois said, "Must be big if they brought you in on this, Detective Bennett."

"C'mon, Lois, no one's bringing in anyone. It's a homicide in Upper Manhattan. If you'll recall, my assignment is to the Manhattan North Homicide unit. I'd get called no matter the circumstances."

"Can you give me any insights?" Lois had pulled a small pad from her purse, which looked more like a duffel bag.

"The best insight I can give you is that cannabis stocks might be a good investment."

"Very funny. Anything about this homicide?"

"Technically, we don't know it's a homicide yet. Until I get up there and look around it's still a death investigation."

"Cut the shit, Bennett. We all know he was shot at long range. Why do you think everyone's out here at this ungodly hour? We want to pick up details about the latest victim of the Longshot Killer."

"Did you come up with that name, Lois?"

She beamed for a moment. "Why, yes, I did."

"Well played. Descriptive without being too campy. You could give lessons to the *Daily News* or the *Post* about variety and imagination when naming a killer."

"Thanks, Bennett. It would be an even better story if you could give me a few details."

I shrugged. "Don't know what to tell you, Lois."

"We heard the victim was well-known."

I shrugged again. I honestly didn't know anything yet except the victim's name: Adam Glossner.

CHAPTER 4

THE APARTMENT WAS on the third floor, so I took the stairs. When I stepped through the stairwell door on the third floor, the scene was exactly as I had expected. Cops, medical examiner workers, and tenants all milled around the open door to an apartment. A few doors down, sitting in a chair that looked like it came from the apartment, was a distraught doorman. Several crime-scene techs were getting their equipment ready, and a uniformed patrol sergeant kept nonessential workers and gawkers away from the door.

The sergeant looked up and said, "About time someone from Homicide showed up."

I smiled at Sergeant Leslie Asher and said, "We show up as soon as we're called."

"Touché." She smiled and said, "I already sent the imbecile who didn't call you home. What we got isn't pretty."

"Talk to me, Leslie."

"The victim is forty-one-year-old Adam Glossner. Some kind of hedge-fund manager. His wife found the body about two hours ago, when she realized he wasn't in bed. She said he'd been headed out to the balcony when she went to bed around nine. It's a single bullet hole visible on the right side of his head. Looks like he sort of bounced off the French door frame and fell on the floor. The two kids are with the wife in one of the neighbors' apartments. There, you're up to date."

I stepped into the apartment and let the videographer and photographer do their job before the crime-scene techs moved in. The body was still on the floor where it had been found. Someone from the medical examiner's office was waiting outside to take Mr. Glossner.

I paused and said a quick prayer for Adam Glossner's soul. My grandfather always tells me how important it is to take every life seriously. By extension we must take every death seriously. This isn't a ritual I treat lightly. But I wish I didn't have to do it so often.

I felt a pang of sorrow for the victim's children. I've seen too many kids grow up without parents due to homicides. A murder can have ripples in a family for generations.

For a long moment, I stared down at the body and its blood that had seeped onto the gorgeous tile floor. The dark blood clashed with the white tile. It was my deepest hope that Glossner's wife had been able to get the kids out of the apartment without them seeing the remains of their father.

I could see exactly what Sergeant Asher had been talking about. It was clear Glossner had been standing on the balcony when the bullet struck him. I could picture him spiraling through the door and onto the pristine tile.

I looked out the open French doors. The apartment was on a bend in the road that allowed a view of the balcony from at least five different buildings. I tried to get an idea where the shot had come from. I was at a loss. My boss, Harry, had texted me that he already had cops canvassing the area. Maybe someone heard or saw something.

I walked through the apartment by myself. I could see the family had built a life here. Young kids, good job, the American dream. I hoped the victim had had enough sense to appreciate his family and situation. I'd seen many a Wall Street financial manager work so hard they forgot they had a life outside of lower Manhattan.

The other thing I realized as I stared at the wound on the right side of Adam Glossner's head: I was not used to homicides like this. I generally dealt with killers who get up close and personal. Even with firearms. Most people feel more confident the closer they get.

Clearly that wasn't true of this killer.

CHAPTER 5

I'D GOTTEN A decent sense of the crime scene. Now it was time to toughen up and do my least favorite assignment in a case like this: interview the grieving. I nodded to the crime-scene techs filing into the victim's apartment as I walked out and then down the hallway to the neighbor's place.

The door was open. I saw a young female patrol officer sitting on the couch next to Victoria Glossner. The officer had a little boy in her lap as the mom rocked back and forth with a girl I judged to be about six years old.

Mrs. Glossner was a very attractive, fit woman of about thirty-five, probably six or eight years younger than her husband. I don't even notice teary, bloodshot eyes anymore on this job. But I saw how she clutched her daughter and how both the kids looked completely confused. It hit me like a sledgehammer. I remembered talking to my kids when their mother was dying of cancer.

We'd had months to prepare for the eventual shock. What do you do when your whole world changes in just a moment?

The patrol officer looked up and saw me. I nodded. Then I tilted my head to the left and the sharp young officer stood up with the little boy still in her arms. She said to the little girl, "Let's see if we can find something for you guys to drink."

Mrs. Glossner released her daughter to walk with the officer into another room. I sat across from her in an antique, uncomfortable chair. I introduced myself and told her how sorry I was. It wasn't an act. I am always sorry in a situation like this.

She said she was okay to talk. "I watch so many of the police reality shows that I know how important the first forty-eight hours of a homicide investigation can be. I don't know what I can tell you. But I'll answer any questions you have."

I handed her a tissue from a box on the table next to the couch. She nodded her thanks and dabbed at her eyes. She explained to me that she had gone into the bedroom around nine and had talked to her sister on the phone for about forty minutes. Afterward, she'd quickly drifted off to sleep. Her husband had not come to bed by that time.

I asked, "Is it usual for him not to come to bed at the same time as you?"

She nodded. "He liked to clear his head. He loved to look at the river from our balcony. He did it almost every night. He usually came to bed somewhere between ten and eleven." She sniffled and looked like she was about to sob again. Then she gained control of herself.

Victoria Glossner said, "It's just not fair. We had so many plans. We'd been through so much. We were talking about having another baby. How could this have happened?"

I asked all the usual questions. The ones about her husband's friends and associates. If she knew of anyone who might want to harm him. I held off on the questions about potential drug use and gambling. It's surprising how often one of those two vices is behind a homicide in an area like this.

She answered no to all of those questions.

I said, "You said you'd been through so much; was it anything that would've made someone angry enough to do this?"

She quickly shook her head and said, "Just some rough spots in his business. Nothing we were too worried about now. That's what I'm saying. Our life was really good. Or at least about to become really good." She started to cry. Then it turned into a flood of tears.

I waited silently, wanting to expand on what sort of business problems Adam Glossner had been experiencing. Before I could speak again, a tall, well-dressed woman came to the door.

When a patrol officer tried to stop her, she snapped, "I'm going in to get my daughter and I don't care who doesn't like it."

The officer looked at me, and I just nodded. As the new woman marched toward the couch, Victoria Glossner looked up and then moaned, "Oh, Mom. Thank God." She jumped up and hugged her mother.

Her mother said, "Get the kids, and let's go to my apartment. We need to get you and them away from here."

Victoria said, "I was just answering a few questions for this detective."

Her mother didn't even bother to look in my direction. She said, "That can wait until later." Then she took her daughter by the hand and started calling for the kids.

They were all out of the apartment in less than a minute.

CHAPTER 6

VANESSA WRIGHT, A new detective with our squad, brought me the neighborhood canvass summary. She wasn't quite my height of six foot three, but she stood well over six feet and could look me in the eye as she gave me the report.

Vanessa said, "We tried to hit all the buildings to the north, where we think the shot came from. Now we'll swing south for a building or two. Does that sound thorough enough for you?"

I said, "Vanessa, I know you haven't been in our unit for too long, but I'm not used to getting a professional report without some kind of a prank." I saw her wide grin and beautiful, straight teeth. I added, "Someone told you to prank me, didn't they?"

"I won't say who, but it *was* suggested that I should tell you everyone went to get breakfast and would start again sometime around lunch. I knew better than to even joke about that."

I smiled and nodded, letting her know I wasn't an officious

prick. I like pranks and I've played plenty during my career. Instead, I asked her about the canvass they had just completed.

Vanessa handed me a sheet of paper and said, "A couple of people thought they might have heard something. Maybe a pop or a bang sometime around 10:15 last night. One elderly man in a building to the north said he'd only talk to the boss. Claimed he had important information."

Even the neighbor next door to the Glossners hadn't heard or seen anything unusual. It wasn't until she heard a commotion in the hallway this morning that she even looked out and saw the police officers. She knew Mrs. Glossner and the children. "That's why she took them in while everything was going on."

As we came out the front door of the building, I saw Lois Frang still standing there. I had to admire that kind of persistence. She yelled out, "What do you got, Bennett?"

I called back, "I have a slight sciatica problem and arthritis in my hip!"

"When am I going to get a straight answer out of you?"

"When I've got something worth saying."

Detective Vanessa Wright led me to a building nearby, to the third-floor apartment of Walter Cronin, the elderly man who'd claimed to have information. When he opened the door, he was clearly happy to see Vanessa again. Despite having asked to talk to the boss, he didn't care too much about me either way.

I said, "I heard you have some information that might be useful, Mr. Cronin." I spoke a little louder than I normally do. I don't know why—I just assumed an elderly man would have poor hearing.

"You bet I do." He motioned us all the way into his lovely apartment. The eighty-six-year-old retired dentist had apparently had a very lucrative practice. After he made us sit on the sofa, he pulled out a notebook and said, "I've been detailing the shenanigans going on with this building for years. The fees this place charges are out-rageous. There's so much fraud going on I don't know where to start."

I held up my hands and said, "Excuse me, Mr. Cronin, but we're not here about fraud. We're in a homicide unit. A man across the street was shot from somewhere around here. The killer used a rifle."

"Yes, yes, yes, I know. I was just trying to give you some bonus information as well."

"Do you have any information at all about the shooting?"

"Aside from hearing the shot before I fell asleep last night, I don't know anything."

"You're sure you heard a gunshot?"

"You're too young to remember this, but we used to have a draft in this country. I did two years in the Army and heard plenty of gunfire. I know the sound of a high-powered rifle when I hear it. There are no car backfires anymore. There were no sonic booms. Just a single gunshot, not long before I fell asleep. Probably around 10:15 or 10:30."

"Did you investigate the source of the gunshot?"

"Why on earth would I do that? I don't have a gun. What hap-pens if I find a man with a gun? I doubt you're the right man to look into the fraud of this building anyway. Investigate the gun-shot." Mr. Cronin just shook his head as I finished up my notes.

CHAPTER 7

AFTER THE CRIME scene was secured and I'd done all I could to talk to relevant witnesses, I headed to the office. I knew there'd be a lot of questions from my bosses, and I had names and information I wanted to pass on to our squad's criminal intelligence analyst. His name is Walter Jackson, and he's an absolute wizard with computer databases. Give Walter a name and a few minutes, he can tell you every neighbor they've ever had as well as their cell phone carrier, their main bank, and what credit card they use.

I took the elevator up in the unmarked building that housed Manhattan North Homicide. It had been my home within the NYPD for so long I couldn't imagine reporting to a precinct or to One Police Plaza.

It's always comforting to see my lieutenant, Harry Grissom, sitting in his office with the door open. He oversees three staff assistants, two criminal intelligence analysts, and nine detectives, plus a rotating group of detectives trying to get broader experience. And he does it all without losing his temper, getting frustrated, or being petty. In short, Harry Grissom is an awesome boss.

I gave Harry a quick rundown on what I'd learned.

Harry stared at me across his desk without saying a word. It lasted maybe five seconds, but it felt like a week. This is why I never play in Harry's poker games. He seems like he'd be unbeatable.

Absently smoothing his mustache, Harry asked in a quiet tone, "How did the wife seem?"

"The usual. Distraught, near shock. She answered a few questions before her mother swooped in and told me I could talk to her later."

"Did she say anything useful?"

"I did get an odd vibe. It's hard to describe. It's more about what she didn't say. It felt like she wasn't telling me everything about their current circumstances. I don't know if it was a marital strain or something else. But I'll have it in my head if I need to talk to her again."

"You think she was unhappy with her husband and figured a way to have someone shoot him, do you?"

"I don't think so. But maybe. I guess it's possible. Although it did cross my mind that if someone was really smart, they could use the cover of the sniper to have a person shot from a long distance. But I don't think that's the case here."

Harry gave me a folder with some information on the other two homicides involving the sniper. Harry said, "I heard someone call the shooter 'the Longshot Killer.' I guess that's as good a nickname as any."

Harry told me to grab the complete reports off the computer and said I could consider myself the lead detective on all three cases. That might not make me too popular with the other homicide detectives already working them, but I knew better than to say anything. Harry doesn't much care for whining or complaints. His philosophy is simple: *We've got a job to do, so let's go do it.*

Frankly, it does make the work environment here in our off-site office much more pleasant without people bitching constantly about everything.

Harry said, "What kind of help do you need? Besides the usual analytical assistance and help with interviews?"

"I'm glad you asked. As I was standing on the balcony where the victim was shot, I realized I don't know much about snipers. I'm pretty good with figuring out trajectories and bullet wounds inflicted from a drive-by a few feet away, but these long-distance angles and the whole sniper mindset is new to me. Do you think we've got anyone who can help me with that sort of stuff?"

Harry chuckled. Or as close to a chuckle as he ever came. "Mike, this is the NYPD. We got someone who can help you build a plane. Leave it to me."

CHAPTER 8

LESS THAN AN hour later, Harry Grissom forwarded an email to the whole squad. Someone new was going to be around the office for a while. Command staff was sending over Rob Trilling, a sniper from the Emergency Service Unit, to help me on the case. He'd be on temporary duty until we made an arrest, or until I didn't need him anymore. That was about all I could ask for.

As a trained investigator, I like to have as much information as possible before I start anything new. That includes knowing who I'm working with. As soon as I had the chance, I went over to Walter Jackson to get the scoop on this sniper from ESU.

As I stepped into Walter's office, he turned his computer screen slightly so I could see a photograph of a mountain with someone working at the top of it.

I said, "Okay, I'll bite. What's that?"

"Mount Rushmore just as they were starting construction on the monument." A huge smile spread across the big man's face. He had to add, "The beauty of the mountain was un-president-ed."

I groaned. Then I said, "Aren't your daughters making you put a dollar into a jar for every pun you make?"

"Not anymore. I made them another bet. I told them if they could keep a straight face and not groan or laugh at my latest pun, I'd keep doing the pun-jar payments."

"So I take it they lost that bet?" I asked. "Since you're going to tell me anyway, what was the pun?"

"What happened when two artists had a competition?"

I shrugged.

"It ended in a draw."

I gave him a look, not a groan, and said, "Okay, I'll admit that was pretty good." I could envision his little girls giggling at that one. "But the real reason I stepped in here was not to hear more of your puns. I need some information."

"On your new partner?" It wasn't really a question. It was a statement, and it made me realize how transparent I could be.

All I could do was smile and say, "Yes, that's exactly what I'm looking for."

"I was curious myself. Vanessa was the last one to come on the squad, and we vetted her like she was going to the White House. The weird thing is, I can't bring up this guy's NYPD personnel records, but I did get into his military record. I have a contact with DOD who forwarded his electronic file to me."

"Why can't you get his NYPD records?"

"That's like asking me why we don't get HBO on the squad TV. I don't know the specifics; I just know we don't have access to them. This guy Rob Trilling's file is locked. But I know he's on an FBI task force, so that might have something to do with it."

"I thought he was on our ESU as a sniper."

"A couple of quick phone calls to my contacts tells me he hasn't been in ESU since midsummer and has been over at the FBI fugitive task force since then." He turned the screen a little more and motioned me to sit in the chair in front of his desk. He brought up the electronic file he'd received from the Department of Defense.

Before I could even understand what we were looking at, Walter let out a whistle. He said, "Damn, this guy has seen some shit. An Army Ranger. A tour in Afghanistan. He even received a Bronze Star for protecting a medical unit under ambush."

"How the hell did he end up in New York?"

Walter shrugged, never taking his eyes off the screen.

I said, "Was he a sniper in the Army?"

"You'd think, right? I don't see where he was sniper qualified. But if you look at his last fitness report, it lists his rifle and self-defense skills as 'outstanding.'"

"Is that outstanding compared to the general population or compared to other Rangers?"

Walter whistled again and said, "I'm betting it's against other Rangers. That makes him a certified badass." He looked me in the eye and added, "You won't like this part."

"What?"

"Rob Trilling is only twenty-four years old."

"Then how long has he been with the NYPD?"

Walter said, "I told you, I can't get into his NYPD file. But if he was in the Army and is only twenty-four, he can't have been with us for very long."

A voice just outside Walter's office said, "A little over nineteen months."

My head snapped toward the door, where I saw a dark-haired young man dressed in a nice button-down with a blue tie that looked like the one I'd worn to my prom.

The man said, "Hi, I'm Rob Trilling."

CHAPTER 9

I TURNED AND stared at the young man standing just outside Walter Jackson's door. It wasn't just that Rob Trilling had surprised us in the middle of discussing his service record. It was that he *did* look incredibly young. He looked like he could've been one of my kids. Age-wise, he actually could have been.

It was quite a blow to an active cop who tries not to think of himself as getting older.

It was Walter who saved me. While I just sat there with my mouth open, Walter slid out from behind his desk and extended his hand. I was still trying to get my head straight and say something intelligent. I couldn't even really judge Trilling's height because six-foot-six Walter towered over him, like he did over most people.

Finally I stood and introduced myself.

"Nice to meet you, sir."

"Please call me Mike."

Trilling nodded but didn't say anything else.

I said, "We'll be working together."

"Yes, so I've been told."

"I'm looking forward to it. I could use a perspective on long-range rifle shots." I took a moment to study the young man as we all stood there. I guess I'd expected him to say something in response, but he just stood there quietly.

Walter suggested I introduce the new guy to the lieutenant and the other detectives on the squad. It didn't take long to walk him around the office. I noticed he had extremely good manners and didn't say much. He used "sir" and "ma'am" a lot but generally waited for people to ask him questions before he said anything.

When all the introductions were done, I led Rob Trilling to our conference room. I shut the door so we would have some privacy. I brought over a folder with reports giving a broad outline of all three cases and what had been determined so far about where the shots had originated.

I tried to put Trilling at ease and said, "Can I get you some coffee?"

"No thank you, sir."

"Call me Mike."

Trilling just nodded again. He wasn't at attention, but it was close. There are a lot of former military members who continue their public service as officers with the NYPD, but it's usually not this easy to spot them. They typically slip into a more relaxed, civilian mode. This guy seemed like he was still a Ranger.

"Why don't you tell me about yourself?"

"Not much to tell. I was in the Army and now I'm with the NYPD. That sums things up pretty well."

29

"Are you from this area originally? I can't place your accent."

"I'm from just outside Bozeman, Montana."

"How on earth did you end up in New York City?"

The young man just shrugged and didn't say anything.

I stood there in awkward silence with this twenty-four-year-old former Army Ranger. After almost a minute of dead air, I had to say something.

I said, "Look, I moved us in here so we could have some privacy. I'm getting the sense that you don't like the idea of working on this case with me. Talk to me, cop to cop. Nothing either of us says will leave this room. What's going on?"

It took almost a full ten seconds before Trilling looked me in the eye and said, "It feels like I've been assigned here so you can keep an eye on me. I don't need a babysitter."

"No one said you did."

"That's the problem with the NYPD. No one says *anything*. They move you around or send you someplace new, but no one ever explains why they do it."

"I'm not sure I follow."

"The military lets you do your job. If you screw up, they tell you. Here, it seems like they dance around issues, and it doesn't help with accomplishing the mission."

"What do you think our mission is?"

"To protect people."

I couldn't argue with that.

CHAPTER 10

I SAT AT my desk after Rob Trilling had left. I was at a loss. My initial meeting with my new partner had been a little tense and awkward. Altogether less than spectacular. Less than encouraging, even. Veteran cops have a natural inclination to want to help younger cops along. Pass on some advice, maybe a few decent quotes. It makes you feel like you've done your part.

Rob Trilling was not making me feel that way. He'd seemed happy to scoot out of the office and grab the gear he needed from the FBI task force. I'd told him we'd start early the next morning. I hadn't given him a time on purpose. I wanted to see what his idea of "early" would be, what kind of a work ethic the young man had.

But he'd left me with a number of questions. Questions that made me uncomfortable but I had to get answered. You can't be with one agency for as long as I have been and not have a list of contacts that could fill up three phones.

I wasted no time jumping on my phone. I was able to reach exactly who I was looking for. Sergeant Alane Eubanks was an old friend who was now working as some kind of liaison to the federal agencies and a task force coordinator. It was a desk job after she'd been ambushed by young men claiming to fight fascism. They'd fired sixteen shots at her and hit her three times. The three bullets had put Alane in the hospital for more than two months. She'd fought her way back on the job. The shitheads had taken a generous plea offer and were now in jail upstate.

Alane sounded like her usual cheerful self when she answered the phone. "Bennett, you old dog, how's it hangin'?"

I couldn't hide my smile, hearing her sound like her old self again.

Alane made me fill her in on the family. She's one of the few people who can remember the names of all ten of my kids. I remembered how Alane once told my daughter Bridget that the next time a particular boy started to pester her, she should punch him right in the nose. No boy is going to admit that a girl clocked him hard in the face, Alane said. But she'd left out one detail: she'd forgotten to tell Bridget not to do it in front of a teacher. Bridget may have scared away a bully, but she spent a week in detention for it. Secretly I was still proud of her.

After we made it through the family roundup, I was finally able to ask Alane, "How are you feeling now?"

"Not bad. Few aches and pains. One of the bullets damaged my bladder and I feel like I have to pee all the time. I guess it's better than the alternative."

I set her up for one of cops' oldest jokes. "What's the one thing you never want to hear anyone say again?"

"'It comes with the job.' I swear to God I will punch the next asshole who thinks being shot is part of a cop's job description." Every cop hears that every time they're punched in the face or stabbed or shot. Then Alane said, "So what prompted this call out of the blue?"

"I got assigned a new partner named Rob Trilling. Most recently he was over at the FBI fugitive task force."

"The really young guy? I remember him. Good-looking too."

"That's him. I was just wondering if you had any insight into why he's been shuttled around even though he's been on the force less than two years."

"The FBI says he's a real go-getter. They like him."

"He made it sound like he had been sent here as a punishment." I noted the long silence on the other end of the phone.

Finally Alane said, "I know they pulled him from Emergency Service a couple of months ago and sent him to the FBI. Our command staff had put him into ESU without the usual time in grade, and enrolled him in sniper school immediately. He got moved to the FBI without much notice."

"Do you know why?"

"No, not really."

"Can you guess?"

Alane had a slightly harsher tone when she said, "You're the devil, Michael Bennett. I'm trying to be a professional."

"And I'm trying to make sure I'm not being saddled with a problem partner who could get me killed."

She started slowly. "Okay, this is only conjecture. Command staff must be worried about him for some reason. Either some kind of complaint or a weak allegation against him. It's easy to shuttle someone off to a simple task force. Looking for fugitives. What could go wrong?" There was a pause before Alane asked, "Why the hell is he working in Homicide?"

I explained the case and his expertise.

She said, "That makes sense. He'd be the right guy to talk to. I can tell you, all his assessments are very good. But you know how people around One Police Plaza get nervous and overreact about every little thing."

I really did know.

CHAPTER 11

I MISSED DINNER but somehow managed to make it home before everyone was asleep. When you have ten kids, it takes a while to greet everyone properly.

I finally found myself alone in the kitchen with Mary Catherine. The fertility treatments had become a little less jarring to her physically. She looked good and seemed to have a pretty reasonable handle on the household. I felt bad that I hadn't been more help. Some people might say it's crazy to try for an eleventh kid. I understand that. But with ten adopted kids from my first marriage, I also understand Mary Catherine's desire to have a baby.

I filled her in on my first conversation with my new partner. I tried to paint a realistic picture. She picked up that I was concerned the meeting had been tense.

Mary Catherine said, "Invite him to dinner. That way you get to see a different side of him, and he gets to meet your wonderful family. Including your beautiful new wife."

I chuckled. "Having someone over for dinner seems to be the Irish answer to every problem."

"Because it tends to solve every problem. No one can be upset over a good brisket with onions and carrots."

"Let's give it a little more time. I'm not ready to give up an evening to this guy just yet." Then I did a little math and realized I'd only said hello to nine children. I looked at Mary Catherine and said, "Where's Jane?"

"Juliana said she's at the library working on something super-secret."

"Sounds like her."

From the dining room table, where she was drawing with crayons, Chrissy yelled, "I bet she has a boyfriend."

Mary Catherine was quick to point out that my youngest daughter should mind her own business.

Chrissy innocently said, "Isn't my sister my business?"

I stepped out into the dining room and kissed the top of Chrissy's head. "That's a pretty good answer. Is that what you think Mary Catherine meant by her comment?"

Chrissy shook her head and said, "Nope."

I glanced into the kitchen to see Mary Catherine smiling. We are definitely on the same sheet of music when it comes to raising these kids.

I went back to the kitchen and nibbled on the kids' leftovers. I guess that's a dad thing, no matter how gross everyone thinks it is. There were no other immediate problems on the horizon with the kids, so I decided to venture into a slightly more controversial topic.

"When is the next appointment with the fertility doctor?" I asked. Now I knew to keep my voice a little lower.

"Day after tomorrow. And we may get some concrete information one way or the other."

"Have you given any more thought about when we should bring it up with the kids?"

Mary Catherine looked at me and shrugged. "Trying to find the right time with at least a quorum of the kids has been hard. I think I'd rather wait till we have some real news. No reason to get them excited—or upset—by spilling the beans too early."

"What do you mean 'upset'? None of them would be upset by a new baby in the house."

Mary Catherine gave me a look like I was an eight-year-old trying to use physics for the first time. "It's hard to tell how people might react to big news like a new baby. I'm thinking specifically of Chrissy, and maybe Shawna, because they're the youngest. Chrissy's used to being treated like the baby of the family. I don't know how she'd react to being replaced in that role."

"We've raised those kids right. I guarantee they'll support any new addition."

"I hope you're right. I agree that we've raised them to support one another and the family as a whole. But you know that doesn't mean there aren't some squabbles every once in a while."

Thank God I'd found a woman who understands dynamics like this much better than I do. Tough family discussions like these make me realize the relative safety of work once in a while.

CHAPTER 12

I HAD A quick goodbye with the kids and Mary Catherine as I rushed out the door before 7:00 the next morning. I wanted to set an example for my new partner, so I arrived at work at about 6:50. I had plenty to do around the office anyway.

I stepped into the quiet squad bay, glad to see a light on in Walter Jackson's office. I needed a little time with Walter, the earliest riser on our squad. I don't know that anyone has ever beat him into the office. I'd have to hear a few puns, but I'd get a lot done.

I felt a twinge of anxiety about mentoring Rob Trilling. He was so young yet had more experience than I had in the military and in combat. That could sometimes translate to a good police career, but sometimes it didn't. I had seen it go both ways. The strict discipline of the military helps with the transition to police work. But the job requires an incredible amount of flexibility. I was worried about whether he'd be open enough to listen to my suggestions. Most people think cops are trained to investigate. That's not untrue—they do go to classes for it—but the real learning happens on the job. What worried me was that there was nothing Trilling had done with the NYPD that told me he understood investigations. Sure, he had moved into Emergency Service quickly and they had obviously wanted to take advantage of his military background. But working patrol and a fugitive task force wouldn't prepare you for homicide investigation.

I shuffled toward Walter's office with a list of things I needed. I could hear Walter's deep voice and assumed he was on the phone. I heard him laugh about something. Then, just outside the door, I stopped.

Walter wasn't on the phone; he was chatting with someone in his office.

I stepped through the doorway and was surprised to see Rob Trilling laughing and nodding his head. They both looked up.

Walter said, "Mike, you didn't tell me the new guy could hold his own with puns." He looked at Trilling.

No one can resist Walter, so Trilling said, "I love the way the Earth rotates. It really makes my day."

Walter almost fell out of his chair laughing. I smiled and nodded. It was a lot more than I had gotten from the young officer.

I avoided asking what time Trilling had arrived. He'd obviously gotten here before me, and I didn't want him to think I really was keeping tabs on him. It was clear the young man had some drive and ambition. I liked that.

I looked at Walter and asked for the backgrounds on each of the victims in the case.

Walter said, "Rob's already got them all. He even showed me a few more public records databases we can access for free. Just another way to look at things."

Trilling kept his mouth shut, as usual. He looked up at me and shrugged. He finally said, "A little trick to supplement the FBI info on fugitives. They never look too far into social media or anything like that."

I nodded and mumbled, "Good. You ready to head out to Queens? We gotta go look at the site of the first shooting. We're also going to have to come up with a list of potential snipers who live in the greater New York City area. There can't be all that many."

Trilling said, "Military snipers are relatively rare. I was a Ranger, but not a sniper with the Army. The NYPD also put me through the weeklong sniper class."

"Why? You could already shoot."

"A lot of people grow up with guns and are really good shots. That doesn't mean they'd be good snipers. There's a lot more that goes into sniping. Tactics, movement, and decisions on the ground are just as important as having good shooting skills."

"Do you think the list is a good idea?"

"I think we can use it, but I wouldn't depend on it. I talk to guys at the VA all the time. I'll see if they have any ideas."

I nodded. "Sounds like we do need to get you over to look at the first crime scene. I've never read a good account of exactly where the shot could have come from."

We were in my car and headed to Queens a few minutes later.

CHAPTER 13

IT WAS STILL pretty early, so we stopped at a little café on Kissena Boulevard in Queens, not far from the address where the first victim of the sniper was killed. I was hoping to use a little quiet time to get to know Trilling better and maybe smooth over our rough start.

We sat outside at a tiny table with our coffees and breakfast sandwiches. I sprang for both of us, hoping it might loosen up the young former Army Ranger. After five minutes of sitting there silently, sipping coffee and watching people stroll by on the wide sidewalk, I realized Trilling wasn't going to say anything unless I started the conversation. He seemed quite content to keep his mouth shut unless compelled otherwise. Normally, I'd consider that a great characteristic in a relatively new cop. In this case, I needed to try and reach him.

Out of the blue I said, "Where do your folks live?"

It was as if he had to gather his thoughts even on a simple question. It took a full five seconds before he said, "My mom still lives just outside Bozeman. I don't have any contact with my dad."

I would've liked to explore that more, but his tone made it clear that was all he was going to say about it. Instead, we were interrupted by a young, pudgy guy walking by, wearing the uniform from one of the local grocery stores. His name tag said, CHIP.

Chip stopped near our table, looked right at me, and said, "What's coffee run these days? About five bucks?"

I just nodded.

Chip said, "And you probably have at least ten cups a week, right? That's fifty bucks a week. That's about twenty-five hundred dollars a year. Think about it! In the last twenty years of coffee drinking, you would've saved enough to buy a decent boat."

Trilling looked at the man. "Do you drink coffee, Chip?"

Chip seemed psyched to say, "Not at all."

Without missing a beat, Trilling asked, "Where do you store your boat?"

That flustered Chip, who decided he was in over his head. He kept walking down the street.

I smiled and filed the interaction away, realizing there was a lot to this young man that I hadn't seen yet.

It was about eight thirty in the morning by the time we pulled up in front of a nice single-family home with a small front yard and a beautiful garden in a raised patch by the front door. The place was tidy but could've probably used a new coat of paint and maybe someone to pressure clean the walkway and front door.

I'd been a little disappointed by the lack of details about the victim, Marie Ballard, in the reports from the homicide detective, but I knew that her two adult children and one grandchild still lived at the address.

Trilling and I stood on the sidewalk for a moment as I let him soak in the neighborhood. I was about to tell him where they'd found the victim's body, but he beat me to it.

Trilling said, "I looked through the crime-scene photos. She had been gardening and was found at 5 p.m. in that raised bed just under the bedroom window. That means"—he looked up and down the street—"most likely the shot came from that direction."

We took a couple of steps into the front yard when the door opened and a muscular young Black man stepped out onto the porch with a baseball bat in his right hand. He slapped it into his left hand to show us it was heavy and he meant business.

CHAPTER 14

I WASN'T HAPPY to see a man using a baseball bat in such a menacing way. But I wasn't panicked either. The young man was about Trilling's age but a little bulkier. I knew from reports his name was Duane Ballard, and he was the victim's son.

Duane was still a good thirty feet from us. I was more interested in how Trilling might react. If he drew his gun, I'd be a little concerned. I know there's no rule about cops retreating to safety instead of defending themselves, but retreating isn't a bad tactic either. Certainly not in a nice neighborhood like this where crime isn't the central problem.

Trilling stayed absolutely still. He gave no reason for the son to get more upset. I was impressed.

I pulled out my badge and identified myself.

Duane eased up. He set the bat on the small porch with the handle leaning against a brick wall. We cautiously worked our way up the walkway, and he came down the three steps to meet us.

He said, "I thought you were more reporters." He looked at Trilling, then at me. "I guess neither of you look too much like those douchebags who try to get photos inside the house or take pictures of my sister and her baby."

I said, "I'm glad we passed your test."

Duane said, "Y'all doing anything to find my mom's killer? You're the first cops I've seen in a month. Once that fireman in Staten Island was shot, it was like you forgot about us. Even the media attention all shifted to him. Now some rich dude in Manhattan gets shot and I figured you'd ignore us."

"We're trying to narrow some things down."

"I'm not even sure I want you guys at our house. No one from the NYPD has shown much interest in solving the murder of a single Black woman."

Now Trilling stepped toward the young man and spoke for the first time. I tensed, hoping he didn't try to do this the hard way.

Trilling said, "Man, I'm so sorry about your mom. I don't know what I'd do if I lost my mom."

I hadn't expected that.

Trilling stepped even closer to the young man. "You staying in touch with friends and family? That can drop off when you're grieving. It's really important."

Duane tried to answer but got choked up. He just nodded as he looked down at the ground.

I was surprised to see Trilling scoot to the side of the man and put a comforting arm around his shoulder. He said in a low voice, "Now, can you walk us through what happened? Maybe you could tell us what you think the other cops have been missing."

Duane started slowly. He sniffled and wiped his nose on his arm. But he showed us how he'd walked outside to find his mother lying in the garden with blood pouring out of a hole just above her right eye. He hadn't heard any shots or seen anything suspicious. I knew all this already from the reports, but I think it was good for Duane to let it out again.

"Someone killed her while she was just out here tending her favorite plants, like she did every single weekend at that time." Duane looked off as he remembered his mother. "She was nice to everyone. And everyone loved her."

I watched as Trilling followed the young man across the yard to the garden. Standing in front of the house, his eyes tracked from every position, and I realized he was looking at the crime scene from an entirely different perspective than I did. I didn't know what this young officer knew about investigations, but it sure looked like he understood long-range shots. I still didn't know how he'd ended up with the NYPD, but I was suddenly grateful we had people with his expertise in our ranks. Officers with this kind of specialized experience are what make the NYPD so effective.

Trilling said to Duane, "Give us a few minutes to walk down the street and we'll come back and talk to you. I'm sorry we disrupted your morning."

Duane nodded and stuck his hand out for Trilling to shake.

Trilling shook, then started walking away from the house, and I had to quickstep to catch up to him. Now I felt like the trainee as I trailed behind Trilling. We finally slowed down about four houses away from the victim's house.

Trilling looked at the corner of one house and the thick bushes all around it. "The sniper fired from right there, under the bushes."

I looked and didn't see anything specific. "Okay, you're going to have to explain that one to me."

"Because that's where I would've shot from. This house is empty."

I hadn't even noticed.

"There's a clear view to the victim's house, but no one would see the shooter. He could have been lying under those bushes for hours. And a single shot fired is very difficult to locate just by the sound." Trilling's head swiveled in every direction. "Really, there's nowhere else the sniper could've shot from."

I looked up and down the street and decided to take Trilling's word for it.

CHAPTER 15

AN HOUR LATER, Rob Trilling did almost the exact same thing when looking from the balcony of Adam Glossner's apartment. The doorman, whom I'd already interviewed, had walked us up to the apartment but refused to come inside. He believed the apartment had bad karma and he didn't want it rubbing off on him. Victoria Glossner and the children were still at her mother's place.

Trilling stood on the balcony as I explained what the forensics people had told me about how they thought the body had fallen into the apartment. Trilling leaned on the railing. He pointed to a building down the street to the north, just visible from the balcony. The little curve in the road gave the other building a perfect view of this balcony.

Trilling pointed and said, "The killer shot from that building. Probably from the second or third floor."

"Again, you're going to have to walk me through your reasoning," I said. "I interviewed an elderly man in that building who thought he heard a gunshot the night Glossner was murdered. He couldn't tell me much else."

Trilling took me a little too literally and we left the apartment and started walking to the building. I don't know why I was still a little skeptical after my new partner's impressive review of the first crime scene. Once again, he didn't say anything as we walked toward the building. When I thought about it, I realized he didn't say much most of the time.

When we walked up to the front of the building, I was surprised to find the door propped open by a stool. There was no doorman. I called out but got no answer. Trilling walked right past me to the stairs and went up to the second floor. It was almost like he was in a trance.

I followed my partner up the concrete stairs to the second floor. He turned and walked to the front corner of the building and didn't hesitate to knock on the door of apartment 2A.

When we got no answer, Trilling tried the door handle and found it unlocked. Before I could even object, he'd opened the door and stepped inside.

The place was completely empty. Not even any furniture.

Trilling walked through the apartment to the balcony. The sliding-glass door was open an inch. He grasped the door high up on the frame, in case there was any forensic material we could get from the door handle, and slid it back.

As soon as he stepped onto the balcony and looked toward Adam Glossner's apartment, Trilling said, "This is definitely where the shot was taken."

I stepped out onto the balcony behind him but couldn't

picture exactly what he was talking about. I could see the building where the Glossners lived, but I didn't understand how Trilling was so certain the shot had come from here.

Then we heard a sharp voice from behind us, in the apartment. I turned to see a heavyset, middle-aged man holding a bucket. It had to be the super.

In a thick Russian accent he said, "The realtor has to show the apartment. You can't just walk in."

I badged him and identified myself.

The Russian superintendent said, "That badge don't give you no right to walk in any apartment you want."

"We tried to find someone when we entered the building. Your front door was propped open."

"Don't give me no excuses. I hate the cops. You guys don't do nothing."

Trilling turned to the man and said, "This is a crime scene. You're going to step out of this apartment and wait until we're done processing the scene. Your shitty security allowed someone to enter in here and shoot someone in the building down the street. That's on you. So you can take your attitude and shove it up your ass. We've got a job to do."

I knew I was smiling as I stared at my new partner, but I couldn't help it.

We didn't wait long for the Crime Scene Unit, but unfortunately they didn't find much to help us. They couldn't find any fingerprints on the doors. They took some DNA swabs but weren't hopeful.

I turned to Trilling and said, "Let's start putting together a list of potential snipers and see if any tips came in from the hotline."

Trilling said, "I have an appointment."

That was all he said, and then he was gone.

CHAPTER 16

IT HAD TAKEN a meeting of the minds from our squad to come up with a decent investigative plan for the Longshot Killer. (Even our lieutenant was using the nickname.) My idea of putting together a list of snipers in the greater New York City area wasn't realistic. But I did still think that if we coupled that idea with tips coming in on a phone line, we might get lucky and connect an unknown sniper to the killings.

We'd already gotten a lead involving a guy who lived up in Newburgh but had been traveling back and forth to the city. The tip said he'd trained as a Navy SEAL.

That's why in the early morning the next day I picked up Rob Trilling in front of the Three-Three in Washington Heights. It was the precinct closest to the George Washington Bridge so we could race up Route 9W to Newburgh, about a ninety-minute drive north.

When he hopped into my Impala, I asked Trilling if he knew anyone from the Three-Three. All he did was shake his head. It wasn't a surprise he didn't know anyone at the precinct. Usually you actually have to speak to people before you get to know them.

We found the guy in Newburgh quickly, and it took only about a minute of talking to him to realize he was a straight shooter, so to speak. He had washed out of SEAL training, but he had worked with the shore patrol afterward. Now he was some sort of half-assed, unlicensed private investigator. He'd been trying to find a missing husband and was able to show us a couple of receipts and reports that convinced me he was telling the truth.

I couldn't face another hour-and-a-half ride without any conversation. I engaged Trilling immediately as we got back in my Chevy.

I said, "Those SEALs can really shoot well. Don't you think?"

Trilling *did* think about it for a moment. The silence stretched close to ten seconds, then he said, "They're good with a lot of different weapons. Only a few SEALs are sniper certified. Most of them are trained to move and shoot."

"How well do Rangers stack up against SEALs or other special forces with long-distance shooting?"

"It doesn't really work like that. Every unit and situation has different dynamics. I'm proud to have been a Ranger, but I would never denigrate any other position in the military."

"Okay, I'll make it more personal. How well can *you* shoot from a long distance? Maybe that would give me a baseline and I could figure out something about our killer."

That must've made sense to Trilling. I saw him smile. I realized it was probably the first time I'd seen it.

The young officer said, "We're about twenty minutes from West Point and it's hardly out-of-the-way on our drive back down to the city. One of my old platoon leaders has a six-month assignment to the academy. He could get us on one of their rifle ranges and I could show you. Maybe it'll give you some insights as to what goes into a shot like that."

I liked that idea, and I also liked the opportunity to see the military academy at West Point up close. Trilling made a call, then turned to me and said, "Captain Hawks said to drop on by and he'd work out the details."

I noticed an even broader smile on my new partner's face.

CHAPTER 17

DOING THE MATH, I realized Trilling had been only twenty-two years old when he left active service and joined the NYPD. I knew from his service record he was now a sergeant in the Army Reserve. But someone thought highly of him. As we pulled up to the front gate, a tall Black captain stood right by the inspection point.

Trilling jumped out of the car and saluted the captain as he approached, then they gave each other a big hug. I didn't even want to think what these two might've gone through together to forge such a strong bond.

Trilling led the captain over to my car. "Detective Michael Bennett, this is Captain Isaiah Hawks. He was just a lieutenant when he ran my platoon in Afghanistan. He's also one of the most trustworthy men I've ever met."

Captain Hawks gave me a big smile and stuck out his hand,

saying, "Is Trilling causing as much trouble at the NYPD as he did in the Rangers?"

Trilling certainly hadn't learned interpersonal skills from the friendly captain. I just grinned and said, "He's been a great resource on this sniper case we've been working."

The captain let out a laugh. "We're just grunts. We don't know shit about snipers." I wasn't sure what the inside joke was, but I laughed along with the two of them.

I parked my Impala, then jumped into a Toyota pickup truck along with the captain and Trilling. Hawks gave a quick tour as we drove down toward the ranges. The campus really was spectacular. He pointed out historic and beautiful spots, like Washington Hall with the giant parade field in front of it. But I was mainly interested in seeing Trilling on the range.

We rode past ranges for all sorts of ordnance. Range 1 was called Argonne, after the US Army campaign of World War I, and was for hand-grenade training. Range 3, called New Orleans, was the combat pistol range. We drove all the way out to range 11B, called Normandy. This was a long-distance range for rifles.

Captain Hawks took a hard-sided case from the rear of the truck. He opened it and pulled out a rifle equipped with a short scope on the top rail. The captain handed the rifle to Trilling and said to me, "This is an M4, the Army's main infantry rifle."

We stepped back while Trilling readied the rifle to fire and stretched himself out on the ground. He moved with authority and speed. This was clearly a weapon he was comfortable with. I was starting to suspect that Trilling might be more comfortable with rifles than people.

When Captain Hawks and I were out of Trilling's earshot, the captain turned to me and said, "I worry about him. Is he doing well with the NYPD?"

"I've only worked with him a few days. To tell you the truth, he's awfully hard to read."

The captain chuckled. "That won't change. The one thing I could count on was Rob Trilling doing the right thing."

"How do you mean?"

From the firing station, Trilling yelled out, "Eyes and ears, the range is hot!"

The captain handed me a tiny packet with earplugs inside. Then he also handed me heavy plastic goggles.

Trilling looked over his shoulder at us to make sure he could fire. Then he looked through the scope and paused.

The captain said, "We have a paper target set up at two hundred yards. He's going to zero in the scope on a metal target about a hundred yards downrange."

Trilling fired once. Then he turned the knobs on the scope. He fired a second time and then sat up. "I need a minute to tighten a few things."

The captain nodded, then turned to me. "He's meticulous. That's an example of doing the right thing. You won't ever accuse Trilling of being sloppy. But more importantly, he follows the mission. For instance, when we were in Afghanistan, the fighting was being done mostly by Afghans with our support. One day Trilling was security on a medical call for an IED victim. Not far from the Pakistani border near FOB Fenty in Jalal-Abad. Turns out it was an ambush. A medic and a Black Hawk crew member were hit immediately. They were grounded with insurgents firing from several nearby buildings. Trilling didn't wait for orders or reinforcements that would be too late to help. Instead, he slipped off to a side street, flanked the shooters, killed two and captured three more.

"He was standing with the prisoners near the building when a squad of Afghan soldiers rolled up in an old deuce and a half. The leader of the squad marched up, gave a short bow of appreciation to Trilling, then kicked the closest prisoner. Trilling knocked the Afghan squad leader off his feet, stood between him and the prisoners, knocked out two other soldiers with some kind of martial arts moves, then held the rest at gunpoint until US troops arrived and flew everyone out.

"Once Trilling knows his mission, nothing will stop him."

I was almost in shock at the story. Then Trilling yelled again. "Line is hot!"

He fired once more. I could hear the ping of the bullet hitting a metal target downrange. Then he shifted slightly in his prone position and fired a steady stream of a dozen shots.

He stood up, showed the captain that he'd removed the magazine from the rifle and that the chamber was empty. He said, "Let's take a look."

As we strolled downrange, the captain explained that the range wasn't in official use so there was no one on hand to run the target back.

Trilling said, "Remember, this was just a scoped rifle, not a true sniper rifle."

It didn't matter. All the bullet holes were basically in the center printed on the paper target.

I got the idea and looked at Trilling in a new light.

CHAPTER 18

I FELT I might understand my new partner a little better now. It took some serious concentration to have the sort of shooting skills Rob Trilling possessed. I had to look past his reserved nature and quiet demeanor. It was almost unsettling. But on the ride back from West Point, he was a little more animated and interested in talking. Maybe it's because I'd let him take me into the world he knew so well.

Before we were even halfway back to the city, Walter Jackson called with a new tip that had come in, one he thought was pretty good. Walter had done the background himself. It was for a Marine veteran named Anton Hobbs, who'd had several violent outbursts and been referred to mental health officials three different times by NYPD officers responding to his apartment in Harlem. The tipster said the guy was sullen and surly.

I had a feeling that one of Anton's nervous neighbors had

made the call. Of course, that was just a guess, but a guess backed up by years of experience dealing with this kind of thing.

Walter had retrieved a fitness report on Anton from his contact at the Department of Defense. The report said that the former Marine had excellent rifle skills even if he wasn't officially a sniper. I wasn't sure what that meant in relation to my criminal investigation, but Anton was someone we could talk to. It was also another chance to evaluate how Rob Trilling dealt with the general public, one of the single most important skills a New York police officer could develop. He'd certainly impressed me so far, but I knew firsthand that not everyone had those skills.

We went to the address Walter had given us, an apartment in a six-story building. Anton's mother answered the door and told us he'd moved out a few months ago to his own apartment a few blocks away. She said her son visited her frequently at this address. That narrowed down who had called in the tip on the former Marine.

The middle-aged woman held me by the forearm and said, "My baby's not in trouble, is he? He gave so much to this country, and he's not gotten a lot back."

That was a lot of pressure. Anton's mother was the sort of sincere, hardworking person who could keep a whole neighborhood from spiraling down the drain. Young people would usually listen to a woman like this, and her tone and manner told me she'd been putting out a lot of fires in this neighborhood for many years.

I said, "We just need to ask him a few questions. I don't think you have a lot to worry about. And I promise we'll be careful and respectful."

The woman said, "You have kind eyes. I believe you. Don't let me down."

We drove two blocks east to an apartment building almost identical to the one we'd just left. Maybe it was a little more run-down. As we stepped out of the car, I had an uneasy feeling. This really could be *the guy*. It's easy to get complacent in this job, but I've learned to listen to my gut feelings.

I took a good look at the building and this time I noticed several apartments with plywood instead of windows. There were some broken bottles along the sidewalk. No one was looking out for kids around here. There was nowhere to play safely.

Walking up to the third-floor apartment, I saw that the floor of the stairwell was covered with trash. Empty Gatorade bottles; ice cream wrappers; old, soggy magazines; and fast-food containers from every possible chain.

There was no one in the third-floor hallway as we emerged from the stairs. I found the Marine's apartment just about in the middle of the hallway.

I knocked on the door.

We heard someone inside call out, "Go away."

I spoke to the door after identifying myself. "Anton? We just need to talk to you for a few minutes."

From behind the door, Anton said, "Am I under arrest?"

"No, sir."

"You have a search warrant?"

"No, sir."

"Then I stand by my earlier comment. Go away. Right now."

I was at a loss. We needed to talk to this man, but he was right: we had no legal paperwork on him. I noticed Trilling writing something on his business card. Then he leaned down and slid it under the door.

Trilling motioned me away from the door and we then stood

down the hallway silently. I didn't even ask Trilling what he had written on his card.

About forty-five seconds later, the door opened, and a tall Black man pointed at Trilling. He said, "You the one who slid the card under the door?"

Trilling nodded.

Anton said, "You can come in. Tell your buddy he has to wait."

CHAPTER 19

I REACHED OUT and held Rob Trilling's arm for a moment. I said in a low voice, "I'm not sure I want you alone in a room with that guy."

"I'll stay alert and keep him in front of me at all times. We need to talk to him, and this is the fastest, most efficient way to do it."

"I'm gonna wait right here. Make sure he doesn't lock the door. If I hear anything out of the ordinary, I'm coming through fast."

"I hope so."

Anton waited at his open door, not even trying to hear what we were saying. He kept glancing up and down the hallway. I wasn't sure what to make of that.

Finally I just nodded, and Trilling stepped into the former Marine's apartment. The door closed behind them.

Aside from being nervous about Trilling inside the apartment, I didn't mind waiting in the hallway. Although the wait was a little longer than I'd expected. I nodded hello to residents who hurried past me nervously. One young lady muttered something about the police. It didn't sound like a compliment.

After a little while, a small boy popped out of the apartment I was standing next to. He looked at me and said, "Why are the police here?"

"Why do you think I'm the police?"

"You're white and you're not collecting rent."

I had to laugh at that. I said, "I'm waiting for my friend, who's just talking to someone in another apartment."

"He talking to Anton?"

"As a matter of fact, he is."

"That won't take long. Anton don't say much."

"Neither does my friend."

The door to the Marine's apartment opened, and I was surprised to see Trilling chatting amiably with Anton. The man who'd wanted to be left alone now laughed at something Trilling said, then slapped him on the back like they were old friends.

Trilling and the Marine shook hands and Anton shot me one last suspicious look before he shut the door.

We took the stairs back to the ground floor. Trilling said, "He's not our man. He had a plane ticket showing he was out of town during the Staten Island shooting, and he was at a group therapy session the night before yesterday, when Glossner was shot in Manhattan. I'll follow up with his therapist to get the details, but I could tell this guy hasn't shot anyone in New York."

I asked, "What did you write on your business card that convinced him to open the door?"

"Just my Ranger background and the date I deployed. I also wrote down that I understood. That's what most people want to know: can you step into their shoes and understand their circumstances."

If Trilling knew that, he'd already discovered one of the most important lessons of being a good cop: understanding where people are coming from and having some compassion.

Maybe I'd been a little harsh in my initial judgment of the former Army Ranger.

CHAPTER 20

I DROVE TRILLING back to the Three-Three to pick up his car. When I pulled into the lot, I was greeted by a couple of cops I'd met over the years, as well as a few of the precinct's administrative people who knew me from past assignments.

Trilling sat silently as I shook hands and gave hugs to the people walking past the car. It was a little like dealing with a surly kid. He clearly didn't care about meeting anyone new. I tried to make introductions a couple of times but then sort of gave up when he barely acknowledged the other person.

I considered calling him out on the rude behavior. Something told me that a guy with Trilling's good manners would take being called "rude" to heart, though, so I decided to keep my mouth shut instead. I felt like we had made some progress today with our interpersonal relationship. I had to weigh the risk-to-reward ratio of calling him out on something as petty as not being friendly enough.

Once we were alone, standing between my car and his, I said, "I was very impressed with how you handled the Marine. I'm glad you're on the case and I hope you feel the same way."

As usual, I had to wait for some kind of response. Unlike what I've seen before with a lot of young cops, Trilling didn't spend any time getting puffed up with the praise and bragging about how he handled the situation. Trilling just smiled, nodded his head, and mumbled, "Thanks."

I was starting to appreciate my new partner, quirks and all.

I glanced over at the Ford Taurus he was driving. "Is that an NYPD car?"

Trilling shook his head. "The Bureau said I could keep it from the task force since I was only working here temporarily. I haven't been assigned a car by the NYPD."

That made sense. Officially, Trilling was still a patrol officer. Based on what I'd observed so far, though, it was clear to me he'd make detective pretty quickly. That was another one of the reasons I wanted him to start meeting people at different precincts. Contacts are what separate good detectives from great detectives. Knowing where to go to get information or who to ask for help. That is stuff absolutely no one can learn in the Police Academy.

I checked my phone for the time and discovered that it was earlier than I'd thought. I gazed out over the parking lot and surrounding streets. Traffic still wasn't too bad. "We got another couple of interviews we might be able to knock out quickly."

Trilling turned from his car and said, "Sorry, I have an appointment." That was all he said before he climbed into his Ford Taurus and pulled out of the lot.

I was still standing there, just staring at the rear of his car as it disappeared down the street. It wasn't often you saw a junior officer blow off a senior detective with a line like that. Especially twice in two days.

I couldn't make too big of a deal about it. There *were* a couple of interviews to knock out, but I was also supposed to meet Mary Catherine in two hours at the fertility clinic. I'd planned to give Trilling a present by cutting him loose a little early. Apparently it wasn't early enough.

I decided to swing by my apartment and act as chauffeur to my wife.

CHAPTER 21

THE APPOINTMENT AT the fertility clinic was uneventful. I listened, but beyond that they were still monitoring all aspects of Mary Catherine's treatments, I didn't really understand everything that was going on. The important thing was that Mary Catherine did. She had already scolded me for asking too many questions and making our appointments go longer. That's why I held my questions until after we were free of the confines of the upscale clinic in Midtown Manhattan.

After the appointment, Mary Catherine and I decided to sneak in a quick, private dinner since my grandfather, Seamus, was looking after the younger kids tonight. The Bennett clan is definitely an Upper West Side kind of family. Between our apartment, Holy Name School, and all of the kids' extracurricular activities, it felt like we were rarely east of Columbus Avenue.

Tonight we ventured a few blocks north of 72nd on Second

Avenue on the Upper East Side to a place called Up Thai. I liked the ambience of the narrow little restaurant. It looked more like a popular bar than anything else. I saw several plates of appetizers strung out among the young couples and professionals crammed in at the bar. Mary Catherine and I were in a corner at a tiny table just for two. It was a nice change from needing a giant table just for thirteen.

I said, "Is this what quiet feels like?"

She giggled, then said, "Is this what conversation is like?"

I smiled. It did feel like we spent a lot of time at home either giving orders or shouting for someone's attention.

Mary Catherine said, "What should we do about Fiona's struggles with algebra? Maybe a tutor?"

"I'd recommend we discuss it tomorrow when we're not on a date."

"That's a fine idea." She smiled and said, "How's your new partner?"

"He's still odd and I definitely don't want to discuss him. Either now or tomorrow." I gave her a grin to let her know I was kidding. Sort of.

Mary Catherine replied with a spectacular smile herself. "You're right, Michael. This one time I'll admit to being incorrect."

"Wrong?"

"Ha! Don't push it. I'll only admit to 'incorrect,' or maybe poor timing."

I reached across and took her hand on top of the table. We started to chat about everything. The kids, our life, our future. There really was no way to compartmentalize our lives when we shared so much.

We both sat appreciating the moment. I gazed across the small table at my wife's beautiful face. Her light hair—which was varying shades of strawberry blond—framed her cheeks and brought out the blue in her eyes.

Mary Catherine said, "We Irish have a saying about love."

I cut in. "Don't the Irish have a saying for everything?"

"As a matter of fact, we do. The first one is, never interrupt someone when they're trying to be romantic." She gave me what she liked to call her Irish glare. It felt more like a loan shark's threat.

When Mary Catherine was certain I'd learned my lesson, she continued. "Love is like a friendship caught on fire."

I just sat and thought about that. It captured us perfectly.

Mary Catherine said, "And a baby would only make the flames grow."

I guess Mary Catherine had no lingering doubts whatsoever about having a baby. There was no hesitation at all.

CHAPTER 22

ROB TRILLING DIDN'T like leaving his new partner so abruptly to handle his personal business. But he hated to miss appointments, and he'd barely made the one today.

At least now he was on his own time and not responsible for anyone but himself. It hadn't taken long for Trilling to learn that a cop, like a member of the military, rarely had time when he or she was completely "off duty."

Trilling had considered going home and getting some rest. But he knew that was a foolish idea. He was lucky to doze off for an hour a night without taking some kind of medication. And the fact that he required stronger and stronger medication was starting to scare him. Lying awake in bed wasn't the way to relieve his anxiety. But he could definitely feel the lack of sleep catching up to him.

Trilling hesitated at a curb. Maybe he was paranoid, but he

didn't really want anyone to know where he was going or what he was doing. That's why he figured it was safer to park farther away and walk to the building he needed to reach.

It was just getting dark, and he could feel a stab of hunger in his stomach. He tried to eat at places he trusted. He didn't know Midtown that well and decided he could find something healthy to eat at home later. It was tough to stay healthy *and* stay on a budget in New York City. No matter how many times his mom had warned him it would be almost impossible to live comfortably in the city, he was still surprised at the prices. A hamburger in this neighborhood could cost as much as a hardcover book. Trilling considered that his only serious vice: collecting books. His mom let him store half a dozen boxes at her house in Bozeman, Montana. He had another hundred or so books stashed around his apartment.

He started walking the four blocks to the bar he was looking for. The walk gave him a chance to think. To clear his head. Something he was able to do in Montana easily. New York City had proved to be a little more of a challenge when he wanted some space and perspective. He found that was a problem with a lot of New Yorkers: they had no perspective. They just assumed the rest of the country was good with whatever they thought was right. After living here for almost two years, he kinda understood both sides of that problem.

When Trilling first moved to New York, all he'd thought about was his time in the military. Now it felt like most of his time was spent contemplating the politics and landscape of the New York City Police Department. He was starting to warm up to his new partner, Mike Bennett. The detective was intimidating even if he didn't mean to be. The guy was an absolute legend in the department. He'd caught some of the most high-profile killers the city had ever seen.

It wasn't Bennett he was so concerned about, though. It was the police department itself. This latest move to pull him off the FBI fugitive task force had thrown Rob for a loop. He didn't mind being assigned somewhere else temporarily. But there was one fugitive case he did not intend to give up. A real dickwad named Lou Pershing had gotten under his skin.

Pershing was wanted for drug trafficking, but Trilling's interest came from interviewing the fugitive's former girlfriend: an attractive young lady who now wore a glass eye because Pershing had punched her so hard during an argument, he'd popped her real eye. Back in Montana, a guy who did something like that would've been beaten by the other citizens. Trilling had decided after meeting Pershing's poor girlfriend that he was going to bring this man to face a judge no matter what.

Pershing had been arrested several times over the years, but age and some effort on his part had changed his appearance drastically. All Trilling had to go on was a blurry photograph that the girlfriend had provided, and reports that Pershing had a tattoo on his right biceps of a Muslim being hung. Maybe it had something to do with his employment as a contractor in Iraq and Afghanistan.

Trilling found the little bar he was looking for. To say it was a hole-in-the-wall was an insult to holes everywhere. It literally looked like some sort of storage area in the corner of a building. There were no markings over the door and only a little sign on the wall that simply said, MUG AND BOTTLE. This was where Lou Pershing was supposed to hang out. Rumor had it that the bar was also where business off the grid was conducted. Its location was relatively convenient for anyone from the Bronx all the way down to SoHo. A good central spot.

Rob Trilling had been here twice before, looking for Pershing. Even for this expensive neighborhood, the mediocre drinks were wildly overpriced to make up for the small number of patrons who came through the place. Everyone paid without complaint because they needed an establishment like this that they all knew and trusted.

The place was busier than Trilling had ever seen it. Over a dozen patrons. Most of them rougher-looking, middle-aged men. Three attractive women were sitting with a man in a dark corner. A couple of men were watching a hazy TV, trying to keep up with some soccer match in Europe. A few younger men played darts, and the rest were chatting quietly at the bar or one of the few tables. And one guy in the back who could be Pershing. He had a thick, untrimmed beard and hair slicked back with some kind of product.

Trilling made it a point to not even look the man's way as he eased toward the bar. He wished there was a mirror at this dive so he could covertly look at his suspect, but there was just a bare concrete wall with no decorations behind the bar. He couldn't risk a direct confrontation here, especially in case the man wasn't Pershing.

The pretty bartender didn't fit with the place. She was chatting with a tall guy at the end of the bar and showed no interest in seeing if Trilling wanted a drink. That was fine with him. After his childhood, he barely drank more than a single beer when he went out. It had been tough in the Army, but now he just avoided invitations to go out with people from the NYPD. Easier that way.

CROSSHAIRS

As Trilling stood at the bar, something whizzed past his left arm. He looked down at the noise it made as it thunked into the bar itself. He had to squint to make sure what he was really looking at: a dart was buried deep in the mahogany.

It definitely had been intentional.

CHAPTER 23

ROB TRILLING STARED at the dart that someone had thrown dangerously close to his arm. It was a cheap green plastic dart with a brass head. The attractive bartender glanced at the dart and then at him but didn't say a word.

Trilling worked hard to maintain his composure and not snap his head around. That would give too much satisfaction to whoever had thrown it. He turned his head slightly and looked instead at a framed poster leaning against the wall. In the reflective glass of the frame, he caught a glimpse of two young men laughing at their handiwork. They were both about his age, with a little more muscle and weight than him. He knew guys like these in the military. A lot of time at the gym, the rest of the time bothering people.

Trilling turned his head slowly and smiled at the two men. They were both still smirking. He firmly gripped the end of the plastic dart with his fingertips and jerked it from the wood.

He stood there, watching the men in the poster frame while he held on to their dart. He wondered if it would interfere with their game to be missing one of their darts.

Then he heard a voice behind him say, "Little help?"

Trilling glanced over his shoulder at the two men. He didn't say a word.

The taller of the two, a guy with shaggy hair and a half-assed goatee, said, "That dart don't do you much good unless you're going to clean your fingernails with it. How about tossing it back to us."

Trilling didn't hesitate to wing the dart as hard as he could at the table in front of the two men. The man with the shaggy hair and goatee was leaning on the table and the dart landed pretty close to between his hands. That wasn't what Trilling had intended, but he'd let it ride. That was as good a throw as he was going to make. He risked a quick glance to the back of the bar to make sure the man who might be Pershing was still sitting alone. He was.

The shaggy dart player stood up straight, showing that he was a good six foot two. "Think that's funny?"

Trilling smiled and let out a laugh as he said, "Yeah, kinda funny."

"How'd you like it if I shove that dart up your ass?"

Trilling kept his broad smile. "Your mom tried to do that last night. Can't you think of anything new?"

He let the man rush him. It was almost like when he used to wrestle with his brother. The man was slow and cumbersome. With the smallest of movements, Trilling stepped aside and grabbed the man's right arm. Facing the nicest part of the lounge—the mahogany bar—Trilling guided the man's head directly into the wooden bar top. The resulting thud was the only sound from the encounter.

Trilling felt the man's legs go weak and shoved him so that he landed on a stool in a dazed lump.

Now he gave a hard stare at the man who'd been playing darts with the groggy one.

The second man lifted his hands and backed away to show that he wanted nothing to do with this.

Trilling scanned the bar one more time to make sure his potential fugitive hadn't walked out. Clearly no one here cared if there was a fight going on or if a semiconscious man was sitting on a stool. Only a few people even looked up.

Trilling's eyes darted to the rear of the bar.

The table where his suspect had been sitting was empty.

CHAPTER 24

IT WAS A nice surprise when Mary Catherine and I got home to find that all the kids had already eaten and were just finishing up the dishes. I'd like to think my grandfather had something to do with it, but I knew Ricky would have done the cooking, while Seamus was sitting at the end of our long dining table, teaching the twins which hands would win in poker.

My grandfather may look like a kindly old priest, and he is, but he sowed a lot of oats before taking his late-in-life vows.

I was still feeling great after a wonderful meal with my wife. My resilient and understanding wife. The one who wanted to have a meeting to discuss the possibility of bringing a new baby into the family. God, I hoped she was right about a family meeting.

I spent a few minutes chatting with my grandfather, which drew the attention of a couple more of the kids.

Seamus said, "What an easy task it is to babysit these angels."

I cocked my head. "Okay, that doesn't sound like you. What's wrong?"

"Nothing, my boy."

"I can make someone squeal on you if I have to."

"Are you always a cop?"

"Cop, parent—not that different. Now spill."

My grandfather leaned in a little closer. "Bridget may have caught me finishing off your cabernet."

"Not the last bottle of the 2019 Caymus."

"That's just it, boyo. I didn't realize it was the last bottle until it was gone and I couldn't find any more." He gave me a smile like a kid who'd been caught in a fib. I just laughed. No one could get angry at an elderly priest who was still mischievous.

When Mary Catherine and I decided we were ready for the family meeting, six of the kids were already in the dining room: the two oldest, Juliana and Brian, who were both starting to find their way in the world as young adults but still living at home for the moment, thank goodness; Eddie and Trent, our younger boys; and Bridget and Fiona, the twins.

I had to call in Shawna and Chrissy, finishing their chores in the kitchen, and Ricky, playing on his phone in his bedroom.

I started counting heads and got to nine, but before I could ask where Jane was, the front door burst open and she rushed in, apologizing for missing dinner.

Mary Catherine said, "Where were you? Holy Name has been closed for hours."

Jane looked at Mary Catherine, then at me. "I said I was sorry. I'm working on a project and have to spend some time at Butler Library up on the Columbia campus. Sister Mary Margaret worked it out so I have a Columbia ID and everything so I can use the library."

I said, "What's the project about?"

A sly smile spread across Jane's even features. Then she said, "Can I keep it a surprise? I think you'll like it."

How could a father deny a request like that? Plus, she was using her sweet tone, not her disillusioned teenager tone. It was enough to convince me.

I turned to the room and raised my voice in a mock shout, saying, "We're going to have a family meeting!"

The only one who seemed happy about that was Chrissy. "Do I get to vote?"

I said, "Everyone gets to vote. Except, as always, my vote and Mary Catherine's count as two each." That earned a few groans and comments from the older kids, who started to make excuses and wander off.

Without confronting anyone individually, Mary Catherine clapped her hands one time. Everyone froze like we were in a *Twilight Zone* episode. In reality, it was just years of conditioning: when the kids heard Mary Catherine give that single hard clap, they knew they'd better listen.

Mary Catherine said, "Your father doesn't ask that much of you. One meeting to clear something up will help us all. Everyone take a seat at the table."

I stood there dumbfounded as, without another word, each child sat down around our long dining room table. Mary Catherine hadn't raised her voice. She hadn't even issued a threat. That was power. There's no way I could've done that.

I took a breath and started telling the kids about our appointments with the fertility clinic, what the doctors had told us, and that we hoped Mary Catherine might soon be pregnant. I finished by saying, "We were hoping to get your honest reactions to this news."

There was dead silence.

My heart sank.

Then Brian started to clap. The others all joined in. Shawna and Eddie added a couple of shouts and hoots. It was a shower of applause.

Juliana was the first to speak. She looked at Mary Catherine and said, "I was worried you were sick. I knew you were going to a doctor, and you seemed so tired. This is great news."

I let out my breath. Juliana was the oldest and remembered the early days of Maeve's, my first wife's, cancer diagnosis. I should've been more aware of that.

That opened the floodgates. The twins jumped up from each side and hugged Mary Catherine. Suddenly our dining room echoed with raised voices and squeals of surprise.

Then I noticed one kid wasn't joining in. At the middle of one side of the table, sitting quietly and looking like she was about to cry, was my youngest, Chrissy. The baby of the family.

I said loud enough to make everyone calm down, "Chrissy, tell me the truth. How do you feel about this?" I was anxious about her reply. One unhappy kid could sour this whole endeavor.

Chrissy's head snapped up like she hadn't been paying attention. She said, "I just, I mean, I…" She started to cry and tried to wipe her eyes on the sleeves of her blouse.

I felt disappointment lurch through me. Mary Catherine's smile fell right off her face.

Then, through her tears, Chrissy wailed, "I'm so happy I can't stop crying. I'll finally have a little brother or sister! This is the best day of my life."

I was correct; we had raised these kids the right way. Next thing I knew we were in a giant hug around Mary Catherine.

CHAPTER 25

ROB TRILLING DIDN'T want to make it obvious that he'd been watching the man in the corner. He knew the guy hadn't gone out the front door, so he must've slipped out the back. Trilling didn't burst through the back door and race into the alley looking for him. Instead, he eased away from the semiconscious man on the stool and casually strolled toward the rear door.

Out of sight of the bar patrons, though, Trilling picked up the pace, sprinting down the alley and onto the street. He'd like to say it was his keen instincts that led him to turn a corner and catch sight of the man he thought might be Lou Pershing, but that wasn't true. It was just luck. The same way luck could determine who survived the battlefield.

The suspect walked with a determined pace, but Trilling had no problem staying half a block back. He had to remind himself he was on his own and couldn't call in help. All he had to do was see the disgusting tattoo on the man's right biceps and he'd have his best fugitive arrest.

Trilling followed the man onto the 6 train, but almost lost him when he got out of the subway at 116th Street. East Harlem was an unfamiliar neighborhood for Trilling. The crowds in Midtown made it easy to blend in, but here there wasn't nearly as much foot traffic, and he found it much more difficult to stay unnoticed.

Trilling watched as the suspect met a wiry Latino man. The Latino man introduced the suspect to a young woman. She looked *really* young. Dressed in knee-high boots and a skirt too short for the cool temperatures.

No matter what happened, Trilling decided he couldn't ignore this. He watched as the Latino man walked away and the suspect and woman continued north to a questionable-looking building that resembled an old-time SRO — single-room occupancy. Trilling had heard places like this were all over the city thirty years ago but rare now. The nine-story building looked run-down and had no style. Trash blown from the street gathered around a few dead bushes at the entrance.

Trilling raced half a block just as the suspect and the young woman entered an elevator. He flew up the stairs, jumping out of the stairwell at each floor to see if the elevator had stopped there. He kept pushing himself to the next floor. All the way to nine.

Trilling burst through the stairwell door in time to see the suspect step into a room twenty feet away from the elevator. He took a breath and sprinted to the closing door. He blocked it from locking.

There was no turning back now.

The man turned as Trilling pushed completely into the room.

Instantly Trilling realized how formidable the suspect was up close. He stood a little over six feet and had to have forty pounds of muscle on Trilling.

"What the hell?" the man said in a gravelly voice, reaching down with his right hand and grabbing a pistol from his beltline. He had it out and aimed at Trilling's nose in an instant. Trilling didn't think he had ever seen someone draw a pistol so quickly.

There was at least six feet between them now and Trilling knew he couldn't act without taking a .380 slug in the face.

He stayed in place and raised his hands slightly. Then he looked past the suspect to the frightened girl in a corner of the room. He said in an even voice, "You okay, miss?"

The young woman was obviously flustered but managed to nod. She wore a stylish knit cap, and her light-brown hair framed a pretty face.

Trilling knew he needed the suspect to move closer to him if he had any chance of disarming him.

The man was smarter than that and didn't move. He said, "You got three seconds to tell me who you are and what you want."

"Otherwise you'll shoot me?"

"We got a genius on our hands."

He still didn't move any closer.

The man said, "Who the hell are you?"

"My ID is in my front pocket. Do you want me to reach for it or do you want to take it? I don't want to risk you getting nervous with that gun." He could see the man weighing the pros and cons of each option.

Trilling had no intention of telling the man who he was. He just needed him to get about three feet closer.

CHAPTER 26

ROB TRILLING STOOD with his hands raised, ignoring the SIG Sauer P230 .380-caliber pistol and instead looking closely at his suspect. Based on the blurry photo he'd been given, he really couldn't tell if this was Lou Pershing or not. The guy seemed to be a little better built than any of the descriptions of Lou Pershing, but the bushy beard was the biggest impediment to identifying him.

Trilling wondered briefly if the man would show him his right biceps if he asked nicely. That was the most efficient way to handle this situation.

The suspect growled, "Do you have any idea who I am?"

Trilling kept a positive attitude. "Yes. Yes, I have an idea that you're Lou Pershing."

"Who?" The man stepped closer.

That was helpful, but Trilling wished the suspect would come another foot closer. He decided to make use of his training both from the Army and the NYPD. He wanted the man distracted. Thinking about something other than shooting him. Trilling said, "Are you saying you're not Lou Pershing?"

The man shook his head and started to say, "I'm not—"

As soon as he started speaking, Trilling lunged forward, slapping the pistol away, then pivoted and swept the man's legs with his right leg. The bigger man seemed to levitate for a moment then hit the floor with a tremendous thud.

By chance, the man's arm swung past Trilling's face. A metal snap on the cuff of the jacket caught Trilling under his eye, causing a moment of pain. But it was outweighed by the satisfaction Trilling felt as he casually leaned across the man and snatched the pistol, disarming him. He dropped the magazine, pulled the slide of the pistol, and ejected a single hollow-point .380 bullet. It made almost no sound when it hit the thin carpet.

Trilling looked up at the girl again and said, "It's okay. I'm not going to hurt you or anyone else. I just need to check something with this man."

The girl nervously nodded. Her right hand trembled.

He looked back down at the man on the floor. He said in a casual tone, "I need to get a look at your right arm. Slip off your jacket?"

The man looked up at him and grunted. "I ain't taking off nothing."

Trilling shrugged and said, "Suit yourself." He reached into the front pocket of his Wrangler jeans and pulled out the Gerber pocketknife he'd carried with him since he was twelve. Including his time in Afghanistan. He flicked the three-inch blade open with his right thumb.

The suspect's eyes were wide with terror. He didn't say anything. A slight mewling sound creeped out of his throat.

Trilling wasted no time stabbing the knife near the man's right shoulder. With two quick movements, he severed the sleeve without leaving a scratch on the man's arm. He yanked the sleeve off and stared at the man's biceps, partially covered by a T-shirt.

Trilling jerked the sleeve of the T-shirt all the way up even though he now knew he wasn't going to see anything. He stared at the man's arm, which had no tattoo at all. In frustration, he rolled the man to one side and pulled out a wallet from his rear pocket. He checked the man's ID. Albert Craig from Jersey City. *Shit.*

Trilling stepped away from the man on the carpet. His hand came up and touched his cheek under his eye where the man's jacket had struck him. It was a little tender but nothing serious. Then he turned his attention to the girl, now sitting in the single chair.

Trilling said, "How old are you?"

"Twenty-two."

Trilling gave her a good look. The way he'd looked at his sister when he'd catch her coming in late and she'd given some lame excuse.

Without further prompting, the young woman said, "Eighteen."

"Is this meeting consensual?"

The girl said, "What does that mean?"

"You agreed to meet this man voluntarily?"

This time she nodded. "Yeah, for two hundred bucks."

The man on the carpet said, "You going to tell me what the hell is going on?"

"Sorry, building security. I'm going to take your gun and you can get it back from the doorman when you leave. You might not want to mention this to anyone since you're carrying an unlawful firearm within the city limits."

The man nodded but didn't say anything.

Trilling took the elevator to the lobby. It was still empty as he calmly ambled through, disassembling the pistol in his hands as he walked. He dropped the slide into a garbage can on the sidewalk. He dropped the main body of the pistol down a storm drain and kept walking.

He'd find another way to locate Lou Pershing. He had the name of a Pershing associate who might even be a decent suspect in their sniper case.

CHAPTER 27

I GOT INTO the office early again. As soon as I walked through the door, I realized it still wasn't quite early enough. The first thing I heard was Walter Jackson's deep voice and then a chuckle. I knew exactly who was in there talking to him this morning.

I stepped into Walter's open doorway and said to him and Rob Trilling, "I hope you two are doing something constructive this early in the morning."

Walter said, "You mean in addition to sharing puns and jokes?"

"I'm sure they're hysterical."

Walter was grinning like a little kid. He looked over at Trilling and said, "Go ahead, tell him yours."

"It doesn't look like he's in the mood for puns, Walter."

Walter didn't miss a beat. He looked at me and said, "I have a friend who was raised in England. Over there, they call elevators lifts. We, of course, call them elevators. I guess we were just raised differently."

I'll admit it was cute. I'll also admit it took me a moment to get it. I gave him a pity smile and hoped to move on to business.

Walter, now looking deflated at my response, said, "Rob gave me a potential suspect's name and I've been seeing what we can come up with. Mostly making connections through public records and rental agreements. I'm waiting for confirmation on a couple of things."

I turned to Trilling and paused. There was a tiny cut on his left cheek and his eye was slightly swollen. It almost looked like he had a black eye. I said, "Did you get the shiner at your appointment yesterday?"

Trilling absently reached up and touched his cheek. He said, "I was trying to hang a bookshelf in my apartment. It came loose and smacked me in the face. Nothing to worry about. I'm fine."

He let the whole dig I gave him about his appointment slide.

I decided to let it go. Instead, I said, "Where'd you get the name?"

"He's an associate of a fugitive I was looking for at the FBI. They both are former military and worked for contractors in Afghanistan. The name I have is William Hackford. On some promotional bio he created for their company, Hackford mentioned that he was sniper certified. I'm not sure who certified him or if it's legit, but I thought it was worth a try."

"You're not just looking for a way to find your FBI fugitive, are you?"

I'd been teasing, but for a minute I thought Trilling wasn't going to answer. Then he said, "It wouldn't be a bad thing if we caught the fugitive, Lou Pershing, too. I thought this guy might be a decent interview for us."

That was a good answer. It's hard to argue with a guy who's doing things for the right reasons. It made me think of the Army captain he'd introduced me to at West Point. Captain Hawks had told me Trilling stayed on mission no matter what. Not a bad thing.

Walter started printing out a packet of information for us. He said, "This Hackford guy's got a decent criminal history. Three assaults and one charge of carrying a concealed weapon. The victims dropped the charges in every case. I know some of the military contractor companies will overlook a criminal history if it gets them a motivated worker.

"And he's been ticketed twice in the last month right here in the city. I don't see a home address or even a contact phone number for him, but looks like his name is on the lease to a warehouse up in the Bronx." He handed a folder across to Trilling. "Here's everything I have as well as a Google satellite photo of the warehouse."

I felt a surge of excitement at a new lead. It was hard to tell if Trilling was excited or not, but he jumped up from the chair and moved pretty quickly.

CHAPTER 28

WE TOOK MY Impala north all the way to the New York Botanical Garden. I didn't spend a lot of time in Bronx Park near the Rose Hill campus of Fordham University and was surprised how unfamiliar the area looked to me. Trilling kept a sharp eye out and found the string of older warehouses on a short block at the very north end of the Bronx. None of the warehouses was more than three stories tall, and it didn't look like they were being used much nowadays.

I took a moment to survey the street as we sat in the car. A good cop should know who might be around. I noticed Trilling doing the same thing—although I got the impression he was looking for bad guys more than he was for innocent bystanders we potentially needed to get out of the way. Either way, there was no one around.

At Hackford's warehouse, we nonchalantly took the outside

stairway to the main door. It had to open onto the second floor. I tried the door, which was locked. The two windows in the front had been frosted over from the inside. We found an alley that cut behind the warehouses and tried the rear door at the top of a rickety wooden staircase. It was also locked.

Trilling put his ear to the door and, after thirty seconds, turned to me and said, "I hear noise. There're people inside."

"Think we can use a ruse to convince them to let us inside?"

"I'll bet you lunch they won't even answer the door if we knock."

I didn't give him a chance to back out of the bet. I knocked politely and we waited. Then I pounded on the door with my fist. Still nothing. I turned to Trilling and said, "What d'you think?"

Trilling said, "I don't think you're hitting the door hard enough."

I stepped to the side and said, "Be my guest."

Trilling didn't say a word as he stepped in front of the door. Then, in one smooth motion, he lifted his right leg and kicked the door right next to the handle and dead bolt.

The door flew open, smashing into a wall behind it. Trilling slipped inside before I could say anything. I followed my partner, half expecting to be confronted by an outraged business owner. Instead, there was no one near us. I could hear faint noises coming from another room.

We carefully walked next to the wall toward where we heard noise. When we came to an open door, we saw a catwalk above a main floor that trucks must use to load whatever was held in the warehouse.

Before we stepped through the door, Trilling tapped me on the shoulder and pointed to the far corner of the main warehouse room. There were four or five women working near some tables, all wearing what looked like white surgical clothes. Their faces were covered with N95 masks, but dark hair spilled out and down their backs.

The floor of the warehouse was covered with row after row of heavy, empty shelves. There was a line of cots with blankets on them against the far wall. There was also a refrigerator and microwave by a door. The only activity was in the far corner.

I ducked back behind the wall and leaned in close to Trilling. "I don't see William Hackford. I don't even see any men in that group."

"But you see the drug operation, right?"

"I see what *looks* like five women processing drugs. But if I got on the stand and said that, without going down to check, a defense attorney would rip me in half. That's after we were arrested ourselves for B and E after explaining how we entered without authority."

Trilling nodded, then said, "They got a lot of room here for not much activity. You think they plan to expand?"

"I think the whole idea of this warehouse is that they don't have to worry about noise or anyone paying attention to what's going on here."

Trilling looked over my shoulder. He nudged me to step out onto the walkway. We crept along together, gathering a better view of the operation with every step.

Then I heard a gunshot.

CHAPTER 29

I'D LIKE TO claim it was my police training or my lightning-fast reflexes that saved me from getting shot. The truth is, my new partner, whom I didn't completely trust yet, grabbed me by the arm and jerked me flat onto the catwalk.

I was panting as we hit the wooden walkway. Now I was lying on my belly alongside Rob Trilling. The young former Ranger showed no stress or anxiety. He could have been playing a game with his buddies.

I said, "What the hell? That asshole didn't even offer a warning. Whatever they're doing in the corner is a big deal."

I could just see the far corner of the warehouse floor. The women who'd been working at the tables were now all cowering in the makeshift kitchen. I couldn't see the shooter on the floor of the warehouse. At least not without exposing my head.

I turned back to Trilling as I fumbled for my phone to call for help. Trilling was still as calm as if he were waiting in line. He said, "I'm going to flank him." He was up and moving before I could tell him to sit still and wait for backup.

I scooted back from the edge of the catwalk with my phone in hand. I took a couple of breaths to slow down my heartbeat and tried to *remember* some training that might save my life.

When the dispatcher picked up, I kept my voice low so as not to attract the shooter. In a harsh whisper, I identified myself by name and ID number. "We are in a warehouse in the Bronx and taking fire from an unknown assailant." It took me a moment to recall the address and I barked it out in my hushed voice.

The dispatcher was really sharp, and I heard her already clearing the air to call out, "Officer needs assistance."

Then another bullet ripped through the walkway, about three inches from my face. I sprang to my feet but couldn't see the shooter below me. I knew I had to move. Every footstep felt like a signal of where to aim. I slid to a stop behind some crates piled on the catwalk. I hoped that whatever was in them was enough to stop a bullet.

At least now I could see the entire floor of the warehouse. I finally caught a glimpse of the shooter as he darted from underneath the catwalk and lost himself in some shelving in the middle of the floor.

Then I noticed Trilling two rows away from the shooter. He looked up at me and I pointed past him and held up two fingers to tell him where the shooter was. I saw Trilling crouch down, trying to look under the shelves to locate the shooter.

Then Trilling stood up and put his back to the shelving unit next to him. He started to push. He squatted lower and braced his back against the lowest shelf as he pushed with his legs.

It took me a moment to realize what he intended. I didn't think it was a good idea. The wall of shelves he was pushing tipped dangerously away from Trilling. Then the whole thing tumbled into the next wall of shelves, which immediately started knocking the shelves into the next row.

The noise was unbelievable. It sounded like a freight train had flipped in my living room. I raced to the first ladder coming down from the catwalk to the warehouse floor. I landed and scanned the area in front of me. There was dust in the air as thick as fog.

As I ran toward the toppled shelves, Trilling stepped out of the rubble, holding a man in an arm bar.

Trilling casually said, "Can you collect his pistol? It's about twenty feet down the aisle."

CHAPTER 30

TRILLING AND I turned the prisoner and the pistol over to detectives from the local precinct. The Narcotics guys couldn't believe they had just made a seizure of sixteen kilograms of heroin right at the edge of the Bronx.

For as much noise and damage as we'd caused inside the warehouse, it had had no effect whatsoever outside the four walls. No one had heard the gunshots or the deafening sound of the shelves crashing, or had seen anything unusual.

That was exactly why William Hackford had rented this place. There was no one around to see or hear anything. God knows how much heroin had run through it in the eight months Hackford had leased it.

I looked over at Trilling, who was trying to comfort the five women who'd been working with the heroin. They were all Pakistani and had been smuggled into the US by associates of

Hackford. The women looked amazed that a police officer could be so friendly.

I'd learned that three of them spoke broken English and two could understand basic phrases. They all seemed to be in their twenties. I noticed they all had pronounced forearms, which I assumed had something to do with the work they had been completing every day for the last eight months.

Our suspect was already off the premises. When Trilling brought him out of the rubble of the shelves, I handcuffed the man. Then I said, "NYPD, you're under arrest." I read him his rights immediately and then told him, "You get extra credit if you cooperate with us right now."

The smirk he gave was all I needed. I'd never talk to this asshole again. I didn't care if he had evidence that would bring down the Gambino crime family. That one look told me he assumed he'd be getting out quickly. That someone was going to come up with a boatload of money to get him out on bond, then out of the country. At least that's how I took it.

Some Homeland Security agents showed up for the women. Trilling intercepted them and said, "None of these women are under arrest. They were here under duress."

A tall Black agent, about forty, nodded and said, "That's how I understood it when we got the call."

"So you won't treat them like prisoners?"

"Technically, they're not free to go, so they *are* prisoners."

That seemed to get to Trilling. He looked at me and wiped his face with his bare hand.

Trilling said, "Where will you house them?"

"What are you, writing a book?" The agent turned to his partner and said, "How long till the van gets here?"

Trilling looked like he was getting desperate. "Do they get to see a judge?"

"They sure do. Depends on the roster, but probably not tomorrow—maybe the next morning, first thing, at the annex near the federal building where they hold immigration hearings. The hearings are open to the public."

Trilling rushed back to the women and explained what was going on and that everything would be okay.

Not only did I appreciate that my new partner had saved my life but I also appreciated how he was dealing with these poor women.

Maybe it was time to *show* my appreciation for his talents and attitude.

CHAPTER 31

IT TOOK SOME effort to convince Rob Trilling to come to my apartment for dinner. I had to assure him several times that it would be no bother for anyone in the family. He still seemed unsure, so I told him to do it as a favor to me. Not that he owed me any favors. In fact, he had just kept me from catching a 9mm slug in the head. If anyone owed favors, it was me.

We had a brief conversation before reaching the apartment. I told him, "I've got sort of a big family. Just to let you know."

"Walter said you had a lot of kids."

I smiled. "No specific number?"

"Nope."

"Good. Care to make a guess?"

As always, Rob Trilling looked thoughtful before he answered. Then he said, "Six?"

"Not a bad guess." I didn't commit to anything besides that. I don't often get the chance, but I love to surprise people with the sheer size of my immediate family.

On the way to the apartment, Trilling insisted we stop so he could buy flowers for Mary Catherine and a bottle of wine. He took my suggestion and picked up a bottle of Wirra Wirra Catapult shiraz. Seamus loved the Australian wine, and it wouldn't break Trilling financially.

Once in the elevator to our apartment, Trilling turned to me with a very serious look on his face. "I'm sorry, I have to ask."

"Ask what?"

"How do you live in a building like this? Does your family come from a lot of money?"

I laughed out loud at that. "The quick story is that my first wife, who died of cancer, inherited the apartment from an elderly man she used to take care of who had no other family. He loved her like she was a daughter. He even set up a trust to pay the taxes. Trust me, that's crucial — my entire NYPD salary might not cover the taxes on this place." Obviously the answer satisfied Trilling's curiosity. I had to add, "Why, were you worried I was on the take?"

Trilling shook his head. "That never crossed my mind. Too many people have told me what a great cop you are. You don't get a reputation like that if there was ever any suspicion about your honesty."

It was the closest he'd ever come to giving me a compliment, so I took it with a satisfied smile.

When I finally opened the door to our apartment, the shock on Trilling's face was priceless. Mary Catherine stood with nine of the kids, looking like they were in a receiving line for a wedding. Only Jane was missing, I assumed off working on her secret project. My grandfather, wearing his tab-collar priest shirt, stood next to Mary Catherine, grinning.

Trilling introduced himself first to the crowd, then more formally to Mary Catherine. He just stared at everyone for a moment, trying to take it all in.

For her part, Mary Catherine almost swooned at the beautiful flowers and wine that my handsome young partner presented to her.

Trilling made it a point to shake hands with each of the children. I noticed Juliana lingered and chatted for a moment. She clearly approved of my new partner. Maybe I hadn't realized Trilling wasn't that much older than her.

It's tough to think of your kids becoming adults right before your eyes. Juliana had been doing an internship at Holy Name for a sociology class she was taking at City College. It just felt like she was still at the family school.

Then Trilling found himself face-to-face with my grandfather. Seamus made a show out of sizing up Trilling. The young officer fixed his gaze on my grandfather's collar.

Seamus grinned at the attention. He said, "Are you a man of faith, Rob?"

"Yes, sir. I even attended the first Methodist grade school in Bozeman."

"So you're not a Catholic?"

"No, sir." Trilling paused and finally worked up the nerve to say, "I'm a little confused. If you're Detec…I mean Mike's grandfather, how can you be a Catholic priest?"

I waited for the answer, hoping Seamus didn't lay it on too thick. I was still cultivating this shy young man. Maybe bringing him here to the entire brood was a mistake. My family is a lot to take in.

My grandfather smiled, clapped Trilling on the shoulder, and said, "I entered the priesthood quite late in life."

"May I ask what you did first?"

"I owned a bar."

"Really?"

Seamus put on a serious face, placed his right hand in the air, and said, "Swear to God."

Both men started to laugh at that.

CHAPTER 32

WE WAITED FOR Jane, who burst through the door just as Ricky's pot roast was ready to come out of the oven. Ricky has a talent for mixing cheap red wine, onion soup mix, and Campbell's mushroom soup in a way that would make even vegans want to dig into the meat. It's phenomenal.

Rob Trilling seemed comfortable at the table, though that might've been because Juliana made it a point to sit right next to him. I noticed them speaking quietly whenever they had a chance.

My grandfather opened with a prayer, as usual. "Dear God in heaven, thank you for the many blessings you've given us and for our special guest tonight. Although not a Catholic, he assures me he is a man of faith." The old priest had an impish grin.

Trilling smiled at the comment as well. Maybe he wasn't as stiff-necked as I'd thought.

Mary Catherine asked him a series of casual questions that any CIA interrogator would have envied. I think as soon as she saw Juliana sitting next to him, she wanted to find out everything she could about Rob Trilling.

Mary Catherine was a master. She kept it flowing and never got him overwhelmed. I learned more about the young man in three minutes than I had in the days we'd been working together.

After the initial round of questions, Mary Catherine moved into follow-ups. "How on earth did you end up in New York City from Bozeman, Montana?"

"I spent my first eighteen years in Montana. Then after four years in the Army, I was looking for a change. Plus, my sister and her kids don't live too far away—they're about an hour or two from here, up in Putnam County in a little town called Ludingtonville." He gave the group a charming smile and said, "I used to think Bozeman was a big city."

Mary Catherine asked, "What do you do when you're not slaving away for the NYPD?"

"That's another reason I moved here. I'm finishing up my degree using the GI Bill and a couple of grants that Columbia got to help veterans with their education."

I broke in. "You're taking classes at Columbia University?"

"So far, just one class a semester, except last spring when I took two."

Jane said, "I just came from Butler Library at Columbia." She leaned forward as if in a courtroom. "How does a Columbia student get a black eye?"

I liked how she sounded like a prosecutor about to spring a trap.

Trilling took a moment, as usual. "I was trying to put one of my heavier textbooks on a high shelf and it slipped out of my hand and hit me in the face."

I noted that his excuse for the black eye had changed from when I asked him about it this morning. Clearly he didn't want to talk about how he came by the injury. On the bright side, he was not a particularly good liar. That is a trait I appreciate in people. Good liars can manipulate you and lead you anywhere. Bad liars are usually basically honest people.

Trilling turned to Ricky and said, "This is the best pot roast I've ever had in my life. And our beef in Montana was as fresh as it could be."

Ricky beamed at the recognition from an outsider.

My grandfather said, "How do you like working for the NYPD?"

Trilling hesitated.

I noted it and assured him, "Everything said at this dinner table stays at this dinner table." I looked around at everyone's heads nodding.

Trilling sat up straight and said, "I'm still adjusting. I thought it would be a lot more like the military. Turns out, every unit has a different agenda and different ways of completing that agenda. I like the work. I like continuing my public service. I'm still getting used to the politics."

Mary Catherine said, "Michael says you've been a great help on this case. At least the department is using your military experience."

"I wasn't a sniper in the Army. We practiced with rifles a lot, but like I've been telling Mike, there's a huge difference between a military sniper and someone who can shoot well."

"That's saying something, from a guy who can shoot *very*

well," I said. The conversation moved on from putting Trilling on the spot, and dinner was capped with ice cream for dessert.

I was surprised Trilling was willing to stay after dinner. He played video games with the boys for a few minutes, then continued to chat quietly with Juliana. It reinforced how young he actually was. He was much more comfortable with my kids than with me.

But I continued to gain appreciation for this quiet young man.

CHAPTER 33

I STROLLED INTO the Manhattan North Homicide office the next morning feeling pretty good. Rob Trilling had been a huge hit at dinner. I also felt like I understood the young man much better. Now all we had to do was catch some nut who could shoot long-distance, whom no one had ever seen, and who seemingly chose his victims at random. And we had no leads. Easy.

Harry Grissom was in early this morning as well. I could hear him talking to someone in his office. I was afraid the person might be from One Police Plaza, so I tried to scoot past the lieutenant's door without saying good morning. It didn't work. I heard Harry say, "Mike, come on in here for a second."

When I stepped through the door into Harry's office and saw who was sitting in the chair opposite his desk, I'll admit I was surprised to the point of being shocked. Lois Frang from the *Brooklyn Democrat* was chatting pleasantly with my boss.

Harry said, "Why didn't you ever introduce me to this lovely woman?"

Lois smiled. She had me and she knew it.

Harry said, "You know, she's the one who came up with the nickname 'the Longshot Killer.'"

"Really?"

I hadn't seen this kind of glow around Harry since the last time the Jets made the playoffs. That had been a while ago. He said, "Anything new we can give her?" He turned his head to look at Lois.

I caught Lois's satisfied expression. The reporter had Harry eating out of her hand.

I said, "Not a lot of leads. We're working on it."

Now Lois said, "C'mon, Bennett, at least give me something I can write about."

"I don't know what to tell you but the truth. We really don't have a lot of good leads. It's not particularly exciting and probably doesn't play well in a newspaper column. But that's exactly what's going on."

Lois said, "I tried speaking to some of the victims' families. But no one is talking. At least not to me. The second victim, Thomas Bannon, the fireman from Staten Island?"

I nodded, interested in hearing what she had to say.

"His family is a real piece of work. A couple of them are firemen too. Classic close-knit Irish Catholic city workers. And they don't like outsiders coming into their neighborhoods."

I said, barely concealing my grin, "I'm not sure I can relate to a close-knit Irish Catholic city worker and his family." I did like Lois's insight on the second victim's family. By coincidence, that's where I was heading today. I wanted to talk to the firefighter's widow and see if I could find out any details from her that other detectives had missed.

Harry's glare told me my time bantering with the reporter was over.

I took that opportunity to head in to speak with Walter Jackson. I could see a light on in his office and wondered if he had anything new for us to look at since yesterday. When I knocked on his door, I found the big man involved in a detailed search of records for one of the other detectives. Even so, Walter handed me a folder with all the information on the firefighter's family that I'd asked for yesterday.

He also passed along a new lead on a woman who supposedly worked out at a gym in the Bronx every day around 2 p.m. The woman, Wendy Robinson, was a former Army sergeant who had been part of a special program bringing women into the ranks of snipers. Someone had called in a tip about her and how she'd occasionally brag about shots she'd taken in Afghanistan. The caller said the way she talked about shooting people made them uncomfortable.

I took the folder. It was as good as any lead we had now.

CHAPTER 34

I SAT AT my desk, looking through the folder Walter Jackson had given me and feeling a little uneasy because Lois Frang was still sitting in Harry Grissom's office. Every couple of minutes I heard Harry's cackle. That was not common.

Rob Trilling walked in carrying coffee and donuts for the entire squad. That's a classy move that everyone remembers. After setting down the donuts and coffee, Trilling marched directly to my desk and sat in the chair across from me. He had a serious look on his face.

I said, "When you said you were going to appointments, I didn't realize you were taking a class at Columbia."

"That wasn't the appointments. My class is at night."

That was it. He offered no further explanation about his appointments and why he left in the middle of the day. I decided it was something I'd deal with if it became more of a problem. I was more concerned about the dour expression on Trilling's face.

I said, "What's wrong?"

"That obvious?"

"Even for you who's a sourpuss, as my grandfather likes to say."

Trilling hesitated, then said, "I need to be up-front with you, but I don't want to get anyone in trouble."

I said slowly, "I'm listening."

"Juliana texted me this morning and asked if I wanted to hang out sometime in the next week or two."

It took a moment to digest what he'd just said. My voice was louder than I'd intended when I blurted out, "My Juliana?"

Trilling nodded.

"What did you tell her?"

"Nothing. I haven't replied yet. I thought I should discuss it with you first. Even if she is legally an adult, I'd never come between a father and a daughter."

"I appreciate that, but I'm not crazy about my daughter dating a cop. Though you're right, I try not to dictate to her or Brian what they have to do. They're both old enough and smart enough to make their own decisions."

Trilling thought about that. Then he said, "I'll decline her invitation. That way you don't have to seem like the bad guy. It also avoids any stress in your family."

"I appreciate your mature approach."

"I appreciated you inviting me into your home last night. Your family is so different from mine. I only have one brother, one sister, my mother, and my grandfather."

I noticed he didn't mention his father at all.

Trilling said, "I especially enjoyed speaking with your grandfather. My grandfather raised me. He had a little car lot in Boze-man. But he always had time for my brother, sister, and me. Now he kind of splits time between my sister's house and my mother's house. He's still in good shape physically at seventy-two, but he's been diagnosed with early onset dementia. He has good days and bad. It's scary."

I understood. I worried about my grandfather every day. Every grunt or sigh from him set me on edge because I was afraid it was the start of some terminal ailment. But I couldn't imagine Seamus ever losing that sharp mind of his. That would just kill me.

I tried to cheer up my new partner. I put on a smile, leaned over, slapped him on the shoulder, and said, "You ready to go to a resort?"

"What do you mean? Where is there a resort?"

"Staten Island, my boy. It's an island, so it's kind of like a resort. And we've got people to talk to."

CHAPTER 35

LOUISE BANNON, WIDOW of the sniper's second victim, Thomas Bannon, lived in a nice neighborhood, Dongon Hills, off Hylan Boulevard on Staten Island. The GPS said traffic was bad, even for New York, so we came down through Brooklyn and took the Verrazzano-Narrows Bridge over to the island.

The Bannon house was a cute 1960s two-story. The tricycle turned on its side in the front yard immediately broke my heart. Even with the sun shining and the temperatures comfortable, I felt gloomy when Rob Trilling and I walked up to the house.

As I knocked on the wooden door, I noticed that someone spent a lot of time on the porch. There were stacks of magazines next to a comfortable rocker and a little heater tucked in the corner.

A woman in her late thirties with frizzy brown hair came to the door. A cute toddler and a little girl about five years old stood behind the woman, staring out at us.

I held up my badge and identified myself and Trilling. Louise Bannon didn't say anything for a few seconds, then finally said, "Do you have news on Tommy's killer?"

"No, ma'am. We're working the case and just wanted to talk with you about any details we might've missed."

"You're not even the original detectives. I haven't heard shit in three weeks." She opened the door and shook her head, muttering something about the NYPD.

I knew this wasn't the time to make apologies or excuses. Everything would be forgiven if we could find the killer. To do that we had to ask questions, and I needed her to be open to answering questions. So I kept my yap shut.

After the rough start, we chatted with Louise to get background on her husband. I didn't really learn anything new. He'd been with the FDNY for twenty-one years. He had numerous commendations and was well thought of generally. The whole family had connections to the Fire Department and Staten Island. Thomas Bannon's brother was a paramedic and their father had retired as a captain.

Even Louise Bannon's family was tied to the department. Three of her four brothers were with the FDNY. The fourth worked at a machine shop just a few blocks away from the Bannon house.

After the usual questions, I came in a little hotter with "Did your husband have anyone who could be angry with him? Anyone who felt he did them wrong?"

"Tommy was a good guy. Everyone liked him."

"He didn't have any vices, did he? I mean ones that might draw some attention. I'm not trying to insult your husband's memory, just hoping to find some lead that will catch this shooter."

"But the way you asked that question tells me you are willing to smear Tommy's reputation." Now she set the toddler on the floor and told him to go play with his sister. Louise looked at me and said, "Vices? We all have vices. I don't see what this has to do with your investigation. Tommy was a good guy," she repeated.

Then her phone rang. She pulled it from the outer pocket of the loose cardigan sweater she was wearing. I heard her mumble answers to a couple of questions, then say, "No, the cops are here right now. They're starting to piss me off."

When she looked up at me after ending the call, it was clear she had no use for the police. Louise Bannon said, "Do you have any questions that will catch my husband's killer?" She folded her arms and started to tap her right foot.

I felt like I'd hit a nerve when I asked about vices. It was hard to tell in a situation like this. I turned to Trilling, hoping the charming young man might find a different approach.

Trilling said, "Mrs. Bannon, you read about this latest case in the paper, right?"

She nodded.

"Did your husband or you know either of the other victims? The first one or this latest one?"

She shook her head.

Trilling hit her with a series of decent questions. He was trying to find a connection between her husband and anyone else on the case. I liked the way he was thinking. It was the first time I had seen his natural investigative sense.

I heard two cars screech to a stop in front of the house. Then heavy footsteps on the porch. The front door burst open. Four men, all in their thirties, and all of a decent size, rushed into the room.

I looked up and said, "You must be Louise's brothers."

The tallest one, still in his FDNY uniform, growled, "And if you upset our sister…"

Louise said, "They're asking about Tommy's vices. Making it sound like it was his fault he got shot."

One of the brothers was dressed in a mechanic's uniform with grease smeared across the front and the name LIAM on an embroidered name tag.

I stared at the man, who looked like he was unpleasant in the best of times. "You're not a firefighter like your brothers?"

"Eat shit."

"Oh, I get it. You're too eloquent for the FDNY."

Maybe I should have left the juvenile comments for another time.

The mechanic growled, "We're gonna fuck you up."

CHAPTER 36

I'D NEVER HAD anything like this happen at a *victim's* home. I certainly didn't want this interview to turn ugly. That didn't change the fact that I was standing in the living room of Louise Bannon's house, facing her four brothers, who looked like they were ready to make a physical statement.

The tallest brother, the one in uniform, turned his hips. He looked like he knew how to punch. The two other brothers, presumably the other firefighters now off duty, were heavier and built more like wrestlers. They squared off against Rob Trilling.

The brother in the mechanic's uniform cracked his knuckles as he stared at me.

I said in an even voice, "Don't let this get out of hand, fellas."

The brother in uniform said, "Why not? If the NYPD takes as long to investigate this as it has my brother-in-law's murder, I'll be an old man before anyone comes for me. Maybe it's time you arrogant cops feel a little of the pain the rest of us put up with."

I stole a quick glance over at Trilling. He didn't look concerned. Then again, he never did. One of the brothers facing him said, "I kicked a cop's ass a few years ago."

Trilling smiled and said, "Oh, I doubt that." It took a moment for that dig to sink in. The tubby off-duty firefighter dropped lower, like a defensive lineman ready to knock down a quarterback.

The two brothers facing me took their cue. The tall one in uniform threw a wild roundhouse swing at my head. I juked to the side and then planted a good left directly in his solar plexus. It was the best punch I'd thrown in years. All the air went out of him as he sank down to his knees, trying to catch his breath.

Both of the brothers facing Trilling lunged at him at the same time. Trilling seemed to barely move. He guided one brother into the other, then stepped to the side. It took them both a moment to clear their heads, then, incredibly, they lunged at him exactly the same way.

This time Trilling let one pass him completely, then struck the other brother in the head with his elbow. When the first brother turned to charge him again, Trilling delivered a perfect side kick, right in his lower ribs. The brother bounced off a floral couch that had seen better days and tumbled onto the hardwood floor.

The mechanic charged me with his head down. All I did was bring my knee up as hard as I could, and I caught him right in the face. He stumbled and fell on the floor with a whimper.

Now both Trilling and I backed toward the door. Louise Bannon stood in an archway, staring at her four brothers sprawled across her living room. She cut her eyes to me and said, "I guess they went a little overboard."

I said, "What should we do about it? They assaulted us."

The tall brother had started to catch his breath and come up off his knees. He was clearly the smartest of the group. I suspected he was probably the oldest brother, and the spokesperson. He said, "We're frustrated. We don't hear nothing about Tommy's murder. Then two cops we don't know just show up out of the blue and start interrogating our sister about his life. Maybe we did get a little carried away."

I thought about it for a moment. I didn't like the idea of hitting these guys with an assault charge. At the very least, a couple of them would lose their jobs. I had everyone's attention as they stared at me.

I said, "If we go by old-school rules, I can let this slide."

The mechanic, using his bare hands to try and stop the blood pouring out of his nose, said, "What kind of old-school rules?"

"If no one has to go to the hospital, no one has to go to jail."

We backed out of the house and walked down the pavers to the street.

Trilling said, "I'm impressed. I knew you were smart, but I didn't know you could tussle like that."

"I *can* do it, I just don't like to."

Trilling glanced back at the house, then said, "Real nice folks, you New Yorkers."

I chuckled at that. Then I said, "Ready to head up to the Bronx for what I hope is a calmer interview?"

"I'll meet you at the office at one. I have to run to an appointment right now. Sorry."

All I could do was stare at him. Just when I'd thought I had Rob Trilling figured out, I realized I was wrong.

CHAPTER 37

TRUE TO HIS word, Rob Trilling walked into the office at 1 p.m., just as I finished my Lenwich turkey and provolone sub.

I was still annoyed about our morning workout session with the Staten Island firefighters. I asked, "Did you eat?"

"Not hungry."

A few minutes later, we were both in my Chevy Impala, headed north to the Bronx to interview Wendy Robinson. The tipster had said that Robinson worked out daily at a hybrid boxing-wrestling gym.

The Bronx had evolved over the years. There was a time when people were uneasy going to the Bronx, but in recent years local activists had brought in a number of grants and set up programs for kids. People who don't live in disadvantaged areas often have a hard time grasping the connection, but as a cop, I know how valuable youth programs can be to deterring crime.

We drove through Kingsbridge Heights, looking for the gym. We had to stop for a few minutes in front of the community center while some news crews interviewed a tall, good-looking Latino man. He was dressed in a nicely cut suit and seemed familiar.

Trilling shook his head and muttered something.

I said, "What's with you?"

Trilling pointed at the man speaking to reporters. "You know who that is?"

I took another look and shook my head.

"That's Gus Querva. I looked for his brother, Antonio, on a homicide warrant out of Baltimore. Antonio is supposed to be hiding in the city somewhere. The whole family is a bunch of dirtbags. They organize the gangs up here in the Bronx and then put on the front of trying to help the neighborhood. The whole time they're squeezing businesses for protection money. They haven't helped the neighborhood, they've ruined it. Guys like that make me sick to my stomach."

I rolled down my window to see if I could catch what Querva was saying. He was talking about programs for kids, bringing qualified teachers to the area. I didn't hear anything I could disagree with.

And just like that the impromptu news conference was over. I noticed Trilling's eyes track Querva as he stepped away from the microphones. It was one of the first times I'd seen actual emotion in Trilling's face. Maybe the captain I'd met at West Point was right: Trilling did have passion.

I drove past the community center slowly and let Trilling stare at his nemesis as Querva walked and spoke with several reporters trotting along with him.

I said to Trilling, "We can't fix everything."

"Then what's the point?"

I had to think about that for a few seconds. I felt like I was back in my philosophy classes at Manhattan College. Finally I said, "The point is to do the best we can with what we have. There's another side to the law-and-order equation. People have to work with us. People have to want things to get better."

"That's why things always stay the same. Bullies bully, thieves steal, and no one's willing to do much about it."

CHAPTER 38

IT TOOK LONGER than I'd expected to find the gym where Wendy Robinson worked out. The reason we couldn't find it was because the gym had absolutely no advertising. There weren't the usual bay windows where you could look in and see people getting fit. There was no sign on the door or on the side of the building.

We had parked and were walking down the sidewalk when I saw a homeless man sitting on the steps of a closed business. I thought I could take a moment to show Rob Trilling one of the tricks of being a detective in New York City: make use of all available information. Homeless people generally spend their time outside. Usually that's in one neighborhood. That makes homeless people experts on who comes and goes and who belongs in certain neighborhoods.

It was hard to tell how old the man sitting on the steps was. Somewhere between forty-five and sixty-five. His gray hair was cut short, but his beard traveled the length of his chest almost to his belly button.

Trilling whispered to me, "He's holding a leash. Make sure there's not a dog that could surprise us."

I appreciated Trilling's sense for detail. He wasn't wrong. But somehow I didn't see a German shepherd jumping out from behind the steps at us. Still, we approached carefully.

I smiled and gave a wave to the man as we approached. I said in sort of a loud voice, "Hello. How are you today?"

The man nodded and said, "Pretty fair, today. That's not the way it always is."

Trilling casually leaned around the steps to see what was at the end of the leash. Then he jumped back a foot.

It was the first time I'd seen Trilling agitated and it was obvious in his voice. He said, "That's not a dog. That's the biggest rat I've ever seen in my life."

The homeless man started to cackle. He pulled on the leash. I was astonished to see a huge rat scurry out onto the sidewalk. The leash ended in a harness that went around the rat's back and chest. It was probably made for a Chihuahua or poodle, but it seemed to fit this super rodent pretty well.

The homeless man reached down and stroked the rat. It was clear the rat enjoyed it, and it snuggled up closer to the man's leg. The man said, "Nothing to be afraid of, Nigel."

Trilling said, "You named a giant rat Nigel?"

"I originally was going to name him Cecil, but it just didn't sound right for a rat."

I wasn't sure if the homeless man was just having fun with Trilling. Either way, it was good for someone from Bozeman, Montana, to get a different view of New York.

I asked the man if he knew where the gym was, and he pointed to the building across the street. We were making progress. When I saw how closed off the building was, I decided to show the man Wendy Robinson's photo. I had her New York driver's license photo and the description from the tipster who'd said she was tall and athletic-looking. The man nodded and said, "She's in there most days. But she's done something with her hair. It looks funny now."

I chatted with the man for a few minutes, partly as a way to conduct surveillance without drawing attention but mostly because I was interested.

The man said, "You know all those sad stories about businessmen who lost everything or veterans who ended up on the street?"

Both Trilling and I nodded.

"I ain't none of that. I started drinking beer and really liked it. When I was twenty-eight, I got a job at the port, then hurt my back. The pills they gave me mixed pretty good with beer, and I discovered I had no interest in going back to lifting heavy things off boats. A year later I'm living with my mom. Two years after that she kicked me out. I've been on the street sixteen years. No rules, no one telling me what to do, and no schedule. Aside from freezing my ass off in the winter, I do all right. Me and Nigel are making it together."

When I looked up from the homeless man, I noticed a woman coming out the side door of the boxing gym. She fit the general description of Wendy Robinson except her hair was dyed red and blue. There was some white on the tips in the back. Then I realized she was trying to wear a US flag as a hairstyle.

Trilling noticed her at the same time as I did. I stood up and reached in my pocket to find any loose bills to give the homeless man. Before I could come up with a five, I noticed Trilling hand the man a ten-dollar bill.

My new partner was starting to make me smile more and more.

CHAPTER 39

WENDY ROBINSON HAD a fast stride. Even at six foot three, I had to scramble to catch up to her. A detective learns early in his career not to call after someone. Especially someone who could be a suspect. If I shouted, *Hey, Wendy Robinson, I need to talk to you!* she could easily break into a sprint and I might never see her again.

It was Rob Trilling who made the smart move. He called out, "Sergeant Robinson, is that you?"

The woman stopped and turned. I saw she had a pretty noticeable shiner on one eye. "Do I know you?"

Trilling said, "I'm Rob Trilling, 75th Ranger Regiment."

"Nice to meet you, but how did you know who I was?"

Trilling pulled his badge from the inside pocket of his windbreaker. "I'm with the NYPD now. I was wondering if you had a few minutes to talk to us."

"What's this about?" She tensed, then looked up the street to see if anyone was closing in on her.

It made me think we might be on the right track. The little action of turning her head and bending her knees told me she was thinking about running. That meant she was a legit suspect.

Trilling said, "We have a few questions about your rifle skills we'd like to ask you."

That had a profound effect on the former Army sergeant. Instead of looking to flee, she turned to face us fully and said, "Ask away."

I tried to put her at ease by introducing myself, then said, "I guess my first question isn't necessarily official. How did you get the black eye?"

A smile spread across her face. "You don't work out at a boxing gym without taking a few knocks once in a while." She looked at Trilling and said, "Why does it look like *you* have a black eye?"

"Nothing interesting. Just clumsy."

"Why on earth do you want to talk about my rifle skills? Is the NYPD that desperate? I have an arrest for disorderly conduct and feel like I've already performed my public service."

I appreciated the way Trilling took over the interview, sensing a connection with Robinson. He put her at ease by chatting with her about their shared military service in the Army. Not only did I learn some of Wendy Robinson's interesting background but I also saw a different side of Trilling. He was relaxed and friendly. They made inside jokes that both of them laughed at.

Finally Trilling asked her how she became sniper certified in the Army.

It seemed like the question energized Robinson. Now she pulled me into the conversation. She had an expressive face and talked with her hands as well. "I applied for every interesting school that came available. It turned out they had a special program where they were testing out female snipers." Now she looked directly at me and said, "There's a big precedent in history for female snipers. Especially during World War II with the Russians."

Robinson explained to us how she passed every test they threw at her, physical and mental. "It felt like every sergeant along the way assumed I was going to fail. Everyone thought I would be on a bus back to Fort Belvoir or some other base to wait out my time. But I fooled them all. And along the way I became addicted to serious exercise." She looked back at me and repeated, "Now will you tell me why you're interested in my rifle skills?"

I respected her frankness. I decided to match it. "Will you tell me why you were going to run when you realized we were the cops?"

There was a slight hesitation. Just enough for me to notice and leave a little spark in my brain. "Isn't everyone nervous around the police? You've got a good eye to pick up on the fact that I thought about running. Just an instinct."

I nodded and said, "Fair enough. And we're interested in your rifle skills as part of our investigation into the series of murders by a sniper." I purposely decided to leave out the part where someone she apparently knew had phoned in a tip about her.

Robinson's eyes got wide and she said, "You think I might be the Longshot Killer? That is so cool."

"I'm assuming you wouldn't think it was cool if you were really the killer."

She cocked her head, a lock of blue hair tumbling into her face. "I don't know how to answer that because I'm *not* the Longshot Killer. I suspect that if I was the Longshot Killer, I'd still find it kinda cool you *thought* it was me."

"I'm pretty sure you're telling me you're not the sniper who's murdered three people here in the city."

She gave us another big smile. "I like the way you frame questions. You're correct. I am saying I am *not* the Longshot Killer."

I opened my notebook and showed her a single-sheet printed calendar, each day in the last two months clearly laid out in its own individual square. It was an old trick I'd learned before there were calendars on phones and tablets. I had circled the night Adam Glossner had been shot on the balcony of his Upper West Side apartment.

I said, "Can you tell me where you were this night?" I tapped the circled date with my finger.

Robinson studied the calendar carefully, then looked up and said, "I was in a study group. I'm enrolled at City College. Math is giving me some problems."

"Can you give me some names and phone numbers of the people in your study group?"

She shrugged. "Truthfully, they're all so much younger than me that I haven't bothered to get to know any of them. I know a few first names, but that's it."

I went through the same exercise with the other two dates. As I suspected, they were too far in the past for her to remember where she was.

We all chatted for a few more minutes. We made sure we got her current address and cell phone number.

Wendy Robinson looked at me and said, "You must have a lot of experience. And you seem like the kind of guy who has fun in life." Then she looked directly at Trilling and said, "You don't need to call me just for questions. You can call me anytime."

I enjoyed seeing Trilling blush.

CHAPTER 40

NOT LONG AFTER our interview with the interesting female sniper, I pulled into the parking lot of One Police Plaza. Surprisingly, there was someone else at headquarters we could interview about our sniper case.

As we climbed the steps toward a side entrance, Rob Trilling smoothed out his hair and flattened his windbreaker against his shoulders. He said, "I'm uncomfortable here."

"Join the club."

"Shouldn't we be wearing ties?"

"The only people who wear ties here are the people who *want* to work in this building. We're just coming in to talk to this guy, Joseph Tavarez."

Trilling said, "Do you really think an NYPD officer could be the sniper?"

"First, I always try to keep an open mind. Second, if we make a case on someone else, the defense is going to ask if we checked other potential suspects. This will show that we're diligent. Third, and most important, it wouldn't hurt to get another perspective on the case from a guy who was an actual sniper with the NYPD."

"Why is this guy working an admin job if he's a qualified sniper?"

I stopped in the doorway and turned to Trilling. "He took a shot as a sniper about two years ago. A guy with a gun was holding a convenience store cashier hostage. All the negotiations had failed. The robber had been surprised by a patrol officer who happened to pull in front of the bodega just as the robbery was going on. The robber was more and more frantic and drew blood from the victim's temple by pressing the barrel so hard against her head.

"Tavarez got the green light and made a phenomenal shot. The cashier was saved and the robber had a bullet in his brainpan."

"So what happened? Did Tavarez freak out and ask to be on desk duty?"

"They had to pull him off the street because of a lawsuit from the robber's family, pressure from the media, and insurance liability. It sucks that he did his job perfectly and still got punished for it."

I let Trilling think about that as we worked our way through the maze of hallways and secure entrances of the NYPD headquarters. I nodded hello to half a dozen people who passed us in the halls. After all these years, I still didn't like getting caught in this building.

We found the unit where Joseph Tavarez was assigned. The

unit was basically comprised of nine intelligence analysts handling information, similar to Walter Jackson's job, with Tavarez and a lieutenant running the whole thing. As I understood it, Tavarez's job was to review intelligence reports to see if there were crimes that needed to be investigated or referred to other agencies. Not a job I'd care for at all.

When we walked through the door, I saw the pool of analysts working in cubicles and a man with dark hair, wearing civilian clothes, working at a desk over to the side. He looked up and noticed us, stood from his desk, and walked over to us.

The man said, "You're Michael Bennett."

"Have we met?"

"Are you kidding me? I'd know you anywhere. If not from the newspapers, from some of the NYPD news briefs. I'd recognize you before I'd recognize the commissioner." He stuck out his hand and said, "Joe Tavarez. Nice to meet you."

"You're just who I wanted to talk to."

CHAPTER 41

THE FIRST THING I noticed about Joseph Tavarez was how similar he seemed to Rob Trilling. Not only in his demeanor but also in his appearance. He was ten years older but had the same lean frame and short, dark hair as Trilling.

I introduced Trilling.

Tavarez said, "I know your name too. You're on ESU, right? You came on after I was reassigned."

Trilling nodded. "Yes, sir. I'm not assigned to the unit at the moment. I'm working with Detective Bennett for the time being."

"Don't sweat it. There are worse assignments."

The two of them chatted comfortably for a few minutes until Tavarez looked at me and said, "I know you didn't come by here just to keep me company. Is there something I can help you with?"

I let Trilling explain what we were working on.

Tavarez said, "The Longshot Killer? You guys are working on

the most interesting case I've seen in a long time. I've been following it closely in the media and in homicide reports. You know, the exciting part of police work."

I decided to handle this sensitive part of the interview. "We have to eliminate potential suspects. You were a sniper in the Army, and according to Trilling, military snipers are rare. You were also a sniper with the department. So I've got to ask you where you were on a couple of dates."

Tavarez just eyed us silently. Clearly he didn't expect to be considered a suspect. Even the way I'd worded it, by telling him we were *eliminating* suspects, didn't ease the insult. He was a guy who'd spent his whole life in public service and it looked like the only reward he'd gotten was a shitty job at headquarters and now someone suggesting he was a potential killer. I gave him some time.

Tavarez said, "I'll talk to you, even though we both know it's never a good idea to talk to the cops. This is bullshit."

"No one is accusing you of anything. You know all the hoops we have to jump through. I'm just trying to be thorough." Then I did the calendar trick with him. He said he'd been off duty for the most recent murder, at home with his wife. He gave us her phone number.

"You can call Cindy right now to make sure I don't try to coordinate my story with hers." Joe still had a touch of annoyance in his voice. "I'll give you her office number too. She works over at the FBI as an analyst. Kinda what I'm doing here. In fact, I know I have a similar schedule to FBI intake analysts because I got a buddy of mine from the service a job over there, and we have almost identical schedules. I work ten hours a day, two evening shifts and two day shifts a week."

I said, "Was your buddy a sniper in the military too?"

"Looking for another suspect?"

"No, just curious."

"His name is Darnell Nash. He was my spotter in Iraq. He might not have been a certified sniper, but he's really good with the rifle. He lost a foot to an IED."

"Sorry to hear that."

Trilling asked, "Why is your buddy an analyst if he has military experience? Clearly he must have a college degree or the FBI wouldn't have hired him."

"An FBI analyst's job is not too bad."

Trilling and Tavarez started to talk about different veterans' groups and causes they were involved in. I respect the bond military people feel toward one another.

As soon as we said our goodbyes and were heading to another unit in the headquarters building, I made a quick call to Cindy Tavarez to verify what her husband had told me about his alibi. She backed it up, and even provided a few details about what they'd had for dinner and watched on TV.

CHAPTER 42

I TRIED TO advise Rob Trilling about the importance of making contacts everywhere he went. That included headquarters. There's no way a detective can know all the things that are needed in big cases. Between electronic surveillance, witnesses, forensics, and so forth, it's just too much for any one person. That's why it's important for a good detective to know who to call if he or she has questions.

Trilling was so quiet and reserved, I worried that establishing that kind of network might end up being one of the hardest aspects of the job for him.

I turned to go up to the fourth floor and meet Rebecca Swope, one of the sharpest analysts at headquarters. She also had a direct connection to every college and school in New York. We needed to verify a few things.

As we started up the stairs, I heard someone coming down from the third floor. As we turned for the next flight, I saw the wide figure of my old friend Greg Stout. Greg was a little overweight but liked to tell everyone that he felt it was important his body match his surname. And he was known for being a resourceful and determined investigator. That, coupled with his writing abilities, had moved him up through the ranks to sergeant in charge of major investigations. He also had a joke for every possible occasion.

As soon as he saw me, Greg broke into a wide smile and said, "Mikey boy, what brings you to the king's castle? Someone figure out your degree in philosophy is bogus?"

"My biggest fear, but that's not the issue today."

"How's that big beautiful family of yours?"

"All good. And yours?"

He shrugged.

I knew not to ask any more questions. Stout was frustrated by his twentysomething slacker son who believed every wacky conspiracy he read on the internet.

Stout changed the subject. "Seriously, why are you here? We want to escape, and you come here willingly?"

"Need some expertise and I'm headed up to see Becky Swope."

"If she can't figure something out, no one can." He turned his attention to Trilling and said, "Who's this?"

"He's working on the Longshot Killer case with me. Greg, this is Rob Trilling. Rob, this is Sergeant Greg Stout."

He patted his belly and said, "No jokes. I'm the only one allowed to make jokes around here." Then he took another look at Trilling and said, "God damn, how old are you? You even made an arrest yet? I mean, for anything."

Trilling stayed silent. In fact, he did a pretty good job of ignoring Stout altogether even though it was just the three of us in the stairwell.

Greg looked at me and said, "Seems a little touchy. Maybe he needs to learn some manners."

Now Trilling spoke very evenly. "Where I'm from, manners are something we use every day. With everyone. My grandpa told me to ignore loudmouths."

That was it. Trilling didn't have anything else to say. He continued to ignore the sergeant but looked at me like he was waiting to see what I was going to say. Obviously Trilling followed his grandfather's advice. And he was pretty efficient too.

I said, "Lay off, Greg."

"What's the matter, rookie can't defend himself?" When that didn't get Trilling's attention, Greg Stout reached out and flicked Trilling's ear.

Trilling moved so smoothly I barely noticed as he swept the sergeant's legs out from under him, then held his arm to ease Stout's drop to the metal landing in the stairwell.

Trilling calmly looked at me and said, "I'll meet you up on the fourth floor." Then he started taking the stairs casually, one at a time.

I helped my friend to his feet. He wasn't hurt. Trilling had made sure he wouldn't be.

Greg Stout said, "He really *is* a little touchy, isn't he? I was just joking around."

I looked at him and said, "You were out of line. He's not a rookie anymore. And he's starting to impress the shit out of me. He could've dropped you on the floor like a sack of potatoes. But he grabbed you and eased your fall. It was as good a message as I've ever seen sent."

Greg Stout gave me his goofy grin. "Everything you're saying is right. I guess I deserved that. I'm glad the kid went easy on me. The last thing I need is back problems."

I said goodbye and started up the stairs to catch my partner.

CHAPTER 43

REBECCA SWOPE WAS tucked in her own office with the only sign on the door saying, INVESTIGATIVE SUPPORT. Other analysts and detectives worked in the same squad bay, but the only reason anyone ever seemed to come up here was to talk to Becky.

She'd spent a decade developing contacts at every local college from NYU and Columbia to some of the lesser-known private colleges on the outskirts of the city. There was no registrar she couldn't call and get a straight answer from about something. The trick was to catch her when she wasn't overwhelmed by other detectives looking for similar information.

I stood in her doorway for a moment as she worked on her computer. She raised her eyes and smiled. I didn't know her age, but I knew she had adult children. One of them worked at the NYPD garage as a technician.

Becky said, "I got the name you sent me and checked with City College."

"And?"

"Wendy Robinson was enrolled there but only took one class, two semesters ago."

Rob Trilling stepped into the doorway next to me. He was frowning and I knew why. We'd both bought a lie.

I said, "Becky, this is my partner, Rob Trilling."

Becky said, "Trilling? I don't know that name yet, but if you're working with this guy, I'm sure I'll start seeing it in reports in no time."

Trilling said, "I just started working with Detective Bennett a few days ago, ma'am."

Becky let out a laugh. "'Ma'am'? I'm not used to good manners from most of these guys. I'm going to take a wild guess and say you're not from New York."

"No, ma'am. Montana."

"I love Montana. We took our kids there on vacation probably fifteen years ago. We had a great time. I hope it's nothing like the TV show *Yellowstone*. That makes the locals seem awfully violent."

"Like everywhere else, we have some problems. But don't worry. It's nothing like that show."

Becky got back to business. "Walter Jackson ran Wendy Robinson's name past the Department of Defense. He told me to give you this folder with everything in it. It shows she's not at City College anymore, and it's got a summary of her military fitness reports."

Trilling stepped forward to take the folder Becky handed across her desk so she didn't have to reach too far.

I said, "Anything interesting?"

"Oh, your suspect, Wendy Robinson, saw a whole lot of trouble in the service. Her fitness reports say she had anger issues and she did not work well with people who annoyed her. Which apparently was about half the Army. She has impressive reports on her determination in training, her fitness level, and her participation in some special sniping program. But I wouldn't call her warm and cuddly."

"I didn't get that impression either when we met. But she outright lied to us. That makes her a decent suspect."

Trilling asked, "Why would she lie about something as simple as a study group?"

"Exactly. She could've given us any number of different alibis. She could've said she was home alone and we would never have been able to disprove it. But I'm thinking we surprised her. And now we've got to track her down again." I looked at Becky and said, "Thank you for all this help."

"No problem at all. But in return you need to tell Walter Jackson my price: the next time we're together on a training, he can't tell me puns for a solid eight hours."

"That's a deal."

CHAPTER 44

I CAME HOME that evening absolutely exhausted. After leaving One Police Plaza, Rob Trilling and I had run down every lead we could find on Wendy Robinson. We talked to one former landlord who wasn't particularly happy with the fist-sized holes she'd left in his apartment. She wasn't even connected to the address she had given us.

Trilling said he'd run by the gym where Robinson worked out to see if he could find anything. That was fine with me. My day was over. A few hours with my family and a decent meal would do wonders.

Or so I thought.

As soon as I stepped through the apartment door, I could hear high-pitched yelling that had to be coming from one of the younger girls.

I hurried through the entryway to the dining room. Bridget

and Fiona had squared off with Jane across the dining room table. The usually calm Jane looked ready to spring across the table and crack someone's head. Bridget, normally much more interested in arts and crafts, was screaming that Jane had violated her civil rights.

I could already tell that this was a story I was not particularly interested in hearing. But I was a dad. That left no room for me to just walk away.

I said in a loud voice, "Everyone to a neutral corner." That at least got the girls' attention and stopped the screaming. They all turned and stared at me like I'd interrupted a debate. Then I asked, "Where's Mary Catherine?"

Jane spoke first. "She took Ricky and Shawna to the Museum of Natural History so they could do some kind of report."

That made sense. There's no way these girls would ever get into a fight like this with Mary Catherine around. I made everyone take a seat. As usual, the twins, Bridget and Fiona, sat right next to each other. Across the table, like opposing counsel, Jane sat by herself.

I said, "Does someone want to tell me what this is all about?"

Jane took a breath and said in a reasonably calm voice, "I think it's best if we handle this ourselves."

"Somehow I doubt that. Plus, I'm not sure if my medical insurance can cover what you guys might do to each other." I gave Fiona a hard look. It's wrong to say, but she is always the first to crack in any situation like this. A lot of people talk about knowing which parent to ask permission for different things. The flip side of that coin is that most parents know which kid to question when there's an argument. In this case, my basketball star Fiona was the weak link.

She cracked even faster than I'd expected. She blurted out, "Bridget and I were just fooling around. Jane's the one who freaked out when we took her little notebook. She pulled my hair." Fiona pointed to a few strands of hair on the table. It didn't seem that serious, but it backed up her comment.

I didn't even have to turn my head toward Jane before she started on her defense. "Dad, I told you, I have a big project! It's driving these two nuts that I won't tell them what it's about. So they grabbed my notebook. I'm sorry we were so disruptive when you came through the door."

"Wow. That's a good explanation." I looked at the two younger girls. "Is what Jane said accurate?"

Both the girls nodded their heads. It was satisfying to see my girls tell the truth. Especially after I was already feeling bad about having bought a lie from Wendy Robinson and wasted my afternoon. Then we heard the front door open.

Bridget said in a low voice, "Please don't tell Mary Catherine." The other two girls were nodding their heads vigorously. Was *I* the pushover? Was my new wife the disciplinarian in our family? This was something I'd have to think about.

I looked at Jane. "I appreciate your honesty. The only thing I'll ask is that you guys find a less aggressive way to work out problems. Also, I need you to keep your phone on all the time when you're out of the house, Jane."

"Dad, when I'm in Columbia's library they're really strict about us keeping our phones off and not using them."

"They're probably strict about turning the volume down. But you can answer texts."

Mary Catherine came in and gave me a hug and a kiss as Ricky and Shawna raced by with a quick "Hey, Dad!" But my wife's Irish sixth sense took only a second to read the temperature of the room. She said, "What's wrong?"

I smiled and said, "Not a thing, now that you're home."

I noticed the three girls' smiles as I covered for them. I didn't like to lie, but this one seemed like a good cause.

CHAPTER 45

I WAS AT my desk the next morning before seven. One minute later I was bothering Walter Jackson. I'd given him Wendy Robinson's name and told him we couldn't find her anywhere. That was usually enough for our super analyst to come up with a few addresses no one would think of.

Before I could say a word, Walter asked me, "Do you know why the man who invented the Ferris wheel never met the man who invented the merry-go-round?"

I just shook my head.

As usual, Walter couldn't contain his wide grin. He said, "They traveled in different circles."

I chuckled and tried to be polite as I asked about Wendy Robinson's information.

Walter handed me a sheet of paper with a few more addresses.

He said, "The address up in Brewster is her mother. I think that might be a good place to start."

I lost track of time as I went through notes and answered phone messages. Trilling still hadn't shown up when I broke out of my tunnel vision. I dialed his phone but got no answer. A few minutes later, he sent a text. I'm at an appointment. Then I have to run by my apartment. I'll meet you at the office.

Trilling's lateness was the sort of thing that an administrator like Harry Grissom should handle. But I didn't want to get my new partner in trouble. I just wanted to find out what the hell was going on with him. On the other hand, it was closing in on noon, and I wanted to get on the road and talk to Wendy Robinson's mother in Brewster. It would take about an hour to get up to the little town near the Connecticut border.

I decided it was time for bold action. I found Trilling's home address in Queens and headed over there to catch him when he came home. According to his text, he was headed there before the office. This way we could save some time.

It wasn't hard to find his apartment building after I came over the Queensboro Bridge. It was a two-story building just off Northern Boulevard. I slipped into a spot on the street nearby.

About twenty minutes later, Trilling pulled up in his FBI-issued Ford Taurus. He didn't seem shocked to see me.

All I said was "We need to talk."

Trilling nodded. He said, "Wait here. I'll be right back." A couple of minutes later he was back on the sidewalk with two Miller Lites and a bag from a local deli.

Trilling said, "Sorry. Apartment's a mess. I'll share my roast beef sandwich with you if you don't tell anyone about having a beer in the middle of the day."

I took the beer and half a sandwich. We leaned on the hood of my Chevy. I was a little curious to see how a young man would decorate an apartment in Queens but decided to worry about it later. "You ever going to tell me where you disappear to?"

"Is this a private, off-the-record conversation?"

I nodded impatiently. I wanted answers and then we needed to get back to work.

"And you want to know about my appointments."

I nodded silently.

Trilling took a few moments. He let out a sigh and finally started slowly. "I see a therapist at a VA outpatient center in Manhattan. I've been having a few problems adjusting to civilian life, and my therapist is concerned I have a form of PTSD. I talked to the NYPD medical staff and told them what was going on. That's why I was pulled out of Emergency Service. It's also why they shipped me over to the FBI fugitive task force. They thought it would be a good place to hide me so no one would ask questions."

I tried to process what he was telling me. As a member of a large government agency, I knew that this sounded plausible on every level. If I told someone on the street about this, they'd laugh and say it was part of a prank. But I could see the anguish on Rob Trilling's face. Now I understood why he was skeptical about the NYPD.

Trilling said, "I'm not ashamed of having issues after combat. Just feel like it's my business and it shouldn't be advertised."

"It is absolutely your own business. Sorry I ambushed you at your own apartment. Just needed some answers. Why didn't you tell me sooner?"

"I don't know. You just seem to have it all together. Great

reputation, beautiful wife and family. Maybe I didn't think you'd be able to understand."

"I don't pretend to understand PTSD. But I understand people trying to do what's right. Both for themselves and for the community. We could work it so our schedule isn't as rigid. You can make your appointments easier."

Trilling looked at me and said, "If we're being completely honest, I didn't have a therapy session this morning."

"Are you comfortable telling me where you were?"

"Immigration court. I sat in on the hearing for the five women we rescued from the warehouse in the Bronx."

"And what did you learn?"

"That no one gives a damn about human smuggling."

CHAPTER 46

OUR RIDE TO Brewster, New York, was uneventful. Somehow I'd hoped that by Rob Trilling telling me about his PTSD and treatment, communication would open up between us. But I was starting to realize that Trilling's natural state was quiet and thoughtful. It didn't do much for a ride through the Putnam County landscape.

Calling the area "rural" was like saying Shaquille O'Neal is tall. This was what we city dwellers would call the middle of nowhere. It looked sort of like the area where I imagined Ted Kaczynski had once lived. Quiet, isolated, and, to a New Yorker like me, a little on the creepy side.

The mailbox on the main road had the name Robinson handwritten on it, and the address matched what Walter Jackson had given me. Wendy Robinson's mom, Bev Robinson, had lived at this address for more than thirty years.

A long driveway seemed to wind up the heavily wooded lot. I thought a driveway like that would've led to a mansion. Instead, what stood at the end was a modest, one-story, middle-class house landscaped with manicured ornamental bushes and well-trimmed grass. It was the sort of place you'd expect a teacher or a mechanic to live in.

Trilling asked, "What do we do if Wendy is here?"

"We question her."

"I mean, tactically, one of us should stay by the car."

He was right. I try not to argue with anyone who's right. Trilling stood at the rear of the car as I walked up the short path, onto the porch, and knocked on the front door.

As I waited, I looked down and saw the doormat. It said, ALL WHO ENTER THIS HOUSE ARE LOVED.

A woman in her sixties with short gray hair answered the door with a smile. I could tell right away that she was Wendy Robinson's mom by her eyes. They were almost exactly the same as Wendy's.

I introduced myself and showed her my ID. Trilling stood by until I gave him a signal.

Mrs. Robinson didn't ask the usual *What's this about?* She knew what this was about. From this small but important detail, I could tell the cops had been here about Wendy before. Mrs. Robinson invited us inside, and I motioned for Trilling.

I waited at the front door for him. As he stepped onto the porch and saw the welcome mat, he smiled and asked, "Are we sure this is the right place?"

It was true. Wendy Robinson had warmed to us but hadn't exactly given off "love everyone" vibes. I said, "Kids don't always reflect their parents' traits."

Trilling said, "Thank God. Otherwise, I'd be in prison too."

I did a double take at this revelation from my partner, but he didn't elaborate.

Mrs. Robinson called out from the kitchen, telling us to make our way to the living room. She put on a pot of coffee for us without even asking. That was old-school polite.

The interior of the house was exactly as I'd expected: neat and orderly to a fault. It took us a moment to settle onto the couch with a low coffee table in front of us.

Mrs. Robinson came in and said, "What has my Wendy done now?"

I had told Trilling I wanted him to start the interview. When he said, "Mrs. Robinson—" she interrupted and said, "Call me Bev."

Trilling gave her a charming smile, shook his head, and said, "I'm sorry, ma'am. I'm afraid I can't. I have too many memories of my mom pinching me for not using proper manners."

She smiled and said, "Good boy."

"That's what my mom would say." He paused for a moment, then said, "Why do you assume we're here about Wendy?"

"I have four daughters. Each exceptional in their own way. But only one of them draws the attention of the police. She can be a wild one. She joined the Army to avoid a battery charge. You're not the first police who've made the trek up my driveway to talk to me about my daughter. I'm afraid I haven't seen her in over two months. And I'm afraid I'd rather not know why you're looking for her. I just want to make sure you won't hurt her."

We assured her it was in everyone's best interest for us to find her daughter. We checked to make sure we both had the right phone number for Wendy. Then we even asked Mrs. Robinson to call Wendy herself, to see if she could figure out where her wayward daughter was staying. Just like our calls, she got no answer.

Mrs. Robinson said, "Last time she was here was to practice with a rifle. There are no other houses around, and she said there were no ranges in the city."

Both Trilling and I leaned forward. Mrs. Robinson didn't know where Wendy's rifle had come from, but she told us it wasn't here at the house. Then she took us into the backyard and pointed out to us where a large old sheet of plywood was propped up against some trees in the distance.

As we walked toward it, I saw groupings of bullet holes in four different parts of the four-by-eight-foot sheet.

Trilling said, "Wrong caliber. These holes are likely made by .223s. We're looking for maybe a .308."

"That doesn't mean she only has one rifle."

We couldn't find any bullets to dig out of trees for forensic examination, but we told Mrs. Robinson that we might be back.

She walked us to our car, where I handed her a business card with both of our cell phone numbers. She agreed to call us if she heard from Wendy. Then Mrs. Robinson said, "Can you help her?"

"She may not need help. Right now we just want to talk to her. She lied to us, and we need to know why."

Mrs. Robinson shrugged. "You can never tell with Wendy. At one time, she wanted to be a teacher. She even took a few classes at City College. But she's content to take on odd jobs around the city and exercise at that gym of hers."

Once we were in the car, I turned to Trilling and said, "Doesn't your sister live close by?"

"Yeah, Ludingtonville. About ten minutes from here."

"We can count that as our lunch break if you want to visit."

He didn't answer immediately. He was even more thoughtful than usual. Trilling turned to me and said, "You introduced me to your family. I guess I should introduce you to mine."

CHAPTER 47

ROB TRILLING'S SISTER lived in the middle of the tiny town of Ludingtonville, in a nice two-story house that was kept in good order. A Dodge Ram 1500 pickup truck with Montana plates sat in the driveway.

Trilling casually said, "My mom and grandpa have been here visiting for a few months. They're helping my sister with the kids because my brother-in-law is a long-haul trucker."

He said that his mom, who was named Mona, and his grandfather, Chet, would be there watching his sister's toddler and infant while she worked as a bookkeeper at an auto-parts store in the next town.

A woman I took to be Mona Trilling opened the door as we walked up the driveway. I don't know why it surprised me to realize that she was only a couple of years older than me. She had black hair and wide, dark eyes. She hugged Trilling like she hadn't seen him in years, instead of only six days ago, which he had just told me was when he last came up to visit.

Trilling's grandfather, Chet, came to the door behind Mona. He was a distinguished-looking older man, just under six feet tall with neatly trimmed gray hair and clear, dark eyes.

Chet asked, "Who's this, Rob?"

Trilling said, "This is my partner, Michael Bennett, Pops."

"Partner in the Army?"

"No, Pops. I work for the police now."

The old man smiled and nodded.

They welcomed us into the living room. I chatted with Mona Trilling about the differences between New York and Montana. She told me how happy she was that two of her kids had ended up living near each other, so she could visit both of them at the same time. I gathered that Trilling's older brother was running the grandfather's car dealership back in Bozeman.

I said, "It's nice that you and your father can drive across the country together to visit your children."

"Oh, Pops isn't my father. He's my former father-in-law."

"From what I hear you take really good care of him. I just assumed he was your dad."

"No, but we're close. After my husband left, Pops stepped up and really helped with the kids. I don't know how much Rob has told you, but his father was not a good man. Anyway, Pops has always been very kind to me. And I intend to stick with him through the troubles I know are coming. Right now it's just a little memory glitch. We've been told it'll get much worse and he'll start to act erratically. That'll be tough on Rob. He loves his grandfather."

I just sat there silently. That hit me hard. I couldn't imagine my grandfather, Seamus, having those issues, even though he was almost ten years older than Pops. I listened to the banter between Trilling and his grandfather. In short snippets, you couldn't tell there were any problems at all. They joked with each other. The elderly man brought up incidents from years before with perfect clarity. And it all made me a little sad.

Learning that Mona looked after an ex-in-law, I started to understand my new partner a little better. Apparently everything I'd seen on the job where he cared so deeply was no act. He had learned lessons about looking after other people, and I could see exactly where he'd picked up those traits.

Trilling and his grandfather went to the rear bedrooms to check on the napping children. As soon as they were out of the room, Mona Trilling turned to me and said, "Is my boy doing all right in the big city?"

"Everything I've seen says he's caught on to life in New York pretty well."

"You have no idea how I worried about him the whole time he was deployed. When he told me he was leaving active duty, I felt such relief, I didn't know what to do. Then he goes and joins the New York City Police Department and I start to worry all over again."

"He's got a good head on his shoulders. And he knows how to take care of himself. I wouldn't worry too much."

"Do you know if he's dating at all? I don't want him to be lonely. He brought a young woman by in September for a visit. They were coming back from some weeklong VA retreat in Albany. Her name was Darcy and I think she worked for the VA. She seemed like a nice young lady, but I never heard anything more about her. And Rob is so private, I hate to ask him direct questions about his dating life."

I thought about my own daughter texting Rob Trilling to ask him out. I looked at Mona and said, "I think Rob will be okay. We're working a lot of hours right now while we're on one case. Like every job, we have busy times and slow times. He'll have time to figure out what he wants to do and who he wants to date."

That seemed to satisfy his mother. Just then, Trilling stepped from the hallway, holding an infant, while his grandfather held the hand of a toddler.

Chet looked right at me and asked, "Who's this?"

My heart broke a little bit for the whole family.

CHAPTER 48

BEFORE WE'D EVEN driven back to the city, Walter Jackson had texted me a new possible address for Wendy Robinson. Rob Trilling insisted we look for her right now.

Trilling said, "I'm just thinking about the groupings we saw on the plywood behind her mom's house. Robinson knows what she's doing with a rifle. I don't like being in this gray area where we don't know how strong a suspect she is."

"You'll get used to it in Homicide. It feels like everyone's a suspect sometimes. Let's run by this address in the Bronx and see what we can find out."

"I'll tell you the truth, I hope she's not the killer. I know what it's like readjusting to civilian life. She might just be having a few problems. She seems like she's trying to straighten her life out."

"By lying to us and ignoring her mother?"

Trilling didn't respond. If I'd never met him, I would've said he was brooding.

We found the address Walter had given us and sat in my Chevy down the block from the building. I casually said, "Where do you think she keeps the rifle she used up at her mom's?"

Trilling thought about it. "If I were her, I'd have a place to keep it up in Putnam County. It's too hard to move it around in the city without people noticing."

We'd been sitting on the apartment building for only about five minutes. I was trying to think ahead and wondering if we needed assistance. When a cop does a surveillance like this, they never know when it will end. I've been on surveillances that lasted more than twenty-four hours.

My thought processes were shut down when Trilling tapped my shoulder and I looked up from my phone. Wendy Robinson was walking out of the apartment building, carrying an oversized gym bag.

I said, "Could you hide a rifle in a bag like that?"

"If the rifle broke down, you could. The oversized bag is good camouflage." Trilling started to shift in his seat and reach for the door handle.

I said, "Hang on just a minute. Let's follow her and see where she's headed. Maybe we'll learn something. If we start to lose her, we'll end the surveillance and interview her on the spot."

We waited until Robinson was almost at the end of the block, then Trilling and I hopped out of the car. He jogged up the block when we saw her turn at the end of the street. I remained behind her while Trilling crossed the street to follow her from another angle.

We followed the former Army sergeant six blocks. It only took a minute for me to realize she was headed to her boxing gym. I sent a quick text to Trilling so he could get ahead of her.

I started to catch up to her when she reached the block where her gym was located. I noticed the homeless man with the pet rat, Nigel, sitting across the street, keeping an eye on the entire neighborhood.

I saw Trilling a block ahead of me. Then I hesitated. Wendy Robinson walked right past the entrance to the gym. Trilling picked up on it and stayed out of sight as he casually walked on the other side of the street.

He met up with me as she turned on the far side of the gym.

Trilling said, "What's the plan?"

"We stay on her. Now I *need* to know what she's up to."

We hustled around the building in time to see our suspect speak to a tall man wearing sweats, then follow him through a door at the rear of the building.

Trilling and I walked up to the door. He gave me a questioning look, so I shrugged and tried the handle. We both walked through the door with confidence and were surprised to find ourselves in a warehouse crammed with dozens of people. No one paid us any attention. I worked my way through the crowd and saw that a square area on the floor was being lined with heavy mats.

When I looked across the open area, I saw Wendy Robinson taking off her sweatshirt and flexing her arms and shoulders. The tall man she'd walked inside with stepped onto the mat across from her.

Trilling inched up next to me. "What the hell is going on?"

I was about to say I wasn't sure. Then I heard the ding of a bell and Robinson rushed out onto the mat to meet the man in the sweatsuit. There was no introduction or announcement. She just started swinging.

CHAPTER 49

WHEN WENDY ROBINSON stopped her wild swings and squared off against her opponent, I took a closer look at the man she was bare-knuckle fighting. He was well over six feet tall. He had some bulk to him as well. I figured him to be around thirty-five years old. He had a long, droopy mustache that reminded me of Harry Grissom's impressive facial hair.

Trilling started to step past me, his instinct to stop something like this too strong to ignore. I put my hand out and caught him by the chest. I leaned over and said into his ear, "This isn't her first rodeo. Give it a minute before we do anything stupid."

"We can't let this keep going."

"We can't fight the forty people in here either."

Trilling nodded but didn't look happy about my decision. We both turned and watched the fight. Robinson knew how to move. The tall man landed one glancing blow off her shoulder. Then she stepped to one side, cocked her right arm back, and caught the man on the side of the chin with her bare fist.

I could tell by the way his head snapped that the fight was over, even before I saw his eyes roll back in his head. Then he dropped to his knees and fell face forward to a round of cheers from the entire crowd.

Wendy Robinson had hardly broken a sweat. She checked to make sure her opponent was okay. Several men from the crowd had him sitting up and were checking his eyes. The man gave her a thumbs-up and she turned to walk away.

Trilling and I intercepted her as she was headed into the crowd to watch the next fight. As soon as Robinson noticed us, she turned on the ball of her foot and tried to cut through the crowd to the rear door.

Trilling raced ahead and was waiting at the door.

Once I reached the door, we all stepped outside into the relatively quiet alley behind the gym-warehouse. The place was a perfect camouflage for these illegal fights. Even from inside the gym you couldn't tell there was a rear warehouse section of the building.

We stood on either side of Wendy Robinson as I said, "You haven't been enrolled at City College for almost two years. You lied to us."

She smiled. "I lie to everyone. I have to just to stay sane. My mom wants to know my every move. The VA wants to make sure I stay on my meds. And cops asking questions just makes things worse. I didn't want to tell you I was involved with these guys. You'd shut them down."

I said, "So it's like the movie. First rule is not to talk about it."

"What movie?"

"Fight Club."

She just gave me a vacant look. "Our first rule is to make sure no one gets hurt. It just adds a level of realism to our training, and the owner of the gym makes a little extra from people coming to watch the fights. The VA would never sanction this sort of therapy for PTSD. I swear to God it's the only way to deal with living here."

I said, "Now that I know your alibi is bullshit, I need to know where you were the night Adam Glossner was shot on his balcony." That was the date we knew she had lied about.

She made a sour face and said, "C'mon, guys. You can't figure it out? I was right here. I'm here two or three nights a week. Your detective abilities don't seem that sharp to me."

I looked at Trilling and he nodded as he went back inside to verify her story. He'd find the manager easily enough.

I looked back at Robinson. "We visited your mom. She seems very nice."

"She's the best. Except she expects everyone to live their lives the same way she has. I don't want to end up in a little town with a house full of kids running around."

"Where's the rifle you used at her house?"

Another smile slid across her face. "So you're saying I shouldn't confide any criminal activities to my mother. She showed you my little range, didn't she?"

"To be fair, she didn't know why we wanted to talk to you."

"The rifle belongs to one of my buddies who lives near my mom. I just wanted to feel a rifle against my shoulder for an hour or so. It's too expensive to shoot anymore. Ammo costs a fortune. I liked it a lot better when the government provided me with bullets." She gave me a sly smile. She wasn't worried about a homicide charge.

After a while, Trilling came back out. "Robinson's story checks out. The manager even showed me some video. He says she's a regular and never causes any trouble."

Robinson did a little curtsy. "That's me, just a good little girl." She pointed at the building. "I guess you could say this whole thing is my anti-anxiety drug. Please don't shut us down."

"Answer your phone if I call you again and we won't bother this place. Ignore me and I'll make a call that shuts this place down for good. Do we have an understanding?"

She held out her right hand and shook mine. "You have my word." She turned to Trilling and stuck her hand out again. When he reached to shake it, she pulled him close and planted a kiss right on his lips. "That's just to show I'm serious about my work."

Watching Trilling blush never got old.

CHAPTER 50

I'M USED TO calls in the middle of the night. Every homicide detective is. The only thing that surprised me about this one was the caller. Instead of Harry Grissom calling to give me an assignment, it was my sometime partner, Terri Hernandez, directly from a scene in the Bronx. Usually Terri handled the homicides up that way. Then she dropped the bombshell: it looked like the sniper had struck again.

Mary Catherine was just conscious enough for me to give her a kiss on the forehead as I slipped out of the bedroom and then the apartment. Traffic was light at this hour. I was on the scene in the Highbridge area, half a dozen blocks north of Yankee Stadium, in about ten minutes.

Terri met me in front of a nice apartment building. She gave me a quick hug and asked about the kids. It doesn't matter the situation; you still know who your closest friends are.

Similarly, before I even asked about the specifics of the homicide, I asked after her sisters, Christy and Sylvia.

Terri smiled and said, "My dad is getting used to the idea of their goofy white boyfriends. Sylvia's boyfriend loves heavy metal music and has a dog named Ace, after one of the members of Kiss."

Thinking of how that would go over with Terry's Cuban-born father made me smile. Then I got serious. I said, "What's the story here?"

"Someone used a rifle to shoot a community activist named Gus Querva. The doorman found him about an hour ago. My rough estimate is that he was shot around eleven o'clock from somewhere to the north of the building. It looks like Querva was walking in the front door when the killer took the shot."

I considered that for a moment, then asked, "Is this the same Gus Querva who some people claim is part of a gang that terrorizes the Bronx?"

Terri gave me a sideways glance and said, "Whoever told you that wasn't from any of the precincts around here. We got a very specific memo saying we weren't supposed to talk to anyone about him. We weren't sure if it was because of all of his efforts building youth centers or if the feds were working some kind of big case on him."

Terri had already covered the bases on this homicide. She had people out canvassing the area, talking to doormen, and looking for video surveillance. She asked, "Where's your new partner?"

I was more than a little annoyed to notice that Trilling hadn't shown up yet. I had texted him after I got the call from Terri but had gotten no answer. I looked at Terri and shrugged.

She said, "What's with these guys with no sense of duty?"

"That's not Rob Trilling. He's all about duty and responsibility. But I don't know where he is right now."

A couple of local TV news trucks came down the street and stopped just outside the police perimeter. I figured one of the doormen had made the call. They'd learned there were some perks to tipping off the media to things like this.

A green Toyota Camry rattled to a stop behind one of the news trucks. I couldn't help but smile when I saw Lois Frang pop out of the beat-up car and start marching toward the perimeter. When she waved at me, I felt obliged to walk over and talk to her.

I said, "Tell me who tipped you guys off. I'm just curious."

Lois let out a quick laugh. "No one ever gives *me* tips. I work for the *Brooklyn Democrat*. What could I give them in return? I rely on a good old-fashioned police scanner. It catches your general traffic, and I could tell something was going on."

"You were up listening to a police scanner at this hour?"

"Insomnia. It's either a gift or a curse." She looked past my shoulder and said, "I thought it might be the sniper again. Seeing you confirms it. Can you tell me anything?"

"Not much." In the silence that followed we both heard the TV reporter next to us practicing his introduction.

"We're at the scene of a murder, possibly committed by the sniper who has been terrorizing the city. The victim is Gus Querva, the man responsible for bringing countless youth centers and community advancements to the Bronx."

Lois snorted.

"What's funny?"

"These journalism-school grads who believe anything that's fed to them. Everyone with half a brain knows Gus Querva was able to live in a building like this by running a protection and extortion racket. There's hardly a bodega in this part of the Bronx that doesn't pay one of Gus's crew a cut every week just to be left alone."

I nodded and made an excuse as I headed back to find Terri Hernandez. I checked my watch and called Rob Trilling. I told him to call me as soon as he got my message.

I thought about how upset Trilling had been when he saw Querva talking to the media. He'd said the same things about Querva that Lois Frang just had. I felt a sharp sting of anxiety in my stomach as I thought about my partner's comments regarding our latest victim.

CHAPTER 51

ROB TRILLING SHOWED up at the crime scene in the Bronx at almost exactly seven in the morning. All his new partner said when he arrived was "You need to live next to your phone when you're working in Homicide." Trilling nodded, knowing more would be coming later. He'd had his ass chewed by professionals in the Army. So far, no one in the NYPD scared him too much.

Trilling tried to make sense of the scene and what each of the team members was doing. Uniformed police officers kept the media and gawkers behind the police line. Crime-scene techs took photos near the front door where the body had fallen. Detectives were searching for potential witnesses. And Trilling took it all in. He wanted to understand how a smart guy like Mike Bennett could figure out the details that led to an arrest. He knew that was always the key to any mission: details.

Trilling stepped over to Bennett and asked, "When did the M.E. take Querva's body?"

Bennett stopped what he was doing, turned to face Trilling, and said, "How did you know the victim was Gus Querva?"

"It's on the news. I heard it on my way over here." Trilling didn't like the look Bennett gave him. He stayed put while Bennett started to march through the crime scene, checking on each person doing a specific task.

Trilling wanted to be close to Bennett so he could learn how this shit was done properly. He caught up to Bennett and started to follow him around as he talked to a couple of potential witnesses, including Querva's girlfriend. The former Miss Colombia had been asleep in their apartment. Apparently the doorman had an excused absence for a couple of hours, then came through the rear door, so he didn't notice the dead man by the front door. As soon as he'd found the body, he called 911.

After the initial round of tasks was completed, Bennett turned to Trilling and said, "Let's go sit in my car for a few minutes. It's quiet and I need to think." His Chevy was parked almost in front of the building. Its close proximity to the crime scene discouraged anyone from walking up and talking to him when he was sitting inside. Trilling could understand why he needed to get away from everyone's questions for just a few minutes.

Once they were settled in the car's front seats, Bennett turned to him and said, "We have something we didn't have before."

"What's that?"

"The canvass turned up a coffee shop employee who saw someone walking by with what they thought was a musical instrument case. At least we have a description now. White male, about six feet tall, with short, dark hair. The description that fits maybe five hundred thousand people in the greater New York area."

"I even fit that description." Trilling noticed Bennett didn't say anything.

"You going to be okay working on the homicide of a guy like Gus Querva?" Bennett asked. "You told me you thought he'd ruined the neighborhood and was just putting on a show for the media."

Suddenly Trilling felt like someone was tightening a vise on his chest. He'd never had anyone question his integrity before. In the service, if you completed your mission, no one harassed you.

"It almost sounds like you're trying to accuse me of something. Go ahead and ask me anything you want."

"I just did. Can you work the case?"

Trilling nodded.

"Where were you that you didn't answer your phone?"

Trilling was silent. He stared at Bennett for a moment, then said, "Do I need an alibi? Sure you want to ride around town with me?"

"Making smart-ass cracks right now doesn't help anything. I texted and called you and got no answer. Where were you?"

Trilling didn't need someone looking at him the way Bennett was right now, grilling him over a missed phone call. All he could say was "I was at home, sound asleep. No fancy excuses. I screwed up and I know it."

Bennett sat silently, looking out the windshield. "For a guy who got to sleep last night you look like shit."

Trilling nodded. He knew he had bags under his bloodshot eyes. He could tell Bennett was exhausted. Maybe too tired to pick up on some details of the crime and the shooter.

Trilling said, "I'm here now. Let me take some of the burden off you. What do you need done right now?"

Bennett took a deep breath. He was thinking hard about something. Finally he said, "Coordinate the canvass of the neighborhood. Extend it two blocks south. Maybe someone else saw the man with the large instrument case. Maybe we'll get lucky and he'll be on a security video somewhere." Bennett looked at Trilling. "And tell me exactly where you think the shooter fired from. That's what you're an expert on, right? We'll send a forensics team to you when you find the location."

In the Army, a superior officer would usually tell him, *Dismissed,* when they were done with giving orders. Trilling had the good sense to know when he'd been dismissed whether someone said the word or not.

CHAPTER 52

IT'S SOMETIMES HARD for people to comprehend what goes into a police investigation. I had two things going for me: experience and a really good team. I never took Walter Jackson for granted. He saved me hours of work on every homicide by finding where witnesses lived and worked. Other detectives conducted canvasses for witnesses and checked for other vital information. But the initial period after a homicide is always hectic.

This one was particularly difficult for two reasons: it was the fourth in a string of killings, and I had a disturbing thought in my head about my partner. I just couldn't ignore his very specific comments about Gus Querva. And the fact that Trilling hadn't been around last night made me consider some terrible possibilities.

I made it a point for us to take a break at noon. I'd been on the clock longer than a regular workday and saw no end in sight. I needed some food and made Trilling stop with me at a small sandwich shop in the Bronx.

We were able to grab a tiny table for two in the corner and a bit of privacy. The place was busy enough that our voices didn't carry.

I wiggled on the hard, wooden chair, trying to get comfortable. Trilling stared down at his tuna salad like he was dreading having to speak with me.

Finally I said, "Tough night and day. This is what a homicide investigation looks like immediately after the body's discovered."

"I'll admit, I didn't expect it to be like this. Your phone has rung at least thirty times."

"That was before I put it on silent. I always update Harry Grissom. It's the bosses from One Police Plaza that I tend to ignore. There's always a lot of information thrown at us right after we get the call of a body being found. It never really changes." I waited, hoping Trilling might say something to put me at ease. I was out of luck.

After a few minutes of silence, I said, "Can we talk frankly? I don't really have time right now to beat around the bush."

Trilling smiled and said, "I've never been around you when you *did* have time to beat around the bush."

"Do you want to say anything to me? Do you have any more details you can provide about why you never answered my call?"

It took longer than usual for Trilling to answer. When he looked up at me, I noticed his eyes were bloodshot. He suddenly looked older as well. Then Trilling said, "I don't know what to tell you." He shook his head and kept looking down at his plate.

"Tell me what's going on. Why you look like you've been running from aliens all night. I just want to understand."

Trilling slowly nodded. "I get it. And I can see why you're looking at me funny after what I said about Gus Querva. The truth is, I've had a few issues since coming back from Afghanistan. The worst issue is sleep disturbance. My counselor at the VA got me a prescription for a drug that really puts me out. I mean, I lose eight to ten hours of consciousness. They call it 'sleep.' I call it a coma. Then I wake up feeling weak, tired, and confused. So I can't honestly tell you exactly what I did last night. I started the night lying in my bed, and I woke up in my bed. I've learned from past experience that doesn't mean I didn't do something in between. Once I made a meal when I was asleep. The next morning, I thought someone had broken in and microwaved the Stouffer's lasagna and garlic bread that was sitting on my kitchen table."

"Have you told the NYPD medical staff about this?"

"They know I'm under treatment by the VA. They've been in touch with my counselor. I stay on my schedule for appointments and even have been to a couple of their weeklong retreats. My counselor, Darcy, is the one who came with me to visit my mother. We were on our way back from Albany in September. I let my mom think it was more than just a counseling retreat. That way she didn't keep asking me if I'd met any nice girls in the city."

I appreciated his honesty as I considered everything he had said. But it didn't ease my concerns. I still had that funny feeling in the pit of my stomach. The one that always made me nervous. The feeling that everything was about to be turned upside down.

CHAPTER 53

WE CLEARED UP all the immediate interviews and leads related to the murder of Gus Querva. Rob Trilling looked so rough, I told him to go home. As soon as I said it, I knew ordering an insomniac to rest and sleep was like telling a heroin addict, *Just stop using heroin.* But Trilling didn't complain. He said he was going to do his best.

I called Mary Catherine. She sounded tired.

I said, "Is the fertility treatment getting to you?"

"I don't know, Michael. I thought I was past it."

"Is there anything I can do for you?"

"No, darling, I'm just a little tired. And you've been working since the middle of the night. Is everything okay with you?"

There was so much I could've gone into. Instead, I said, "Just finishing up the last few things for the day. You sit tight and I'll grab dinner on my way home."

Forty minutes later, I barely made it through the door as I juggled four large pizzas in one hand and a dozen roses in the other. The grateful look on Mary Catherine's face made the effort well worthwhile.

Despite a deep-down exhaustion, I enjoyed hearing about the kids' day. It sounded relatively uneventful. Fiona appeared to have finally figured out algebra, Trent used parts from four different computers to make a working one at Holy Name's computer lab, and Brian helped install a giant AC unit on top of a warehouse in the Bronx.

Chrissy was very sweet, making Mary Catherine sit at the table while she rushed around and brought her pizza, then a drink, then moved the roses closer to her on the table.

I noticed Jane huddled with my grandfather at the end of the table. They were looking at a sheet of paper and whispering back and forth like middle schoolers who had just been passed a note.

I waited until after dinner to casually slide next to my grandfather on the couch. He had just gotten his good-night kisses from the younger girls and was patiently watching the boys play a video game. I took the quiet moment to do some subtle investigative work.

"What were you and Jane discussing at the dinner table?"

"I'm not allowed to catch up with my great-granddaughter during dinner?"

"That's not what I said. And I'm too tired to play your crazy word games tonight. Jane's been acting a little secretive and I want to make sure everything's okay. So do you care to tell me what you were talking about?"

"You know that I love you, my boy. This whole family is what keeps me feeling young. That's why I'm sorry to disappoint you when I cite priest, great-granddaughter confidentiality. I'm afraid it's one of those immutable laws of nature that wasn't designed to be broken by an old sinner like me."

"Do you ever peddle this crap down at the church?"

"Every day. Why do you think the monsignor always looks so confused?"

I had to laugh at that and appreciate how my grandfather kept the kids' secrets. Everyone needed someone they could talk to without fear. Maybe that was where I was letting Rob Trilling down. Maybe he wasn't comfortable being completely honest with me. I shook that thought out of my head.

I said to my grandfather, "I just worry about the kids growing up too fast."

"I wouldn't worry about Jane, my boy. She's more likely to be the city's youngest mayor than she is to do something stupid."

"Some people would say running for mayor *is* stupid."

My grandfather smiled. "That's because only stupid people usually run for mayor. Jane will break that trend."

CHAPTER 54

I'D BEEN CAREFUL once I got into the office. The morning had been a blur. I had some serious anxiety about my new partner, but I couldn't just start suggesting he could be responsible for a series of murders. Life doesn't work that way. Once I said it, it could never be taken back. And that would follow Trilling the rest of his career. Assuming, of course, he *wasn't* the Longshot Killer.

I could've used some help from Walter Jackson, but I didn't want to involve him. I gave Trilling a detailed list of things to do on the case. Checking security videos, re-interviewing a few witnesses, and generally tying up his entire day. He didn't bat an eye at the long list of assignments.

Now I found myself in Midtown Manhattan. Trilling had told me he came to an off-site VA clinic here. That wasn't too hard to track down. I recalled that he and his mother had both told me that his counselor's first name was Darcy. A name just uncommon enough for me to think I could find her.

The clinic was on the third floor of a commercial building just a tad on the run-down side, with cheap carpet and scuffed walls. Not high-end enough for law firms and architects to rent office space.

I walked through the door marked VETERANS AFFAIRS, with the *s* faded off the end of the nameplate. In the small waiting room, I found an empty reception desk with a note that said, "Be back in twenty minutes." I had no idea how long the receptionist had been gone, so I sat in one of the five mismatched chairs available. In front of me was a coffee table with magazines I barely recognized. The best I could find was a *Sports Illustrated* that was about four years old. I wondered how many coaches the New York Jets had gone through in that time span.

One of the four doors leading to reception opened, and a young man dressed in a T-shirt and ratty jeans stepped out, followed by a pretty woman in her early thirties with short brown hair. I caught a break when the young man said, "Thanks, Darcy. I'll see you next week."

As the man headed out the door, I stood up. Darcy turned to me and said, "Can I help you?"

"I wasn't sure how long the receptionist would be gone so I waited."

"She's been gone about two and half years. We haven't gotten funding for a new one. I wrote that note myself about six months after she left. Pretty good, right?"

I already liked her. I pulled out my badge and introduced myself.

Darcy cocked her head and said, "And you want to talk to me?

I haven't run afoul of the law since I was a graduate student at Boston University."

I smiled and said, "Couldn't get into City College, huh?"

That made her laugh and put her at ease.

"I was hoping I might talk to you about one of your clients."

"I'm afraid I can't discuss any of my clients with the police. I need their permission, and there would be some paperwork with the VA."

"I understand all of that. And I'm not trying to pressure you. I'm just trying to assess the situation in my office. One of my coworkers told me he comes to see you, and I have some concerns about his psychological stability. I'm worried about him." I could tell by the look on her face Darcy knew exactly who I was talking about. But she was a pro, so she didn't let anything slip verbally.

"I can tell you that the majority of my caseload isn't any threat to anyone. They're just trying to adjust to life back here after being deployed. Our focus here is assimilation. We're trying to keep veterans from withdrawing. That's why so many vets end up homeless. This is one way to try and stop that. All I do is let them talk. I would think you were perfectly safe working with anyone under my care."

I liked her even more. Darcy was trying to help me without betraying any confidences or breaking any rules. "Do you prescribe medications?"

"No, but I'm supervised by a psychiatrist. She can write prescriptions as needed."

"Would some of those prescriptions be for serious sleeping pills?"

"I'm not giving anything away by saying most of my clients have issues sleeping through the night. The most common symptom of PTSD," Darcy said. "As far as the drugs go, I'm a counselor, not an MD. I have a general idea of what each drug does, but I'm certainly no expert."

The door to my right opened and a tall woman in her fifties with a giant ball of bleached-blond hair stopped in the doorway and stared at me like my fly was down.

Darcy jumped in quickly. "Dr. Hendrix, this NYPD detective was just asking about the symptoms and treatment of PTSD. Can you give him any insight?"

The doctor looked annoyed. Clearly Darcy was used to dealing with her on a regular basis. She seemed to have developed techniques of distraction, much like coaxing a reluctant cat into a carrier.

Dr. Hendrix snapped, "Which drug? We prescribe a huge array depending on what the client needs."

Darcy spit out a long, six-syllable pharmaceutical name. I knew immediately she was surreptitiously telling me which drug Trilling had been prescribed. She was able to do it without violating any trust or confidence.

The doctor frowned and said, "That's a very strong sedative. It's also one we prescribe regularly."

I said, "Can you give me an idea of the side effects?"

"It does have a tendency to make the user hazy in the morning for the first twenty to thirty minutes. It's also not uncommon for the user to perform activities while under the influence of the drug."

"What sort of activities?"

"Usually activities related to their everyday lives. They cook. They clean their apartment. I had a carpenter once who built an entire pigeon coop on the top of his apartment building over the course of a month and never realized it."

I asked, "These can be complex activities that the user of the prescription does during the day?"

"That's what I just said." She looked at Darcy. "Several of your clients take it. Even the young cop. The one who sits and doesn't talk? That one worries me with his sullen attitude."

Darcy all but cringed. She recovered quickly and said, "I know who you mean." It was her way of shutting up the psychiatrist.

Dr. Hendrix asked, "You have a case involving the drug?"

I just nodded, trying not to give anything away. The statement from the psychiatrist alarmed me. Her description of the powerful side effects, and their potential impact on Trilling's behavior, sent a chill through my body.

I started to formulate a hypothetical question that might shed more light on my concerns, but I was cut off.

The doctor looked past me toward the exit. "I'm sorry. I have some errands to run. Doesn't the NYPD have someone on staff who can answer these questions?" She didn't wait for an answer. She marched past us and out the door without another word.

Darcy just looked at me. She handed me her business card.

I looked down and saw her last name was Farnan. I said, "Thank you, Ms. Farnan. You've been a big help, and I won't tell anyone I was here."

"I'll keep it quiet too, for now. Can you keep me in the loop if there's anything specific that's worrying you? Of course, I have no idea who, exactly, you're talking about." She had a friendly, mischievous smile.

"I promise. And I hope it's nothing. But I have to be thorough."

CHAPTER 55

I KNEW MY next stop was going to be tricky. I had a love-hate relationship with the Federal Bureau of Investigation. I'd worked with them closely in the past, but always with my good friend Emily Parker. I hadn't had much contact with the FBI since her murder in Washington, DC, a short time ago.

I managed to score a fifteen-minute appointment with Robert Lincoln, the ASAC, or assistant special agent in charge. Usually the ASACs were the ones who actually ran the FBI offices in big cities. The special agent in charge was more likely to meet with the other law enforcement agencies and the media when required. Lincoln and I had butted heads on several different cases over the years. He was exactly what most cops disliked about the FBI: pompous, secretive, and patronizing. The trifecta of pissing off people trying to do their jobs.

But I'd learned that Lincoln was personally overseeing the

fugitive task squad Rob Trilling had been previously assigned to while the squad supervisor was out on extended medical leave. So it gave me an excuse to come find out some information.

My escort was a young man named Jason, who led me through the maze of hallways at the New York office of the FBI to a solid door with the nameplate ROBERT LINCOLN on it. Jason knocked on the door softly and opened it carefully. I saw Lincoln sitting behind his enormous oak desk. He didn't even bother to look up. He mumbled, "Thanks, Jason. You can have a seat, Detective."

I still wasn't sure how I wanted to handle this. I didn't want to get Rob Trilling in trouble. Not if he wasn't doing anything wrong. I thought I'd figured out a way to talk to the ASAC and still accomplish that goal.

Finally Lincoln looked up at me. He was in his late forties or early fifties and still looked fit. I knew there weren't that many high-ranking Black agents with the FBI, so despite our differences, I realized he had to be somewhat on the ball.

All he said was "What can I do for you, Detective?"

"Thank you for letting Rob Trilling come back to the NYPD temporarily to help us on the sniper case. I thought I should give you a quick update that we've tied the latest shooting to the other three. We don't have any specific leads yet, but I wanted to let you know you can call me anytime if you have questions. Or if you'd prefer, I'll come here to your office and brief you."

"I'd *prefer* not to have a twenty-four-year-old police officer on our fugitive task force. I took him as a favor to one of your assistant commissioners. As far as your case goes, I'm not surprised the NYPD hasn't come up with anything. This sniper seems a notch above the level of killers you typically deal with. I have some analysts looking at different information to decide if we're going to get involved or not."

I knew Lincoln said that just to stir the shit. Contrary to public opinion, the FBI couldn't just step in on any case. It would cause too many problems with a major department like the NYPD. I let it slide.

I said, "I was told that the supervisor of the fugitive squad has been out for several months with some sort of medical issue. They said you're overseeing the group."

Lincoln nodded. "Yeah, the supervisory special agent has serious back problems. He might go out on a medical. Is there something specific you want to know?"

"Just doing an evaluation on Trilling. Did he do a good job for you?"

"Surprisingly, yes. I don't usually expect much from local law enforcement. But he seemed to be sharp and determined, even if he's awfully young."

"Anything negative?"

"You understand, supervising a single squad is a sideline for me. I have the entire division to look after. I didn't see or hear about anything that Trilling screwed up, if that's what you're asking. Now, if you'll excuse me, I have actual work to do. Not that I would expect someone from the NYPD to understand that."

Robert Lincoln would never know how much it took for me not to respond to a snotty comment like that.

CHAPTER 56

YESTERDAY, ROB TRILLING had found the sniper's perch one block south of the building where Gus Querva had been shot. Trilling had talked to the crime-scene tech who'd taken the most photographs. The photos were detailed and showed the wound just above Querva's right temple. Trilling admired the shot from a professional perspective.

After looking at the photos, Trilling determined where the body had been found, then stood in that spot and looked down the street in each direction. That's when he knew exactly where the shot had come from. A nice recessed doorway to a small office building was perfect. Trilling got crime-scene techs to photograph it. He didn't ask for any DNA swabs of the area.

Trilling liked working alone and consulting with the crime-scene people as needed. He didn't feel like he was just tagging along behind someone as he usually did with Michael Bennett.

Not that that was a bad place to be. He appreciated how the seasoned detective had gone out of his way to explain how investigations worked and how everything came down to details. There were no shortcuts in a homicide investigation.

Today, Trilling checked security footage from the shops and buildings around the crime scene. He'd just finished looking at the fifth security recording. He was able to find a short clip of a man carrying a long case right after the shooting. The man walked past a camera in an electronics store. The image wasn't clear enough to identify the man, but Trilling could see that he was around six feet with short, dark hair. He didn't appear overweight or really skinny. Pretty similar to the description given by the coffee shop employee.

Trilling wanted to prove to Michael Bennett that he could conduct a professional investigation even if he wasn't sorry that the victim was dead. Gus Querva and his buddies had run roughshod over parts of the Bronx. The media focused on Querva's PR moves, especially the money he'd shelled out for community centers. The irony was, he had taken the money *from* the community before he'd put it back *into* the community. Not one major media outlet seemed to ever question how he'd made his money.

Just thinking about the situation made Trilling angry.

As he was going over his assignment notes, Trilling got a text. He looked down at it immediately. He was surprised to see it was from Michael Bennett's daughter, Juliana, asking if he had time to call her.

Trilling sighed and made the call right then.

Juliana's cheerful voice immediately made him perk up. She wanted to go to lunch. When he said he didn't have time, she settled for ice cream. She gave him a place on the Upper West Side that was on his route back to the office.

As Trilling walked down the block toward the ice cream shop about twenty minutes later, he wondered why he was doing it. No question Juliana was a beautiful, intelligent girl. But the hassles this could cause in his already strained relationship with Michael Bennett outweighed the benefits.

Just as he considered turning around and texting Juliana that he couldn't make it, she spotted him and waved from a table in front of the shop. She wore a simple jacket over jeans and a colorful blouse. Her brown hair bounced on her shoulders as she waved. He couldn't turn around now even if he wanted to.

Trilling ordered two chocolate sundaes. As they sat in the cool autumn air, Juliana peppered him with questions about his personal life. She sort of sounded like his mother.

No, he wasn't dating anyone. Yes, he was eating enough. Yes, he was taking a break from work when he needed to. At least that's what he told her.

Then Juliana asked, "How is it, working with my dad?"

"Educational. He'd be a good teacher."

"I guess he would be. I never thought of it like that. But he does handle ten kids pretty well. That's not something everyone can do."

"It looks like he's done a great job with your family. I can barely keep my own schedule straight let alone keeping track of ten other people's schedules too."

"Mary Catherine gives him a lot of help. She's been part of our lives for a long time now. My youngest sister, Chrissy, even developed her own little Irish accent for a while, not long after Mary Catherine joined the family." Juliana paused and turned serious as she said, "How's the case going?"

Trilling just shrugged. He was tired of telling people they had no leads.

A giant smile spread on Juliana's face. She was almost bouncing in the seat when she said, "Do you want to surprise him and come to our apartment for dinner again tonight?"

Looking into Juliana's warm brown eyes, it was hard for him to make a rational decision. After a full ten seconds, Trilling said, "I don't think that would be a good idea right now."

Juliana didn't ask for any explanation. Trilling had a hard time reading the look on her beautiful face. He couldn't tell if she was angry, hurt, or okay with his answer. Trilling's experience with women was limited. This was another puzzle he'd have to learn how to solve.

CHAPTER 57

I HEADED OUT of the FBI building, still smarting from Robert Lincoln's comments about the NYPD. I passed a squad bay marked INTELLIGENCE ANALYSTS and decided to take a risk. I remembered the analyst at One Police Plaza, Joe Tavarez, telling me that his wife, Cindy, worked a similar job here at the FBI. I slipped into the room, and a woman at the first desk looked up and saw my law enforcement visitor's badge. She asked if she could help me.

"I was hoping to see Cindy Tavarez. I don't have an appointment. I just wanted to say hello." The woman led me to an inner office that held six more analysts.

Cindy stood up and greeted me as I approached her desk. She said, "Detective Bennett? I thought I recognized you from all the newspaper articles over the years. Glad to meet you in person." She had a warm smile.

"Just wanted to make sure no one was upset we were verifying Joe's alibi. I told him we were just trying to eliminate anyone with his kind of skills." Cindy seemed okay with my explanation and invited me to sit for a minute.

As we were chatting, a younger man walked by, and Cindy said, "Darnell, this is Michael Bennett with the NYPD. He knows Joe." She looked at me and said, "Detective Bennett, this is Darnell Nash. He was Joe's spotter in the service."

I shook the young man's hand. "Joe said he had a friend who worked over here."

Nash said, "I would've followed him on to the NYPD if I hadn't gotten a little careless and stepped on an IED." He lifted his left pant leg to display a titanium prosthetic. Then he said, "If it wasn't for Joe and Cindy, I never would've landed this job. I thank God every day for them."

"You got a lot more analysts in one place than us. The NYPD tends to scatter them among the squads."

"The FBI does too. I'm still new to this, and they thought it would be best if I worked down here in intake until I was up to speed on everything. Cindy makes sure I don't get in too much trouble. Plus, I like the 4/10 schedule. Do you ever work joint cases with the FBI?"

I hesitated, then said, "Occasionally. I used to work with an agent named Emily Parker."

Nash said, "I'm sorry. I heard about her murder. It's shocked all of us to the core. I didn't know her personally, but I've heard great things about her."

"She was great. She made working with the feds easy. Sometimes it feels like a lot of your agents didn't get that memo."

Nash handed me his business card. "I'd like to work with other agencies. Especially the NYPD. I met one of your guys working on a task force. Rob something."

"Trilling. He's working with me for the time being."

"We vets tend to stick together. I hope he's doing well."

I just nodded.

Cindy Tavarez excused herself.

When she was gone, Nash asked me in a quiet voice, "Working anything interesting right now?"

"That depends on how you define 'interesting.' I met a man with a pet rat named Nigel. That was interesting."

"I meant case-wise."

I shook my head. "I never think of people being murdered as interesting. Just a job that needs to be done." A job I needed to get back to right now.

CHAPTER 58

THE NEXT MORNING at nine o'clock, I was surprised when Rob Trilling still hadn't come through the office door. I had a lot I wanted to discuss with him. Some of it was professional, some was personal. All of it was starting to eat at me badly. I couldn't be around anyone else. I pretended to be going over reports at my desk so I didn't have to hear any of Walter Jackson's corny puns. Even if they usually made me smile. On rare occasions, I don't *want* to smile. I want to be grumpy. I think that's in the Bill of Rights for fathers. Certainly for fathers of more than three children.

Trilling rolled into the office about 9:30, carrying a stuffed equipment bag and an armful of notebooks. He dropped it all at the desk he'd been using next to mine.

He didn't wait for the question. Trilling said, "Sorry I'm late. The FBI's rotating cars and I had to return my Ford."

"Did they give you a replacement?"

"They said I get a new one when I come back to the task force. I only had about five minutes to clean out the car. I don't like to turn in equipment that's not spotless."

That was definitely a military attitude. I wasn't sure I'd ever seen it as a police attitude. Sometimes it felt like the goal of some detectives was to see how much garbage they could leave in a car they had to turn in.

Trilling looked at me and asked, "Something wrong?"

I looked in every direction to make sure no one had wandered into the squad bay. It was empty, aside from us. Trilling took the chair next to my desk.

I said, "Were you going to tell me about your date with Juliana?"

"It wasn't really a date. It was ice cream in the afternoon. And it was over before four o'clock. There was really nothing to it. I swear to God."

There wasn't a lot to argue about in that reply. I dropped the subject and instead asked, "Did you come up with anything interesting yesterday?"

Trilling said, "Here's a still taken from security video of a potential suspect. I think this is the same guy the coffee shop worker saw after Gus Querva was shot." He laid a four-by-six-inch photo on my desk.

I picked the photo up and studied the grainy image. It wasn't something we could use in court to identify an individual, but at least it gave us a general description. What immediately struck me was that the man with the case looked like Trilling. I felt a ball of ice in my stomach.

Trilling stared at me with his usual silent intensity. He said, "Tell me what you're thinking."

I admitted, "That this could be you. Same height, same hair, same build."

"Maybe I should hang out with Juliana more often so she can provide me with an alibi."

I looked up at Trilling's face. I couldn't tell if he was joking or not. I knew that *I* wasn't in a joking mood at the moment.

CHAPTER 59

ROB TRILLING AND I managed to work together during the morning. We searched through NYPD records and reports having to do with shootings over the last twelve years. The time period was dictated by how long the reports had been computerized. For anything older, we'd have to look at paper files. We were hoping to find a similarity to an earlier shooting. Anything that might help the case.

My mind wasn't completely on the task at hand. I kept finding myself glancing up at Trilling, working at the desk next to mine. It seemed crazy to even think about an active police officer being a vigilante serial killer.

He didn't act like a vigilante. He seemed to be working hard on the case. The fact that he'd so willingly handed me that photo of a potential suspect made me hesitate. If I'd committed a crime and there was a photo of me walking away from it, I don't think

I'd show it around the squad. The flip side was that he might've realized I would probably see it at some point anyway. Bringing it to my attention himself looked less suspicious.

This sort of circular reasoning tied my stomach into a knot. Why couldn't life be simpler? The fact that my daughter had a crush on this young man only made things more confusing.

I thought back to the day I went to Trilling's apartment. The day he'd explained to me about visiting the VA and the appointments he kept having to leave work for. He had been careful not to let me into his apartment. At the time, it had struck me as a little odd. Now it was just one more piece of the puzzle that made me anxious.

What was my next move? Go to Harry Grissom and explain my concerns? Wait till there was another killing? There were no good answers. Harry would be required to relieve Trilling of duty. If no more evidence came in, there was nothing else we could do on the case. And Trilling would be left in limbo, his career shattered. Even if he came back on duty, no one would trust him.

My phone rang. It was a switchboard number so I couldn't see who was calling. I answered curtly, "Bennett."

"Hello, Detective. Robert Lincoln here."

As if I needed to hear his name once I heard his baritone voice. "What can I do for you?"

"You might want to come over to the office. One of our agents was cleaning out the car your man Trilling turned in today."

"And why should I care?"

"The agent found an empty .308 bullet casing. Could that be the same caliber your sniper keeps using?"

I was shocked into silence. That never happens. Then I blurted out, "Where did they find it?"

"Stuck in a gap in the carpet in the trunk."

"Maybe it's just the casing from when he was at the range."

"That's for you to decide. I was just giving you a courtesy call, in case you wanted to place the casing into evidence and have forensics performed on it. Seems like an odd coincidence that an officer working on a case like yours would have a casing like that."

"I'll leave right now and be at your office in the next thirty minutes."

Lincoln chuckled. "Somehow I thought that's what you'd say."

CHAPTER 60

MY TRIP TO the FBI proved to be anticlimactic. Maybe I was reading more into ASAC Robert Lincoln's comments. He was busy and couldn't see me. At least that's what the flunky he sent to meet me said. The agent just handed me a .308 rifle casing in a clear plastic bag. He told me there'd be a report on where it was found and recovered coming to me in the next few days.

I still wasn't ready to just run Rob Trilling into the ground. I called a sergeant on the NYPD Emergency Service Unit. His name was Jeff Mabus. I'd met him at training over the years. He was also one of our defensive tactics instructors. He had a reputation for brutal honesty, exactly what I needed right now.

He agreed to meet me in the back lot of One Police Plaza. My request for the location had as much to do with my tight schedule as my hoping to avoid the command staff so I didn't have to update them on the sniper case. What would I say? *The young officer you sent to help me might be the sniper.* I doubted that would go over well with anyone.

Mabus was about my age and dressed in 5.11 cargo pants and a tight NYPD T-shirt. I guess if I looked like him, that's all I'd ever wear too. Even in cool weather like this. He wore a ball cap over his bald head. A scar from some fight years ago ran across his neck and chin.

We greeted each other and Mabus said, "I slipped out of a training class. Figured if a guy like you from Homicide needs to talk to me, it's more important than learning how to fall properly when someone shoves you." He looked around the parking lot, then at me and said, "What can I do for you?"

"The first thing is that you tell me this conversation is private and unofficial."

Mabus took a moment, then said, "Hard to say okay to that without knowing what you need."

That was the veteran, intelligent answer.

I said, "It's about Rob Trilling."

Mabus was quick to say, "He's not on ESU right now. Last I heard he was over at the FBI on some task force."

I paused, then looked at the lean ESU sergeant and said, "It's about Rob Trilling. But it needs to be off the record."

Reluctantly, Mabus said, "Okay, I won't say a word to anyone. I like Trilling. Is he in trouble?"

"Truthfully, I'm not sure."

"He was a good ESU member. At first, I was annoyed they waived some of the rules to get him on the team so quickly after he signed on with the PD. But he turned out to be a good team member and a pretty good sniper. Never complained. Worked hard. Paid attention in training. His military background was a real positive."

Now I was more hesitant. This had seemed like a better idea when I left the FBI office. Finally I asked, "Do you know the last time Trilling shot a rifle? Specifically, a .308?"

"I can check. But I can tell you for a fact he hasn't been on an NYPD rifle range since early summer. I don't think there's any way he would've fired a rifle since then. I'll double-check our training records and confirm with you."

"When can you confirm it?"

"God damn, this isn't some minor policy violation, is it?"

"I'd rather not say yet."

"I respect that. Like I said, he's a good kid. He gave up a lot for the country. Cut him some slack if you can."

"I hope I can."

CHAPTER 61

I DROVE BACK to the Manhattan North Homicide office slowly. Just trying to give myself a few minutes of quiet to digest everything I'd learned today. My first thought was that it could all be explained. A crazy coincidence.

Somewhere in my brain, I wondered how a sniper who'd been so precise and careful could leave such an obvious piece of evidence for someone to find. The answer was simple: he made a mistake. Everyone makes mistakes. Even the sharpest former military man. The only people who don't make mistakes are in the movies. It didn't make things any easier and I felt a little sick thinking about it, but at least I could wrap my head around it.

Before I even found a parking spot outside our building, Jeff Mabus texted me to confirm that Rob Trilling hadn't officially fired a .308-caliber rifle in seven months. Well before the time he had the FBI car. *Shit.*

The squad bay was fairly empty. Trilling was out on an assignment. I noticed Harry Grissom sitting in his office. I walked in without fanfare, sat on the hard wooden chair he kept in front of his desk, and laid my entire concern out to him. Everything, including the comments Trilling made about Gus Querva, his absence on the night of Querva's murder, my research on the drugs the VA had prescribed him, and, finally, the empty casing the FBI had found in his vehicle. I even told him about verifying Trilling's training records to see when he last shot a .308 rifle.

Harry bit his lower lip. Something he only did when things had slipped from bad to horrible. He sucked in a deep breath and said, "You were right to come to me with this."

"Harry, I looked at this a half a dozen ways. Tell me I missed something obvious. Something that might clear this whole thing up. I keep asking, *Why Trilling?*"

"Because life works out that way sometimes. But we gotta notify the right people. And we've got to do it right now. No delays."

"But if it's not true, the gossip will cripple Trilling's career."

"And the answer is to let a potential killer run around the city?"

Questions like that were hard to answer. No, we couldn't let a potential killer go free. I sat there silently, considering everything that was about to happen. I knew the NYPD could move swiftly when they wanted to. They'd want to get in front of this before there were any accusations of a cover-up.

Harry leveled his eyes at me. He said, "If you had this much on someone you didn't know, would they be considered a good suspect?"

"Yes."

"You like this kid."

"It's kind of tough to call a war hero a 'kid,' but yes, he seems like a good person."

"And you don't want him to be the killer."

"No."

"Tough shit. You're a homicide detective. You go where the evidence and witnesses lead you." Harry picked up his phone. Then he looked at me and said, "Stand by. Whatever we do, we're going to need your input."

CHAPTER 62

THE BAD NEWS from headquarters arrived in the form of Detective Sergeant Dennis Wu. The Internal Affairs sergeant had been on the force about ten years and no one would ever think he was a veteran cop. He wore glasses that made him look like a banker or stockbroker, his usual Brooks Brothers dark suit, and a colorful tie chosen to distract people he was interviewing.

He strolled over to my desk, smiling. "Hey, Bennett, how's it going? I mean, besides your gigantic fuckup?" He let out a laugh and then mumbled, "Classic."

I let him go into Harry's office, confident my lieutenant wouldn't put up with much bullshit. After two minutes alone with the IA sergeant, Harry called me into the office.

When I stepped through the door, Dennis Wu said, "Let's see if I can fix this mess with a good interview."

Harry said, "We don't know if it's a mess yet. We're still trying to figure things out, *Sergeant*."

I smiled. The way Harry had emphasized "Sergeant" was a chance to remind the IA investigator how the rank structure worked.

Dennis said, "From what I've seen, it looks like he's good for it." He glanced around Harry's office, then out to the squad bay. "I thought off-site offices would be nicer than this."

I said, "I thought an IA sergeant would be more professional. Maybe if you'd spent more than a few months in patrol you'd have a better understanding of how things work."

Dennis Wu took off his glasses and nodded. "Is that a shot at me for being moved from patrol to translate a Mandarin wire for the FBI? Clever. So what? I only did a month in the bag. I did five years at the FBI, a few years in general investigations, and I've been in IA for three years. I think I have a pretty good handle on how things work around here."

"What about having concern for a fellow cop?"

"I do worry about cops. And the very few bad cops we have give us *all* a bad name. So why don't we cut the shit and start to focus on the case."

He was right, so I nodded in agreement.

Wu asked, "Did you put the .308 casing from the FBI into evidence?"

"I did, and it is going to the lab for every possible test the Ballistic Information Network can do on it."

"NIBIN?"

"Yes, we've entered the casing into the national ATF database. It'll only be useful if a casing from the same gun was used in another crime. Most shootings with rifles are AK rip-offs or .223s. The local drug dealer doesn't have a .308 lying around."

"And no one ever collected an empty casing from any of the scenes we could use for comparison?"

"There were none."

Wu looked annoyed, like someone had dropped the ball. "And this is not a caliber Officer Trilling has fired in the normal course of his job for at least seven months, is that correct?"

I nodded. Then I started to say, "He's a good—"

Wu held up his hand to cut me off. "I don't deal in good or bad. Can Officer Trilling shoot a rifle well?"

"Yes."

"Are you judging that from range scores on his training sheets?"

"No. He showed me at a range in West Point." I told him the story.

Wu said, "You went on a tourist trip to West Point during work hours? Why would you waste time like that during a serial killer investigation?"

"I wanted to see what went into setting up a long-distance shot. Trilling knew someone at the academy. We had access to a convenient long-distance range. I didn't consider it a waste of time. I consider talking to *you* a waste of time."

Wu smiled. "That statement makes me question your judgment about what is, or is not, pertinent to this investigation. Do we need to replace you with a competent detective?"

Harry Grissom stepped in at that point. "I make those decisions, Sergeant. Don't make threats to officers under my command. Not now and not in the future. Especially to a senior detective who's done more in the last year then you've done in your whole career."

All Wu said was "Duly noted, Lieutenant."

Dennis Wu made a few notes in a leather-bound pad. He

gathered his thoughts and basically acted like Harry and I weren't in the cramped office with him. Then he looked directly at me and said, "I'm going to need you in the interview for your knowledge of the sniper case. Will you be able to help or is this too personal?"

That stung a little bit. It sounded a lot like what I'd said to Trilling after Gus Querva was shot. Then I thought of Juliana. What was her relationship with Trilling? I looked at Wu and nodded. I didn't trust myself to speak.

Wu said, "Command staff wants this done today. No delays, no excuses. We're not NASA. We go on time." He looked at Harry.

Harry knew what the look meant and said, "I texted Trilling to come back to the office. He should be here any minute."

I was still standing by the door inside Harry's office. Wu sat in the spare chair. We just stared at each other for a moment. Then I gave the IA sergeant a little smile. There's nothing more insulting than a smile during a disrespect contest.

Harry didn't even know he was breaking up anything when he said, "Trilling just walked in."

Wu asked Harry if we could use his office for the interview.

Harry said, "I think I should be here."

Wu shook his head. "We might need you to take action if things go bad. It's best if you wait in the squad bay."

I thought it was best if Harry was in the other room to block inquiries from command staff. My stomach tightened when I saw Trilling walk toward Harry. Trilling was actually smiling for a change. That made it worse.

Harry said, "This is Sergeant Wu from Internal Affairs."

The smile dropped off Trilling's face. He looked over at me like a kid who'd just gotten dress shoes for Christmas. He suddenly realized that I really did suspect he was the sniper.

CHAPTER 63

I WATCHED ROB TRILLING'S every movement. It was the first time I'd seen him unnerved in any way. Who wouldn't be? Even a relative newcomer like Trilling had heard of Dennis Wu. He realized this was serious and didn't know what to do. I'd be in the same boat.

The Internal Affairs sergeant was polite and offered Trilling a hard wooden chair in front of the desk. Wu grabbed a plastic chair from just outside Harry's office and sat across from Trilling. That left me with the chair behind the desk. It was Wu's way of telling me I was only there to provide information, not to participate in the interview.

As soon as he closed the door, Wu turned to Trilling and said, "You have the right to remain silent."

Trilling stiffened in the chair and blurted out, "Am I under arrest?"

Wu didn't change his polite demeanor. He said, "No, you are not. I just like to be thorough and careful."

I knew that was bullshit. It was an old IA tactic to read Miranda rights at the beginning of an interview. Even if no one was in custody. It tended to scare people and knock them off balance.

When Wu was done reading the Miranda rights, Trilling said, "What's this about?"

Trilling looked at me, but Wu answered. "What do you *think* it's about?"

Trilling didn't say a word. I was used to the new partner's silence, but I wondered how Wu would react. He waited it out a lot longer than I thought he would. Finally Wu said, "The sniper investigation. I'd say you have some explaining to do."

Trilling turned again to face me. He still didn't say a word. His expression said it all.

After another stretch of silence, Dennis Wu said, "Officer Trilling, do you have an alibi for the night Gus Querva was shot? Or any of the shootings?" Wu only waited through a little silence before he added, "Just so we can be sure you're not the..." He paused for a moment. "What's the media call him? The Longshot Killer."

Trilling finally spoke. "Why don't you ask my partner? I told him where I was."

Wu looked down at his notes and said, "Yes, you said you were home asleep. A single guy alone in his apartment. That's a tough one to verify."

I saw a definite change in Trilling's demeanor. He was no longer uneasy. He was angry. He had a slight twitch in his left eye and a vein in his left temple pulsed. I leaned forward slightly in my chair to get my feet under me in case things turned crazy.

Trilling glared at Dennis Wu. My anxiety level started to

rise. I knew Trilling was remarkably quick and well trained. I let my hands drop to the arms of the chair, ready to jump.

Wu must have realized the changes as well. He shifted his tone completely. He took a friendlier approach and assured Trilling again he was not under arrest. Wu said, "I'm just trying to give you a chance to tell your side of the story. It's a good time to do it. No media, no crowds, just us."

Trilling spoke through gritted teeth. "I already told you my side. I was home asleep."

"So you expect us to believe that a dedicated guy like you, who's done nothing but serve his country and community, wasn't bothered by all the praise a guy like Gus Querva was getting from the media?"

Trilling sat stone-faced.

Dennis said, "Praise of a guy like that doesn't help the mission, does it? The mission is to serve and protect. What better way to protect than by eliminating a predator?"

Trilling started to answer. Then he stopped himself. He calmly said, "I need to speak to an attorney." His right hand dropped and rested behind him.

I tensed, worried that he was going for his pistol. When he moved his hand, I realized he had taken his pistol and holster off his belt. He stood up and tossed it onto Harry's desk. Then Trilling plucked the ID badge from his inside jacket pocket and pulled his police credentials from inside the jacket. They all hit the desk next to the pistol.

Trilling paused like he was waiting for someone to tell him he couldn't leave. When no one said anything, he turned on his heel and marched out of the office, through the squad bay, and out the door.

Dennis Wu looked at me and said, "I think that's all we need. He's good for the shootings."

I stared at the sergeant.

Wu ignored me. And continued. "As of this moment, Officer Trilling is suspended, is an official suspect in the sniper case, and you're going to make the charges stick."

"You can't be serious. All he did was ask for his attorney."

"He asked for an attorney because he had no more weak excuses. What are you upset about? You did a great job." Wu saw I wasn't happy with the situation. He said, "I had orders to convey to you that the brass wants this cleared up immediately. Command staff said you were the right guy to do the investigation quickly and efficiently."

"You can tell the brass that it's going to take a little while to clear this up. I've got a lot of background to do. No one wants to charge the wrong person with this crime."

Dennis Wu smiled. "You put together the homicide case, and I'll take care of the Internal Affairs aspects. But make no mistake, I'm going to tell command staff we have our man."

"And *I'm* going to conduct an unbiased homicide investigation."

The Internal Affairs sergeant said, "That's good. Use that line with the media after you arrest that redneck prick."

CHAPTER 64

I WASTED NO time after Dennis Wu's interview of Rob Trilling. I didn't sit at my desk and pout. I didn't try to convince myself that Trilling was guilty or innocent. I looked at what I knew so far and what I needed to find out. There was a mountain of information I had to decipher. And I needed to do it right away. The NYPD might be telling me to keep it quiet, but I knew how things worked: eventually someone was going to make a comment that got into the media. That meant I only had a limited amount of time.

I used a contact at the FBI to gain access to any reports Rob Trilling wrote while he was working on the task force. I didn't go through the ASAC, Robert Lincoln. I may have hinted to my contact that Lincoln had approved it, but I didn't have the energy or the time to put up with that condescending jerk right now. I explained it had to do with a performance evaluation.

So I was sequestered in a room on the first floor of the New York field office with a stack of reports on the table in front of me. If I wanted copies made of any reports, the FBI was going to make a log of what I copied. They even had someone sit in the room with me while I went through the reports. They didn't seem to trust anyone.

Trilling had been busy during his brief time at the FBI. He was out looking for fugitives every day, even on the weekend a couple of times. And it looked like he usually got who he was looking for. I saw the name Lou Pershing and remembered that he was an associate of the asshole William Hackford we'd arrested at the Bronx warehouse. The guy hadn't yet weaseled out of federal custody yet, mainly because of the amount of heroin found in the warehouse. Like Trilling had said, it was almost as if no one cared about the human trafficking violations, though Hackford had been charged with that as well.

I was looking through a surveillance report from a couple of months ago on a house in Queens. The resident at the house was the mother of a fugitive the FBI had been looking for. I saw the address and felt an icy shot through my system.

I quickly pulled out my phone and brought up a map program. The house he'd been surveilling was only two blocks away from the house of the sniper's first victim, Marie Ballard. It could be a coincidence, but it made me uneasy.

Now I raced through report after report, focusing mainly on the addresses. Trilling had been in Staten Island and Midtown Manhattan. Neither of the surveillances was that close to the shootings, but they did show Trilling had been in the area.

I took a deep breath and tried to figure this out. Of course, on a task force like this, he'd always be riding all over the city, looking for fugitives. But I kept going back to the address in Queens.

I tried again to get into the head of the shooter. I'd been trying since the case was first assigned to me. Why were these victims targeted? What was different about them? Was it completely random?

I had copies made of the most relevant reports. The young woman who was assigned to sit with me looked like she wouldn't care if I told her the case involved the kidnapping of the president. She just filled in the number of each report I had copied and had me sign the bottom of the log.

I needed to bounce a few things off Walter Jackson before he left for the day.

CHAPTER 65

WALTER WAITED FOR me at the office after I texted him. He liked coming in early so he could be home at a decent hour to spend time with his daughters. I know what it's like to fight for time with your family. I hated taking him away from that. But if ever there was a case that was important to me, it was this one.

As soon as I walked in the door, Walter said, "I don't need to be home early today. I already gave my wife a present."

I was confused but managed to ask, "What'd you give her?"

"A little model of Mount Everest." He paused, and when the smile came over his face, I realized what he was doing. "She asked me if it was to scale. I told her no, it's just to look at." His belly laugh lifted my spirits.

I grinned, then quickly got Walter up to speed. I said, "I can't believe the victims are just random choices. But looking at them, I can't find a pattern. It's driving me crazy."

Walter opened a folder on his computer. I could see it held newspaper and internet articles. Some had been scanned, so I could see the headlines. Others were just electronic files in small fonts.

Walter said, "You know I always keep every media report about a case someone on the squad is working. It helps me keep an open mind about cases. I find that occasionally reporters will see something or interview someone that we didn't. They may not know the significance of what they saw. Maybe you'd want to look through these files?"

"Have you seen anything that would be of interest?"

"I haven't had time to do anything but save the articles. But they're from a wide range of media. From straight-up newspaper reports, like the articles Lois Frang has been writing for the *Brooklyn Democrat*, to business journalism covering Adam Glossner's company. There's a lot in there right now."

I had Walter email the files to me so I could look through them.

Walter said, "By the headlines, the media is portraying each of the victims as a hero in their own right. A single mother, a firefighter, a family man, and a community activist."

"The question is, how accurate are those portrayals?"

"You know how the media can twist things to their own narrative. And no one likes to talk badly about crime victims or the dead. Hell, even if someone like O. J. Simpson died, some sports reporter would be talking about what a great running back he was and leave out the double murder and armed robbery. It's just a way to get readers interested." Walter added, "Look at Gus Querva. The media's about to anoint him a saint. But no one's talked about how he extorted businesses and is a suspect in four different homicides."

I thanked Walter for his information and for giving me the chance to just run ideas by him. He had a good head on his shoulders, and sometimes that's all you need to see something more clearly.

I had to find time to read Walter's media reports. That meant I'd have to steal some time away from my family. Just like most cops.

CHAPTER 66

I GOT HOME late and scrounged a few leftovers. The kids had already dispersed to do homework and other projects. Trent and Ricky tried to make it look like they were studying, but I knew they were on their phones playing a game together. I didn't have the time or energy to comment.

Mary Catherine knew I had a lot to do and gave me some space. I was looking down at my iPad, which was usually reserved for watching movies or following New York sports teams. Tonight I was using it to read the files Walter Jackson had emailed me.

I saw what he meant about no one wanting to say anything negative about the dead. Each of the victims was painted in the best possible light. The first victim, Marie Ballard, had worked at the Housing Authority for over twenty years. She also had raised two children by herself—Duane Ballard, the young man we spoke to the day Trilling and I went to the house, and his younger sister. As far as I could tell, she'd done a good job raising the kids.

The firefighter, Thomas Bannon, had coached Little League baseball on his days off.

The *New York Post* shared four different photographs of Adam Glossner with his wife and kids. Anyone would be moved by those family photos.

Most of the articles about Gus Querva were glowing. Only Lois Frang at the *Brooklyn Democrat* was brave enough to mention that Querva had done prison time for strong-arm robbery and had beaten his first wife so many times she fled and stayed at various women's shelters until she could move out of state.

The last thing I read was an older article from a financial journal. It talked about the company Glossner had run, Holbrook Financial. There was a photograph of Glossner at a conference table with six other professionals, but nothing about his family.

Mainly, the article talked about a fine the company had recently paid due to a complaint from the Securities and Exchange Commission. There wasn't much else I picked up from the article other than the attorney's name at the SEC: Chloe Lewis.

Then someone said, "Hey, Dad, can I talk to you?"

I looked up from my iPad to see Juliana standing next to me. "Of course. You can always talk to me." She slid onto the seat beside me. Her eyes looked a little bloodshot. "What's wrong, sweetheart?"

"Did you and Rob have a fight?"

"Why do you ask that?"

"I was texting with him, and his last message said he couldn't talk to me for now until you and him got something straight." She wiped her eyes with her finger. "Was it a fight about me?"

"No, sweetheart, it has nothing to do with you. But it could be a pretty big deal. Maybe try not to have any contact with Rob until we resolve it."

"Can you tell me what it's about?"

"I wish I could. But it has to do with work, and I'm not allowed to discuss it." That may have been the truth, but the look on my daughter's face made me feel like shit for saying it.

I didn't like how threads of this case were getting entwined in every part of my life. Maybe I'd get some clarity tomorrow. I try to keep my work and home lives separate. This whole situation with Trilling blurred that line.

I couldn't focus with the kids that night and slept in fits. All I kept thinking about was whether Rob Trilling could be the Longshot Killer.

CHAPTER 67

ROB TRILLING DIDN'T exactly wake up. He just sort of transitioned from lying in his bed, unable to fall asleep, to standing up and moving around. Even if he didn't have sleep issues, he wouldn't be able to get any rest now anyway. His whole world felt like it was crashing in around him.

He had no idea how seriously the NYPD was looking at him. His ex-partner, Michael Bennett, was probably working the case right now.

Trilling needed some friendly human contact. Some lively conversation. He wasn't going to find that in his apartment. At least not with his current roommates.

He got dressed quickly and slipped out the door. The cool early morning air invigorated him. The feeling wore off before he reached the sidewalk. Without even thinking about it, Trilling hopped on the subway. He was hoping to catch Darcy Farnan at the VA off-site counseling center in Midtown.

There were only five people on his train as it rolled toward 42nd Street. Sitting by himself in the back of a subway car wasn't any way to get his mind off his troubles.

Two men stepped onto the train at the next stop. They were both in their mid-twenties, trying to look cool. Light shirts in the cool weather to show they were tough. Maybe it would be okay on the subway, but the wind in the city would cut right through them. Trilling went back to feeling sorry for himself.

A few minutes into the ride, raised voices caught Trilling's attention. When he looked up from the rear of the car, he saw the two men without jackets were standing over a pudgy guy who'd been typing on his phone.

One of the men looked down and said, "Nice phone you got there."

The other man said, "Give it here. I wanna take a closer look at it."

The seated man was older, maybe forty, with wire-rimmed glasses and a heavy parka like he was in Wisconsin.

This was the shit that drove Trilling crazy. That bullies like this would just take things away from people because there was no one to stop them. A bullet in the head might stop them. Maybe a good thrashing on the subway would too.

Trilling sat up straight and watched the confrontation for a moment more. The man meekly handed his phone to one of the bullies. The bullies just turned and went back to their seats with it, satisfied with their effort.

Trilling stood up and held the overhead rail. He tested its strength to see if he could pull himself up and kick if he had to.

He realized it was a little theatrical and decided that his heart wasn't in the effort anyway.

He watched silently as the bullies got off at the next stop with the man's phone.

Three stops later, Trilling left the subway car. He didn't even give a look of concern to the man whose phone had been taken. Instead, as soon as he came up onto the street level, Trilling called Darcy Farnan at the VA. But he got no answer.

Trilling wasn't sure what he'd say to her anyway. That all he was trying to do was help the people of New York? That his meds and lack of sleep had caused too many problems for him, and he needed more serious therapy?

Maybe it was just as well Darcy didn't answer.

CHAPTER 68

I'D ALREADY BEEN to the office and was out running down leads when my cell phone rang. I was surprised to see that the caller was Lois Frang. I debated picking it up. I really had nothing I wanted to tell her about. But I also knew that she'd met Harry Grissom for breakfast once already this week. If I didn't answer, she might call Harry. I decided to make it a quick conversation.

"Hello, Lois. What can I do for you on this beautiful morning?"

"Wow. That's the best greeting I've ever got from someone at the NYPD."

"Part of our new directives. Spread sunshine, then worry about solving crimes."

"Between you and Harry Grissom, I'd say you guys are working overtime on the sunshine part."

"Was there something specific you needed today, Lois?"

"I'm trying to follow up on some rumors that I heard."

My stomach tightened. Had a rumor about Rob Trilling already slipped out of the NYPD? I didn't even want to think about that.

Lois said, "It's about the second victim in the Longshot Killer case. The fireman named Thomas Bannon. I thought about talking to his family, but I heard they're a closemouthed bunch. You know how the Irish Catholics can be."

"I know all too well."

"Do you know Bannon's family?"

"We've met." I flexed my hand, which had been sore since I'd punched one of the brothers who'd assaulted us at Louise Bannon's home. I added, "What's the rumor?"

"That Bannon was a pervert. That he'd been caught downloading child pornography on a FDNY computer."

"You're not going to run a story like that, are you? It doesn't do any good for anyone."

"I'm not sure where I'm going with it. But I was hoping you might verify the rumor."

"I've never heard anything about that." Even as I said it, I realized I wanted to check this rumor out. It might also explain why Bannon's in-laws and widow got so bent out of shape when I just asked a few simple questions.

Lois said, "I need to hear it verified from a reliable source. Any ideas who might talk?"

"I thought you and Harry Grissom had breakfast yesterday. He's a pretty reliable source."

"We had breakfast today too."

"Did he say anything about the case?"

"Zilch."

I chuckled. "He's a puzzle, that one."

"And I'll figure him out one day. But now I'm looking for someone to quote. Even anonymously."

"That doesn't sound like it's directly related to our case. You couldn't get Harry to comment?"

"As I understand it, you and Harry have been friends for twenty years. Have you ever known him to talk about a case or police work with someone other than another cop?"

"Good point. I rarely see Harry talk to anyone about anything. You should consider yourself privileged."

"He's a lovely man. But now I feel like you're trying to distract me."

"Not really. I've honestly never heard that rumor, and I'm up to my eyeballs with other things to worry about."

All I got was a quick thanks as she hung up.

If Thomas Bannon did download child pornography on a city computer, why was there no mention in any NYPD report? Just one more thing to add to my list.

CHAPTER 69

I HAD NEVER visited the offices of the Securities and Exchange Commission. There's not a huge call for it when working homicides. The first thing I noticed was that the SEC was not among the agencies in the Jacob K. Javits Federal Building just east of Broadway but in the American Express Tower just west of the 9/11 memorial.

This luxurious skyscraper was a far cry from the near-slum conditions of the VA off-site office. The lobby bustled with well-dressed professionals who might take clients to lunch in the array of restaurants on the second floor or show off the unobstructed western views of the Hudson. Not bad for a government office.

I took the elevator up to the fourth floor and easily found the SEC offices. I marveled at the art reproductions on the walls and realized this was one of the few government agencies that actually *brought in* money. The fines the SEC levied on hedge funds and banks who'd skirted the law were legendary.

The polite receptionist took my name and then led me down a hallway. I'd called ahead for an appointment and was surprised I could get in so quickly. The receptionist tapped lightly on a solid wooden door, then opened it for me.

I stepped into the wide office with a view to the north. A young woman behind a giant desk was on the phone but waved me into a chair. I took a moment to look around the office and saw the attorney's personal touches. A full-sized movie poster of Marvel's *Avengers: Endgame* dominated one wall; degrees from NYU, including a law degree, hung on the wall directly behind her.

As soon as she hung up the phone, the woman stood to shake my hand. "Chloe Lewis. Nice to meet you." She had a warm smile that put me at ease.

After we chatted for a few moments, Chloe Lewis said, "What, exactly, can I do for you, Detective?"

I explained that I was investigating the murder of Adam Glossner. I asked her about the article I'd read concerning his company paying huge fines.

The attorney shook her head. "I can't believe they let him get away with just paying fines. Not to speak ill of the dead, but Glossner personally raided several accounts, and if everything had gone right, no one would have ever caught him. He also hid interests in two different companies that he pushed to clients. I referred the case to the FBI. I assumed they'd go after him, not settle without even an indictment."

It was an old story. Not just with the FBI but with most law enforcement agencies. With limited resources and manpower, if a case could be resolved quickly, that was usually the route taken.

Chloe Lewis said, "I guess I just expected more from the FBI. They're nothing like how they're portrayed in movies and on

TV. They let Glossner write a few checks and that was it. I hope he developed an ulcer at the very least." She cringed, then looked at me and said, "I'm sorry. Is that wrong? I mean, with him being dead."

"Did you kill him?"

"No, of course not."

"Then I wouldn't worry about it." I liked her relieved giggle.

The attorney went through a few other issues on the case. I wasn't really listening toward the end. All I could think about was that two victims, Adam Glossner and Gus Querva, may have both had criminal backgrounds. And I needed to look into the rumor Lois Frang had brought up to me about the firefighter. It was the only thing I had at the moment.

CHAPTER 70

I TOOK A moment before I walked into the fire station on Staten Island. After my last encounter with the local firefighters, I wanted to think this through. Despite everything, I would've felt more comfortable if Trilling were with me. Having him around was sort of like having your own superhero walking the streets of New York. My pistol was on my right hip. To be on the safe side, I also had slipped a collapsible ASP baton into my front pocket and a slim container of pepper spray into my jacket pocket. I didn't think I'd have to use them. But I like to be prepared.

The fire station where Thomas Bannon had worked was not far from his family's house. I'd been in dozens of firehouses over the years, and truthfully, aside from a few structural differences, they all looked and felt about the same to me. Big cavernous buildings to hold the fire engines. Echoes from every corner. Millions of dollars in equipment stacked along the walls or in cabinets. And a few easygoing firefighters cooking or doing chores.

This station was no different. The first two firefighters I saw were engrossed in polishing some equipment. They looked up at me but soon returned to what might have been a power saw.

I continued into the administration area, where I found four firefighters sitting in comfortable chairs in a semicircle facing the captain, a tall, fit woman in her mid-forties who was leaning on a counter. It almost looked like they were holding an encounter group.

I waited at the rear of the room until the captain looked up and saw me. I was in an all-weather jacket with no visible police insignia. But the captain was sharp. She said, "Can I help you, Detective?"

I walked closer to the group, men and women in their twenties and thirties, including one man who had to be over six feet tall. All eyes were on me, and I felt a definite hostile vibe.

I had an idea how she knew I was a cop. In my most polite voice, I said, "I was wondering if I could talk with you in private, Captain."

"That's not necessary. We have an open-door policy in this station. Anything you say to me, I'll say to them. In fact, since we're all gathered here, this is the perfect place to talk."

She was a cool customer. Clearly the Bannons had talked about their scuffle with me and Trilling at the Bannon residence. I decided I had to plow ahead. If I went through official FDNY channels, it could take time. I was starting to feel like I had a real break in this case. I wasn't going to ruin my momentum.

I cleared my throat and said, "I'm—"

The captain cut me off. "We know who you are. We also know what you're doing here. Louise Bannon already told us about your run-in with her brothers. We also know the nasty rumors that have been floating around about Thomas Bannon. Am I pretty close to why you're here?"

All I could do was nod slowly.

The captain said, "But he's dead. So the rumors don't mean anything and have nothing to do with why he was murdered. What none of us can understand is why you're trying to smear the reputation of a true hero, instead of trying to find the shitbird coward who shot him."

That comment was greeted with a round of nods and approval from the other firefighters.

The captain looked at the giant man I had noticed as soon as I stepped in the room. She said, "Russ, why don't you show the detective out. And I'm telling you right now you don't have to take any shit from him at all."

When the man stood up, I realized I had underestimated his height. He was more like six foot eight, and probably weighed three hundred pounds. The vast majority of it muscle. All the other firefighters seemed satisfied with the way this situation was being handled. It made sense. If this guy knocked the crap out of me and I filed a complaint, no one else would be in trouble. If I caused a scene here, not only would I have to deal with multiple firefighters, after it was all over, but also they could get their story straight and make it look like I was lying.

I went willingly with Russ. He didn't grab me by the arm or shove me. He just pointed me through a side door, blocking my path back to the open engine bay where I'd entered.

As soon as I stepped outside, I realized exactly what Russ had planned for me. There was a little grassy area between the fire station and a furniture store. No one would notice the empty patch unless they walked around the building. That could be bad news for me.

I turned and faced Russ. All I could say was "You're big."

"I know." He showed a little satisfaction with that statement.

I said, "I don't want any trouble."

"No one ever does."

I said, "You know the old saying 'The bigger they are, the harder they fall'?"

"Yep. Just more fake news."

"I think it'd be better if you just sat down and avoided the fall altogether. Less chance of injury that way."

Russ said, "I'm going to enjoy knocking out a few of your teeth. Why would I sit down?"

"So you don't run into a wall or twist your ankle tripping over something when you can't see."

The giant man said, "What the hell are you talking about?"

That's when I casually pulled my left hand out of my jacket pocket. The can of pepper spray was easily concealed in my palm. I sprayed Russ in the face and stepped back. I'd expected a shout of agony, but the low register and volume were surprising. I watched the giant firefighter stumble around in the grass. I stepped forward, holding his arm as I kicked his feet out from under him.

I said, "Easy does it, big fella," as I eased him to the ground and left him whining and holding his eyes. I made sure he was safe in the grass. "Just sit here for a while and the stinging will go away."

He managed to speak through the sniffles. "Really? How long till it stops?"

"An hour. Maybe less."

Russ moaned as a long string of snot flooded from his nose.

I'll admit I had to keep from smiling as I hustled around the building to my car.

CHAPTER 71

AFTER MY ENCOUNTER session with the giant firefighter on Staten Island, I raced directly to One Police Plaza. Essentially, the firefighters had confirmed the rumors. There's no way they would have reacted like that if there wasn't some fire behind the smoke. Their crude attempt at scaring me off only pushed me to find out exactly what the hell was going on.

Once inside headquarters, I didn't make my usual rounds to say hello to my friends and check in with old partners. Instead, I went directly to a specific analyst who had helped me on cases a dozen times before. His name was Neil Placky, and he had one of those minds that could remember and interpret seemingly insignificant details. All good analysts have that same trait. But Neil had a University of Pennsylvania education to augment it. A fact that he worked into virtually every conversation.

As soon as I stepped into the main analytic room, several

heads turned to look at the door. Once they established that I wasn't anyone of note, everyone went back to work. Everyone except Neil. He stood up from his desk at the front of the room and waved me over.

We shook hands and caught up. But I'll admit I gave him the abbreviated version. Basically, "Everyone's fine." Then I laid out parts of the case I was working on. Mainly, the rumor FDNY firefighter Thomas Bannon had downloaded child pornography on a city computer.

I could tell by Neil's silence that there was meat to this rumor.

After a quiet moment, I gave Neil a hard look and said, "I can't tell you how important this is. Not only to a homicide investigation but for the NYPD as well."

Neil let out a long sigh. He said, "C'mon, Mike. Don't do this to me. I have very explicit instructions not to talk about this."

"I already know Bannon was downloading child pornography. That fact was confirmed by other means. I just want to understand, if everyone knew about it, why wasn't there an investigation? Could it lead to someone taking the law into their own hands?"

It looked like a light went on in Neil's eyes. He now understood exactly what I was asking and why. He said, "We never talked about this, right?"

"I was never even here."

"That's not gonna fly, because every analyst in this room just saw you walk in and talk to me. But we're just catching up. Two old friends. I remember when I was at Penn, I had an ethics class. Thank God I slept through most of it."

"You don't have to give me evidence, just tell me what happened so I understand."

"Okay. We did receive a complaint that Thomas Bannon had downloaded child pornography. Apparently, an administrator who was at the fire station observed it. To avoid a conflict of interest, the NYPD referred it to the FBI. All I know is there was some issue with the chain of custody of the evidence and they cut a quick deal for no prosecution if Bannon retired immediately. His paperwork was in when he was shot. That's all I know."

"While I have you in the right frame of mind, let me ask you about the first victim of the sniper. She worked for the Housing Authority."

Before I could say anything else, Neil asked, "Marie Ballard?"

I stared at my friend. Just by coming up with the answer without knowing the exact question told me everything I needed to know.

I said, "Were there allegations against her?"

"We got a referral from the Housing Authority inspector general. She'd used over a hundred thousand dollars in city money to pay personal expenses. This was over the course of at least nine years."

"And nobody caught it until recently?"

Neil just shrugged. "We referred that one to the FBI as well. That's how I knew her name so quickly. I heard that the mayor had called the FBI directly to keep it quiet. She was on a repayment plan to keep from going to trial." Neil was now speaking in a very low tone. Almost like we were in church. But he was smart enough to know he had pointed me in a new direction in the case. I'd finally found a link between all four victims. They had each committed crimes for which they weren't being prosecuted.

And Rob Trilling would have had access to all those reports while he was at the FBI.

CHAPTER 72

ROB TRILLING HAD to do something to get his mind off his worries. He didn't think it was right to go visit his family up in Putnam County. They shouldn't have to be around someone who felt as low as he did. He didn't even want to think what his negative vibes might do to his niece and nephew. He needed to get out and do something useful, maybe volunteer for a few hours. Usually food banks and soup kitchens posted when they needed people, but Trilling decided to help the community in another way.

He looked down at his phone. There was a text from Juliana Bennett, asking if he was okay. He messaged her back, saying, As good as can be expected. Hope to be able to talk to you about it soon. He didn't risk saying anything else. The last thing he wanted to do was hurt a young woman who'd been nothing but nice to him. Trilling didn't have any idea what her father was saying about him. It didn't matter. He intended to keep on doing the right thing.

He slipped out of the apartment with the idea to look for his fugitive, Lou Pershing. Trilling had searched internet forums having to do with mercenaries and off-the-grid nut jobs. Even if they called themselves "military consultants." Although there was a lot of extraneous crap on the internet, Trilling was able to find a few mentions of Pershing. A few new mentions of Marisol Alba had popped up too, a woman with a phone number that had been linked to Pershing when Trilling was still at the FBI. Intel had said she could be his current girlfriend and she lived in a rented brownstone apartment in Brooklyn. Maybe Pershing would be there too.

Trilling rode the F train into Brooklyn and got out at Carroll Street, then walked south toward the area called Red Hook. He liked not worrying about a car and where to park, though he didn't particularly care for walking. Not that he minded the exercise; it just felt boring to him. He found himself looking at the address about forty minutes after he got off the train.

There was a vacant house a few doors down and across the street. Trilling found a comfortable place on the porch to sit where no one could see him from the street and he could watch the house where he thought Lou Pershing might be living. He appreciated parents walking children home from school and joggers hustling along the sidewalks under the canopy of trees. Somehow this didn't feel like the kind of place a guy like Lou Pershing would live.

Not long after nightfall, Trilling noticed a single light in the upstairs of the house. The way it moved told him it was a flashlight. That looked like someone trying to keep a low profile.

Maybe Pershing and his girlfriend had turned off the electricity so people would think they'd moved away.

Having scouted the area, Trilling was able to walk unseen across the street and down to Pershing's building. He slipped into the building's entryway. It took only a little effort with his pocketknife to slide the single lock from the doorframe.

He creeped through the ground floor and made his way upstairs without making any noise. He paused at the top of the staircase near where he'd seen the light and lowered to a crouch to listen for sounds within the apartment. His plan was simple: grab Pershing and leave him tied up in front of the nearest precinct. He didn't care about getting credit for an arrest. He just wanted to get an asshole like Pershing off the street before he hurt anyone.

Trilling realized he was in the weeds on this one. But if he was already going insane, one more crazy act wouldn't mean much. He stood up and heard his knee pop. When he stepped around the corner, he froze.

The point of a knife pressed against his throat.

CHAPTER 73

IT WAS AFTER dark by the time I arrived at my apartment on the Upper West Side. I had been so busy all day that I'd lost track of life in general. I'd skipped lunch; I hadn't checked in at home like I usually do; I'd jumped from interview to interview. And as soon as I walked through the door, it all hit me at once. I thought I might collapse. But something wasn't right. Some vibe in the apartment felt off.

I stepped through the foyer and still didn't see anyone. I heard some movement in the living room, but no one had come to greet me. That was unusual. One of the big advantages of having ten kids is that there is always someone interested in meeting you at the door.

When I came through the dining room and into the living room, I had to stop and take in the scene. Mary Catherine sat on the couch, propped up on a mountain of pillows. Her feet rested on an ottoman. A TV table was positioned in front of her. All the kids—and I mean every one of them—turned and faced me, grinning like they were posing for a photograph.

I couldn't keep a smile from spreading over my face. "What's this all about?"

Chrissy stepped forward. "We decided it was International Mary Catherine Day. We want to show her how much we love her. And how happy we are about trying to have a baby."

I was speechless. A tear ran down Mary Catherine's left cheek. We really had raised these kids the right way.

I said, "Ricky, does this mean you're making something extra special for dinner?"

My son shook his head. Then he looked across at Chrissy and said, "Jane and I are the official servers. But Chrissy and Shawna are making dinner." The four of them broke off from the group and headed into the kitchen.

Bridget and Fiona took my hands and led me to the couch next to Mary Catherine. They set me up pretty much the same way. Only without the ottoman. They used a chair to put my feet up.

After a couple of minutes, Ricky and Jane walked out with plates. Each plate was covered by a bowl, and they made a show of revealing the meal to us: hot dogs on buns, with mustard, plus a handful of potato chips and a pickle.

Jane whispered to me, "Chrissy counts the pickle as your vegetable serving."

I said, "It looks delicious."

Chrissy came out of the kitchen still grinning and said, "They're even your favorite kind of hot dogs."

"Nathan's?"

Chrissy looked crestfallen. She said, "No, all-beef Ball Park franks."

"I love those too."

Then Shawna said, "We even have the perfect movie for everyone to watch. You don't have to move or anything."

Jane said, "We picked the movie through a democratic process."

Trent moaned, "A really long democratic process."

Jane gave her brother a dismissive look, then added, "We each listed five movies, then we picked three out of that whole group. We kept voting until we came up with *The Princess Bride*."

Mary Catherine beamed. "Brilliant."

It was exactly what I needed. It got me out of my head and only thinking about what was most important in life: my family.

CHAPTER 74

ROB TRILLING STOOD as still as possible. He was afraid to even swallow. He could feel the knife tip dig into the skin of his throat. The idea of his blood spilling onto the floor kept him from doing anything stupid. At least anything more stupid than breaking into a building to find a fugitive while he was suspended from the police force.

Trilling felt a slight tremor in the blade. Whoever held the knife was nervous too. He hoped they weren't nervous enough to make a mistake. In the dim light he couldn't tell who was standing against the wall with the knife to his throat.

Then a woman's voice said, "Who are you?" She had a slight accent.

"I'm Rob. Who are you?"

"What do you want here?"

Trilling decided he had nothing to lose. He said, "I'm looking for Lou Pershing."

"Why?"

He was going to say, *To arrest him,* but at the last moment said, "To turn him over to the authorities."

"You're a bounty hunter?"

"I guess." He felt the knife move away from his throat. Trilling sucked in a deep lungful of air. Then the flashlight turned on and he saw an attractive woman with long, dark hair that needed to be washed. She held a butcher knife with an eight-inch blade.

Trilling said, "Are you Marisol?"

She nodded.

"No power?"

"I have power, but I didn't want to risk Lou thinking I was home. He's been gone a few days, and I'm just trying to get out without him seeing me. I was going to go to Los Angeles, but I can't come up with the money."

When Marisol turned, Trilling noticed bruises around her neck and swelling around her left eye. He felt anger welling up inside him. How could men act like this?

Trilling made a split-second decision. "I know a place you can go where you'll be safe. Pack a small suitcase. Just the stuff you really need."

"I'm wearing everything I really need. Can you actually get me out of here?"

Forty-five minutes later, Trilling and Marisol stood in front of a women's center in Manhattan. Trilling had learned about the center while on patrol his first week with the NYPD.

He stayed with Marisol while she answered a few simple questions from the woman who ran the facility.

As he stood up to leave, Marisol gave him a hug. She whispered, "Thank you," into his ear.

The director said, "I wish every cop paid attention like you do, Officer Trilling. I'm glad you know to bring women here."

"One last thing," Trilling said to Marisol. "Do you by chance have a recent picture of him? The one I have is blurry, and I could really use a better one."

Marisol fumbled for her cell phone. It took her a minute. "I may have deleted them all." But then she stopped, turned her phone for Trilling to see finally a clear image of the man he was determined to find.

"Thanks." He left the center feeling like his head had cleared a little bit. He hoped to find Pershing soon. If for no other reason than to stop him from terrorizing his girlfriends.

CHAPTER 75

I WAS IN the office early again. Despite the great evening with my family, where Mary Catherine and I were pampered like a rich lady's French poodles, I still had an anchor in my stomach when I thought about Rob Trilling.

As usual, the only other person in the office was Walter Jackson. I gathered my notes and went in to talk to Walter, the walking computer whose ease in finding the smallest detail in a case matched his ability in coming up with puns.

I stood in Walter's doorway, waiting for him to stop focusing on the computer screen. He looked up and grinned. "When I heard someone else in the office, I knew it had to be you. Are you holding up okay?"

I shrugged and said, "I'm trying to treat this like any other case. Be thorough and fair. That's what they used to drill into us at the academy." I tried to get a glimpse of his computer screen to see what Walter had been focusing on. "What was that you were reading?"

"A story about glass coffins being all the rage, but I don't know. All I can say is: remains to be seen." He kept a neutral expression for almost five seconds, then his grin came back. That was also about the time his pun clicked in my brain. I smiled and nodded. It wasn't bad, but my mind was elsewhere.

Walter picked up that I wasn't in the mood to joke around. He turned in his chair to fully face me. He said, "Tell me what you found out so far."

I told him about the victims and their criminal pasts. I said, "It's not just the NYPD. The Securities and Exchange Commission also sent a referral to the FBI for Adam Glossner. That means whoever's getting the information is getting it from the FBI."

"And your boy Trilling had been working at the FBI since around the same time the sniper started shooting people." Walter paused and looked at me. "I like him personally too. None of the rest of you ever come up with puns for me. But I can't dismiss him as a suspect because of my personal feelings."

"Neither can I."

"Your theory is sound. He's got the skill, the opportunity, and possibly the motive. I didn't want to mention it, but he's wrapped a little tight. He could have a serious vigilante streak in him. Straight arrows like Trilling hate it when people beat the system. Maybe it pushed him over the edge. Call it whatever you like. PTSD, morally driven, or just plain crazy. Look at how pissed he was about the gang leader, Gus Querva, being treated like a saint. I think he's good for the shootings."

I said, "I know. It's a simple theory to follow. Rob Trilling took exception to people getting away with crimes. I've seen it before, but not to this extreme."

Walter said, "Why does a simple theory make you nervous?"

"Because it is so simple, someone from headquarters could run with it without any follow-up. I think we owe it to Trilling to take it a little more seriously."

"So, what do you do next? Wait for him to snap and maybe shoot a bunch of people at once?"

That made me stop. All I could think was *Holy shit, what if that really does happen?* The thought scared me to my bones.

I hung my head. "I guess I've got to go over to the FBI again. That could be messy."

"Or at least unpleasant. Who can you call over there? That ASAC who has it in for you?"

I shook my head. "I'm not sure. I used to call my friend Emily Parker. She always worked miracles." It hurt to even think about my dear friend.

Walter mumbled, "She was a smart woman. That was a big loss to us all."

Instead of answering, all I could do was nod. I sat there silently, considering my options. Then I had an idea. Possibly a really good idea.

I spun around and aimed for my desk as I thanked Walter. It was still too early in the morning to try this idea, but I knew what call I'd be making as soon as the clock struck eight.

CHAPTER 76

THE OFFICE WAS still mostly empty when I called Roberta Herring. Roberta and I had worked together in the Bronx decades ago, back when we were both rookie patrol officers. I tried to teach her patience and she tried to teach me to use my gut feeling more. The irony is that she left the NYPD and worked her way up the ladder with the Department of Justice Office of the Inspector General. It was about the only agency with any oversight over the FBI. It also forced Roberta to be patient with every case. Investigations into wrongdoing at the FBI were never undertaken lightly and always took far too long.

Roberta picked up on the second ring. I could almost feel the smile as she said, "Mike Bennett, calling me before 9 a.m. My guess is that you need help, or you miss me so badly you couldn't wait until I was a little more settled behind my nice cushy desk."

"Both." We laughed together for a moment. We weren't only

old friends; we were also *good* friends. We didn't need any pretext to call each other, and we didn't need excuses when we called to ask for help. Roberta had helped me through some of the most difficult times imaginable. Hell, Roberta had stood as godmother to my second youngest, Shawna. She had been just about the only choice. Often people just assume that because Shawna is Black, we chose a Black woman as her godmother. That never once played into our decision.

We quickly caught up with each other's lives since I'd last seen her in Washington, DC, where not long ago she'd helped me look into Emily Parker's murder. Then Roberta got right to the point. "What's this call really about, Mike?"

I held nothing back. I told her about the case, Rob Trilling, how even my family loved him. Every detail I could think of. I waited in silence. Maybe longer than I thought I should. Then I realized from the sound of keystrokes that she was looking at her computer. I heard a couple of um-hums and ah-ahs.

Roberta said, "I can see all these referrals you're talking about. None of them are restricted. None of the cases seem particularly high concept or unusual. We both know the city of New York experiences a great deal of fraud. We also know people from all walks of life download child pornography. I'd be surprised to find a serious hedge-fund manager who didn't bend the law."

"So you can find the cases that quickly on the computer?"

"And that means anyone in the New York field office could do the same."

I felt disappointment. I couldn't quite place it at first. But I now realized just how much I didn't want this theory to be possible. Trilling had gone off the rails. I couldn't ignore it. Walter's concern about Trilling snapping popped into my head.

Then Roberta said, "What I'm missing is the psychological makeup and assessment of... What's his name? Rob Trilling?"

"I gotta say, Roberta, he seemed like a really decent young man. I'm afraid Juliana has a little bit of a crush on him. On the flip side, I could see him having a self-righteous streak. He thinks things should be done a certain way. He believes in a mission for the police department. I can imagine him taking things too far. I just don't want it to be true."

"You say he's an Army vet."

"Yeah."

"Sniper?"

"No, a Ranger. From what I gather, a really good one."

"We can't eliminate this being a result of some form of PTSD."

"I've considered that. It doesn't change the fact that he needs to be stopped."

"Does he go to any kind of therapy or counseling?"

"Yeah, I spoke to his VA counselor. She's not all that worried about him."

"Of course she isn't. That's *our* job. And it's a much tougher job when a suspect is likable."

I thought about that, then said, "I guess that's where my doubts spring from."

"Have you started writing the arrest affidavit? That was what always made cases real for me. When I had to put the facts in order and hand it to someone who knew nothing about the people involved. They could read the facts and see that a crime had been committed."

"I've got a few more things to tie up. But I intend to start working on it this afternoon. I'm still piecing together information on the last shooting. The neighborhood activist with a criminal background, Gus Querva. Aside from being a public figure with a dark past, I don't see where the FBI was investigating him."

Roberta typed away for a moment more, then said, "I see it."

I started taking notes on another nail in Rob Trilling's coffin.

CHAPTER 77

I WAITED ON the phone while Roberta Herring checked and rechecked every file she could find connected to Gus Querva.

Then Roberta told me to hang on while she set down the phone. I could hear her on her office phone calling someone to confirm what she'd found on the computer. I had to smile when I heard her tone. Whoever she was talking to must've asked why she was interested. Roberta said, "I'm interested in everything the FBI does. It's my job. I'm not sure what you don't understand about that." There was a pause and then she said, "Thank you for your assistance."

Hearing Roberta Herring dress down someone like that, especially someone in the FBI, made me smile. She'd been a great partner when we worked together in the Bronx. She couldn't stand to see hungry stray dogs, so she always kept dog food in the patrol car. She'd take the dogs back to the precinct and hold them in a back room until she could find someone to adopt them. It worked well until a lieutenant looking for something stumbled upon the makeshift kennel. He would've let things slide, except he'd stepped in a big puddle of dog urine. After that, Roberta kept the dogs she found at a Department of Water facility at the edge of our precinct. One way or another, she always gets what she wants.

She came back on the line, apologized for the wait, and said, "There *was* an official investigation by the FBI into Gus Querva's activities. The New York office had a RICO investigation that included drug distribution, extortion, and murder. The case went on for almost a year until someone blabbed and two key witnesses were murdered. That incident, coupled with the high-profile charity work Querva had been doing, led the US Attorney to decide not to proceed with the case partly for public perception."

"Could Trilling have been able to see those reports?"

"The case was restricted while it was active, but it was closed about two months ago. He would've been able to see the reports. The FBI is weird because they protect the reports like gold but, like in any other agency, everyone talks. Someone must've let something slip. Looks like your boy Trilling cleaned up their mess."

"Roberta, don't make it sound like he's doing a public service."

"You telling me you don't get a little discouraged with the way the courts just spit people out? That's why every cop loved that old Charles Bronson movie series *Death Wish*. Charles Bronson got to do what we dream about doing: killing some of these thugs who prey on people."

"Except this isn't a movie and Rob Trilling isn't Charles Bronson. I'm worried about him as much as anything else. Now I have a definitive link between the four victims. Each had been in the FBI system. Maybe that was enough to throw Trilling over the edge."

Roberta said, "Keep me in the loop, and call me if you need any more help. I'm not sure the ASAC in New York, Robert Lincoln, would appreciate you poking around."

"I guarantee you Lincoln wouldn't appreciate me doing anything."

CHAPTER 78

ROB TRILLING HAD spent the day leaning against a light pole in front of the little dive bar where Lou Pershing was supposed to hang out. The one fugitive he wanted to catch was still out of reach. Hell, Trilling wasn't technically allowed to even *look* for Pershing right now. But he couldn't concentrate on other things knowing this asshole walked free. Technicalities wouldn't stop him from keeping the city safe. It's how he lived with himself.

In reality, Trilling was doing everything he could not to think about his own problems. The alternative to looking for a dangerous fugitive was to lie around his apartment and feel sorry for himself. That wasn't in his nature.

Trilling credited his grandfather with a lot of his attitude. Chet used to tell Trilling and his brother that no matter how low they felt physically, they could always still accomplish something.

So on the few occasions when Trilling was sick and had to stay home from school, his grandfather would make up simple assignments to occupy his mind. Rob would read the entire newspaper, every story, then answer his grandfather's questions. It didn't sound like much, but Trilling knew it helped build his memory and reading skills.

Every time he stopped thinking about Lou Pershing, even for a moment, a feeling of dread washed over him. Trilling felt like his career was already ruined. What would happen if they charged him with murder?

A couple of times he'd even considered the possibility of fleeing. He had options. He could work overseas as a mercenary. Not his first choice. He could go back to Montana and get lost in the wilderness. The idea of not seeing his family again depressed him. So here he was, doing the best he could.

Just then his phone rang. Trilling looked down and saw that it was Darcy Farnan from the VA. He answered it quickly.

Darcy said, "Rob, I saw you called yesterday. Is everything okay?"

"No. Not by a long shot."

"I'm on my lunch hour now, and it's the only free time I have all day. Are you anywhere near Midtown?"

Trilling glanced up at the dive bar's doors, making his decision instantly. "Yes, I'm in Midtown now."

Darcy hesitated, then said, "Rob, there's something I need to tell you."

Trilling didn't like how she'd said that. A quick flash of nerves ran through him. He said, "Why don't you wait till we see each other in person."

"That's probably for the best."

Trilling asked, "Where would you like to meet?" Then he glanced up and froze in place.

He couldn't believe what he was seeing. Lou Pershing, in the flesh, walking out of the bar. How had Trilling not noticed him go in?

Darcy was still talking when Trilling ended the call and stuffed his phone into his front pocket. He fell in behind Pershing, who didn't seem to have a care in the world.

Trilling hoped to change that very soon.

CHAPTER 79

I'D HOPED TO get a little more unofficial background on Rob Trilling's NYPD career so had put in a call to Yvette Morris, a respected patrol officer who'd worked with him in the Bronx. When I got a call back, she told me that she was in training at One Police Plaza today, so I agreed to meet her for coffee in lower Manhattan.

Yvette sat across from me at a tiny café off Church Street. She was in training clothes, which consisted of a T-shirt and 5.11 cargo pants, plus an oversized windbreaker, which covered anything that showed she was an officer with the NYPD. She was about thirty years old, with a soft voice and demeanor, which were incongruent with her hard-edged look of a veteran cop: fit, tall, and with her hair cropped close to her head for practical purposes. She literally inspired confidence.

After we chatted for a few minutes, Yvette said, "I can't imagine why Detective Michael Bennett wants to talk to me."

I said, "This conversation has to be completely confidential. It's about Rob Trilling." I noticed her smile immediately falter. I said, "What's wrong?"

"You're in Homicide still, not IA, right?"

"Yep. Trilling is temporarily assigned to my squad."

"I'm not sure what you want, Detective. Rob is a hard worker."

"I agree."

"Smart, compassionate to victims. He has real potential."

"I sense some hesitation." I noticed how she looked around the café and leaned slightly closer to me.

Yvette said, "He's quick to anger. I mean, he goes from zero to sixty in an instant."

"How so?"

"He won't get in trouble for this, will he?"

I said, "Believe me, any trouble Trilling gets in will be of his own doing."

Yvette took a moment to gather her thoughts. Then she said, "Rob hates to see people beat the system. We arrested a guy for dealing meth twice in one day. The perp got cut loose without any bond the first time. You'd have thought the guy killed the president by Rob's reaction. After we arrested him the second time, Rob walked the perp through booking and then showed up in court on his own time to tell the prosecutor not to release him again."

I nodded. That sounded like Rob Trilling.

Yvette said, "Another time, at a domestic, I saw how Rob hated bullies. The wife and baby were crying, but there were no outward signs of violence. The wife didn't want to press any charges. The husband didn't seem to care one way or the other. Rob led him out of the apartment and downstairs. Supposedly the guy tripped and fell the last flight. He never made a complaint, but it still worried me.

"And then there was a concerning incident of a foot chase of a robber who stole a woman's purse at knifepoint, then shoved the woman into the street, where a taxi nearly ran her over. Rob tackled him hard. Too hard. Broke the guy's jaw and hand in the fall. It made me nervous."

I said, "Did you report these incidents to anyone? This is no comment on you. I'm just curious."

"I didn't have anything solid. No one complained. And he only seemed to react this way to the worst suspects or the ones not facing any punishment. Rob's quirky that way."

I found myself nodding. I wasn't happy to hear anything she had to say. I was almost distraught. But it helped me make up my mind. For a moment I pictured Trilling in prison. The irony wasn't lost on me.

CHAPTER 80

TRILLING FOLLOWED PERSHING east on foot. He thought about calling someone or stopping the fugitive right now, but he wanted to see who Pershing talked to. With Pershing's partner, William Hackford, being held on federal drug and human trafficking charges, there was no telling who Pershing was working with now.

Trilling walked on for a few minutes, assessing his target. Pershing was a big man, over six foot two with broad shoulders. Watching him made Trilling angry, unable to stop thinking about the marks on Marisol's neck or the glass eye Pershing's former girlfriend now had to use.

Trilling had a vague memory of his father. It was really the only memory he had of the man. When Trilling was about four, his father slapped his mother. Hard. Then stormed out. He'd seen his father twice since that incident, but the only thing that had stuck in his mind was the slap. He had no idea where his dad was now. He'd heard rumors. A cowboy in Idaho. Shot by a jealous husband in North Dakota. In jail in a couple of different places. Trilling just assumed it was jail.

Pershing took a corner into a maze of alleys. They were really more like walkways into different businesses. Then Trilling lost him. The fugitive just seemed to vanish.

Trilling looked in every direction. Nothing. Then he started jogging toward the river, which seemed the most likely path Pershing would've taken. Trilling had only taken a few steps when he saw a flash out of the corner of his eye. From around the side of the building a garbage can lid glanced off his head. Trilling ducked and missed the full impact, but it still knocked him a little woozy.

He stumbled back against the brick wall of a building. When he looked up, Lou Pershing was standing in front of him with a three-foot piece of rebar in his hand.

Pershing said, "Who are you?"

"No one."

Pershing let out a little laugh. "Don't sell yourself short, kid. I'm tough to find. I'd say you look a little like a cop. Or you will when you grow up." He looked up and down the alley. They could've been in the Arctic for all the people they saw right now. "Why are you following me?"

Trilling said, "You're a smart guy—you should be able to figure it out."

Pershing slapped the rusty piece of rebar into his left hand. "I'm going to break both of your arms and both of your legs. Teach a cocky bastard like you a lesson."

"I may be cocky, but I knew my dad. I didn't like him. He was a piece of shit who beat his wife, just like you. But at least I'm not a bastard." Trilling canted his body. He'd taken on larger men in his life.

Pershing swung the rebar. Trilling dodged it, then delivered an uppercut. It landed perfectly. Trilling felt a crunch as the punch to Pershing's jaw drove his teeth into his head. Blood spurted from Pershing's upper lip.

Pershing stumbled backward, swinging the rebar wildly. It brushed across Trilling's front, the rough end of the steel rebar tearing open his shirt and breaking the skin of his chest.

They both paused for a moment as each man warily watched the other. Trilling noticed Pershing was panting.

Pershing said, "Let's cut a deal."

Trilling wasn't about to negotiate with scum like this. He raised his left fist. When Pershing tried to block it, Trilling threw a front kick, catching Pershing in the gut.

Trilling heard the air rush out of Pershing and knew he had the advantage. He threw a second kick to almost the same spot.

The blow knocked the remaining air out of Pershing and made him drop the rebar. It clanged on the shoddy asphalt in the alley.

Trilling swung his right hand in a big arc, catching Pershing in the face again. The larger man stumbled back to the wall, but somehow he stayed upright.

Trilling unloaded with half a dozen more punches, until Pershing slid to the ground. He fell on top of Pershing, still throwing punches, then stopped mid-punch. What now? He felt like a dog who'd finally caught the car he'd been chasing. Trilling considered delivering the fugitive to the FBI. That wouldn't work. Too much explaining.

Then he came up with a plan. A plan he didn't like but that made sense.

He stepped away from Pershing. The fugitive was barely conscious, with blood from his nose and cut lips running down his face. Trilling reached for his phone. There was only one person to call.

CHAPTER 81

I WASN'T FAR from downtown when my phone rang with the piano solo from "Layla," the ringtone my kids had installed for me a while back. I was shocked to see Rob Trilling's name on the screen. I thought about not answering the call. I wouldn't take a call from a suspect in any other homicide investigation. I decided to risk it.

I kept it simple. "Hello."

"I'm in an alley. I need you to come here right now." Trilling gave me a couple of cross streets. Then there was silence on the line.

I said, "I'm a few minutes away. I'll be right there." I don't know why I agreed to meet him in person. But something told me it was important. Maybe he'd say or do something that would help me with the case.

Traffic wasn't overwhelming and it was all right turns. I

wondered if I should call Harry Grissom and let him know what was going on. He'd be worried I was talking to Trilling, but at least someone would know where I was. If there was a problem later, a dispute, at least I'd have a boss who knew what was going on. Then I thought about Trilling. The tone of his voice hadn't made me think it would be a trap, or that he was trying to trick me somehow.

I double-parked my Impala and gave a quick wave to an electronics store owner who shouted at me. I raced into the alley and realized it was actually a maze of alleys. I called out, "Rob, Rob!"

I heard him call back, "Over here."

I hustled toward the sound of his voice. I found Trilling sitting next to a big man who was bleeding from a couple of different spots. The man was conscious but not moving too much.

I stared at the scene, and when I didn't get an explanation, I said, "What's this?"

Trilling said, "I told you I'd been looking for the fugitive who was partners with the guy who shot at us in the Bronx."

"The guy who had the Pakistani women to help process heroin?"

Trilling gave me a little smile. "I guess you're not so old that your memory is going completely." He looked over at the man on the ground. "This jack-off is Lou Pershing. He's supposedly the brains of their operation. He's also wanted for heroin distribution and some weapons charges out of Boston."

I stared at the bloody man. Then at Trilling. This was not normal. The sick feeling grew in my stomach. I'd been so focused on trying to find a way to exonerate Trilling that I'd missed his real motivations. He had an intense hate for lawbreakers. By the looks of Pershing, we were lucky we didn't have another homicide on our hands.

Trilling said, "This is your collar now. You've got a major federal fugitive in custody."

"I can't just stroll into a precinct with this mope."

Trilling let out a laugh. "Like anyone in the NYPD is going to turn away the famous Michael Bennett. Or are you too busy trying to pin some more murders on me?"

"Rob, listen…"

Trilling didn't want to hear it. He just turned and walked away.

CHAPTER 82

I TURNED ROB TRILLING'S fugitive, Lou Pershing, over to a patrol sergeant I knew named Chris Zuelie. He was thrilled to claim the arrest. I was still uneasy about the whole event. Trilling was unpredictable, by my estimation. I had to write an affidavit on everything I'd learned about the sniper case, then see what happened from there.

My phone rang. It was Harry Grissom. I answered it, "Hey, what's up?"

Harry jumped right into it. "There's been another shooting."

"Shit." I said to Harry, "Give me the address and I'll head over there."

"No. Keep working on your affidavit and close out any leads you have. I'll supervise our own squad detectives on this and get you the important details."

I blurted out, "I saw Trilling a few hours ago."

276

"Doing what?"

I explained it all to Harry. When I was finished, Harry said, "That doesn't sound good." Harry had a gift for understatement.

"Do you know anything about the new shooting? Victim? Witnesses?"

Harry said the victim was named Scott Dozier. "He's a twenty-six-year-old white male who dropped out of Rutgers. He's got a couple of arrests at protests. One of those antifa folks. He tried to light a patrol car on fire with two cops inside."

"I remember that."

Harry said, "Yesterday, a judge gave him five years' probation. Today, the kid was shot outside his apartment on the Lower East Side."

"Shit." That did sound like something that would get under Trilling's skin.

Harry asked, "What's wrong?"

"That's where I saw Trilling."

I told Harry a few more details of what I'd found and what I was working on. My mind raced with the possibilities. I'd found a pattern among all five victims: each had committed crimes but wasn't being prosecuted. At least we now had a potential motive. Any homicide detective would be excited about that.

As I was about to hang up, Harry said, "One more thing."

"What's that?"

"Dennis Wu is already involved in the new shooting."

"Why?"

"He just showed up. I don't have control over Internal Affairs. Something tells me the guy wouldn't listen if someone told him *not* to get involved."

My phone beeped. I looked to see who was calling, then said

to Harry, "Wu is trying to reach me. I'll call you back in a little bit." I switched over to Wu's call. Before I could even speak, I heard Dennis Wu's voice say, "Bennett, have you heard about the latest shooting?"

"Harry was just filling me in."

"Why aren't you at the scene? What are you, on vacation?"

"I'm trying to finish the affidavit on Trilling. Isn't that what you and command staff want?"

Wu said, "I got something you can add to the affidavit."

"What's that?"

"I came straight to Trilling's apartment after I heard about the shooting. The fat Armenian super said he saw him leave early this morning and he hasn't been back since. Sounds like our boy is on the prowl."

"Could be." I didn't know what else to say. Trilling actually had been on the prowl. That's how he'd found Lou Pershing.

Wu said, "I'm gonna enjoy arresting this prick. Hurry up on that affidavit."

My mind pictured the buttoned-down IA sergeant trying to physically handle Rob Trilling. I doubted he and I together could do it.

CHAPTER 83

IT WAS EARLY afternoon by the time I stepped through the doors of the FBI office in Manhattan. This time, instead of talking to ASAC Robert Lincoln, I linked up with the personnel director, Francesca Scott. All I needed to do was look at Rob Trilling's time sheets, to see if he had been working during any of the sniper murders. I wanted to see if there was any pattern with his work hours as they related to the shootings. I had a warrant in hand, but the director greeted me cheerfully with a big smile and said if I reviewed the file with her I didn't need court orders.

Francesca Scott's office was well located — in terms of reducing my risk of running into someone I didn't want to talk to — on the main floor at the front of the building. We chatted as she led me down a short hallway.

She said, "You're kind of a celebrity, Detective Bennett. I've read your name in the papers a dozen times over the years. I didn't think you would do something as mundane as look at time sheets for an evaluation."

I said, "Rob Trilling is working in our unit. They just wanted me to see what kind of hours he was working over here. You know, the usual."

She had a charming laugh. "I've been the personnel director here for nine years. Everything is usual. I'm happy to get a chance to talk to someone from outside the office. My husband works for ConEd as a supervisor. My conversations with him aren't much more interesting than the conversations around here." She had a twinkle in her eyes that I appreciated.

At first, she wanted me to review the computer-generated time-sheet reports. I explained I needed to see the original, handwritten time sheets. I left out the part where I wanted original signatures because I might need them as evidence.

The personnel director turned her attention to her computer as I started to look through the file of Trilling's time sheets. I flipped through his initial paperwork and noticed that the time sheets were not in chronological order. Great. Luckily there weren't too many of them. Trilling had punctually turned them in every two weeks, and his supervisor at the FBI had signed them.

Then I found a leave request, for an entire week in September.

That made me recall a comment Trilling had made about being at a VA counseling retreat in September.

All I could do was stare at the slip for a moment. Thomas Bannon, the firefighter from Staten Island, had been shot in the middle of that week. This really did change things quite a bit. If Trilling had been out of town at a VA retreat, he couldn't have shot Thomas Bannon.

I had to move quickly. I didn't want to make it seem urgent to Francesca Scott. She'd been nothing but pleasant and helpful. I eased from my chair and asked if I could take a couple of the time sheets as well as the leave slip.

I was out the door as quickly as I could be without making it look urgent or obvious.

CHAPTER 84

I KEPT TABS on the latest shooting. No one had found any witnesses. Nothing to point to a new suspect. Great. It seemed to be typical for this sniper case. Dennis Wu's call had told me Rob Trilling was really in the NYPD's sights. That was no surprise. I couldn't waste any time. I had to verify that Trilling had been in Albany when Bannon was shot. I had to do it in person. And I had to do it right now. By this time tomorrow, Trilling could be at Rikers.

As I headed to my car, I called Walter Jackson.

Walter said, "I'm working on leads from the last shooting."

"Anything useful?"

"Zilch. You still running down other leads?"

I explained what I'd learned at the FBI. I said, "I have to be certain. I'm not sure how else to verify this newest lead from the FBI personnel office. If he was actually in Albany at that time, Trilling can't be the sniper."

Walter had a brilliant suggestion: he was going to expedite getting Trilling's credit-card records from the last three months. He'd already submitted a warrant, like he did on most homicides. It's amazing what credit-card records can confirm. I can't tell you how many cases I've made because I could refute alibis with credit-card receipts.

A few minutes later, I was still in my car when my phone rang again. It was Walter Jackson. His contact with Mastercard had been able to help him immediately.

I said, "I'm guessing you wouldn't have called me so quickly if you didn't find something in the credit-card records."

"That's why you're a detective. You're correct. I have a credit-card receipt from a Holiday Inn in Albany. I'm going to text you all the information, as well as the PDF of the receipt. It looks like Trilling was at the hotel for five days. Thomas Bannon's shooting occurred on the second day of Trilling's stay."

My heart started to beat faster. "I told Harry I was working on the last details of the affidavit. Tell him I'm on a decent lead and will fill him in later. Call me if anything else happens."

"You're not driving to Albany right now, are you?"

"I'm headed into the Lincoln Tunnel as we speak. I hope to be on I-87, headed north, not too long from now."

I felt another pang of guilt for not being at the shooting scene. It's tough to ignore when you're a homicide detective. Like a chef using Hamburger Helper, it just didn't seem right. But clarifying this issue about Trilling couldn't wait. I had to prioritize my anxieties.

I couldn't help pushing my Chevy Impala a little harder once I hit the interstate. I wasn't used to open roads or being able to drive fast in a car. Manhattan is far from Utah's Bonneville Speedway.

I called Mary Catherine to let her know that I wouldn't be home until very late. I didn't go into details. I wasn't even sure what the details were yet. I just knew that I couldn't let this lead wait another day.

I rolled into Albany just about two and a half hours after I'd entered the Lincoln Tunnel. I hoped someone at the hotel could help me even though I hadn't bothered to get a warrant.

The next few minutes could mean a lot to this case as well as to Rob Trilling.

CHAPTER 85

AS I ROLLED up to the address Walter Jackson had given me for the hotel, I realized it was not a Holiday Inn. It was, in fact, called Holliday's Tavern and Inn. It was a fair bit shabbier than most Holiday Inns. It had two long rows of rooms that stretched off the road with the center part of the property holding a restaurant and conference rooms. The dark-green paint looked like someone had slapped it on in the mid-1980s and hadn't touched it up since. The make of cars in the parking lot told me the hotel's biggest attraction was its relatively low rates.

I parked next to a beat-up Ford F-150 pickup truck. As soon as I stepped into the lobby, I could smell a musty odor that would make me worry the place was infested with mold. But I wasn't here to give a review. I was just hoping someone would give me information without needing a warrant. Clearly I had raced out of the city without worrying about legal documents or roadblocks to the investigation. All I could think about was Rob Trilling.

I paused at the empty front desk, avoiding hitting the bell on the counter. I didn't want to annoy anyone I was about to ask for help.

Three men in their mid-thirties stood in the small lobby, not far from reception. I wondered if they were military; all three were in good shape, two of them well over six feet tall, and the shorter one had a Marines emblem tattooed on his forearm. We nodded a silent greeting to one another as I looked around the lobby. After waiting for a little longer at the desk, I called out, "Hello," to the open door behind the counter.

Fifteen seconds later, an older woman shuffled out of the office until she stood behind the desk. She had long, wild gray hair and glasses hanging from a beaded strap around her neck. She looked down at a folder in her hand and didn't even notice me.

I cleared my throat.

The woman looked up at me, startled. "You must be some kind of ninja. I didn't even see you there." She glanced over the desk to see if I had any luggage.

I said, "My name is Michael Bennett. I'm a detective with the NYPD."

The three men nearby all looked over at me as the woman reached a hand across the counter. As we shook, she said, "Margaret Holliday, with two *l*'s. My friends call me Maggie."

I smiled. "That explains the sign."

"I've had a couple of cease-and-desist letters from a hotel chain I won't name. The only thing I ever conceded to was adding 'Tavern' to our title. Other than that, I've run this place for thirty-two years. And I always support the police. I don't think people realize how dangerous your job is. What can I do for a detective from the big city?"

"I was wondering about a veterans' group that met here not long ago. Do you remember that at all?"

"Of course I do. Obviously I support the military too. The VA has encounter groups here at least once a month. I have the perfect conference room for them. Our rates are cheap, and they work around our busy times. Like I said, what can I do for you?"

"Could I look at your registration log?" I slipped her a piece of paper with the exact dates and Rob Trilling's name.

She read the note and said, "I know Rob Trilling. He's here every few months."

Maggie started to type on the computer sitting on the counter. After a moment, she looked up and said, "Got it right here. He was here for four nights and then we let the VA guys stay through the whole day for free—that way they complete a five-day course of some kind and don't have to pay as much."

"Any chance I could see the original registration card with a signature on it?"

That made her pause. "What kind of detective are you?"

"A tired one."

"I like a good sense of humor. Now give me the straight answer."

"Homicide."

The tallest of the three men said, "Hang on, Maggie."

The hairs on the back of my neck tingled. I suddenly had a feeling that I was in for a repeat of my firefighter interviews. I couldn't understand why people wouldn't mind their own business.

The man looked at me and said, "You got a warrant?"

"I'm sorry, who are you?"

"David Klatt. I'm here with the VA and we all know Rob Trilling."

Now I purposely took a step away from the front desk and turned to face the three men fully.

The other tall man in the group said, "Why are you looking at Rob's work here? He does a great job."

"I'm not looking at anything to do with the VA." I tried to stay calm as the men circled me. Each one of them looked like they knew how to fight.

Maggie, the clerk, hadn't left the front desk. She stared at the four of us, no one saying a word.

I said, "Guys, if you're gonna kick my ass, let's take it outside." I needed to buy some time to think. I had a hard time reading the expressions on the three men's faces.

Finally Klatt said, "Kick your ass? Why would we do that? I'm an attorney. I asked about a warrant."

The other tall man said, "I'm an accountant. I haven't been in a fight since basic training."

I looked at the shorter Marine.

He smiled. "I'm an unemployed house painter. I'll kick your ass if you want, but I'm mostly looking to get my faulty key replaced by Maggie."

I turned to Maggie at the front desk. "You confirmed Rob Trilling was here at the time in question. If you could do me a favor and hold the signature card, I'll get a warrant and come back later."

She gave me a cheerful smile. "Sure thing, Detective."

I nodded to the three men. I had to get back to Manhattan and figure things out.

CHAPTER 86

I GOT HOME from Albany late that evening and my effort to be engaged with the kids quickly fell flat.

My mind was racing with the hope that Rob Trilling was not our sniper. But the newest shooting still made me doubt my findings. I'd heard that when Dennis Wu found Trilling at his apartment building hours later, Trilling had refused to speak to the Internal Affairs sergeant. I didn't blame him. From his perspective, there was no upside. Dennis made no secret of the fact that he was trying to pin everything on Rob Trilling. It was still a bad look for Trilling, because without any other suspects, all the attention was focused on my former partner.

The kids and Mary Catherine realized I'd had a long day when I dozed off in the chair in the living room.

I sprang awake the next morning and tried to make amends by preparing a giant breakfast. No one would be at the VA until nine o'clock anyway. I pulled out all the stops. Pancakes, eggs, bacon, and ham. Plus a whole wheat English muffin for Mary Catherine and a bowl of Lucky Charms for Chrissy.

It didn't take long for all the kids to start wandering out to the dining room. Nothing I couldn't handle. Their plates were already made. I realized if the whole homicide investigation thing didn't work out, I might have a second career as a short-order cook.

A few hours later, I was waiting at the VA office when Darcy Farnan walked in. She did a double take when she saw me in the lobby. She turned to a young man with long, stringy hair walking with her and said, "Can you give me a few minutes with this man, Peter?"

The young man nodded, then turned back to his phone. Darcy gave me a quick nod with her head to get me to hustle into the office. As soon as the door was closed behind us, she said, "Please don't tell me anything has happened to Rob Trilling."

"No, it might be just the opposite. I need to confirm something with you."

"I'm sorry, but the same conditions apply as before. He has to give me permission to talk to you. I almost told him you'd been here, but he never met with me after we spoke."

"I get it. I'm not trying to get you to violate any rules or ethics. But I think I can help him. And I already have a lot of the information I need." I gave her the briefest of thumbnails of what I was doing. I explained that Trilling was a suspect in some murders but that I'd gone to Albany, and it looked like he might've been out of town during one of the murders.

Darcy smiled for just a moment. She brushed some hair out of her eyes. "Like I said, Detective, I'd need Rob's permission to confirm that he was at a VA retreat in Albany as both a facilitator and a participant. He would tell you that he was at the hotel the entire time with me and nine other veterans. He would probably also tell you that I saw him every single day." She couldn't hide the smile.

I said, "At some point, probably fairly soon, after Trilling gives you permission, I'll have to ask you about this again."

"After I get his permission, I'll tell you anything you want to know about the week. Even the side trip he and I took to visit his family in Putnam County. I mean, if we really did that." This time she gave me a wink.

CHAPTER 87

I WANTED TO see if there was some way to confirm that Rob Trilling was at his apartment on the night Gus Querva was shot. Things were moving quickly now, and I decided to forgo the surreptitious route and talk to Trilling directly. I had a few more questions to ask him.

I drove directly to Trilling's apartment. The small, older building was just as I remembered from my previous visit. I didn't buzz him. I knew the apartment number and was able to enter the building when another tenant came out. I walked inside and up to the second floor. The stairway's banister was missing six spindles and its carpet was clean but fraying down the center—in need of enough repair that the building was obviously not run by a corporation. I checked apartment doors until I found Trilling's and knocked. I could hear someone moving around behind the wooden door. Maybe more than one person. I hadn't pried much into Trilling's personal life, but I sort of assumed he didn't have a girlfriend. At least that's the impression I'd gotten from my daughter Juliana.

I waited about fifteen seconds, then knocked again. I called out, "Rob, it's Mike Bennett. I gotta talk to you for just a minute." I heard some more rustling in the apartment. Now it sounded like there were half a dozen people in there.

The door opened about two inches, and three separate safety chains caught it. I took a step to the side to look into the apartment. All I saw was a veil of long brown hair.

Without thinking, I called out, "Juliana?" I couldn't see her face. She moved away from the door quickly. I took a step back from the door. Maybe, somewhere in the back of my head, I was considering kicking the door in. You never know how you'll react if you think your child is in some sort of dangerous situation. This time I called out a little more forcefully, "Juliana!" I really couldn't tell if it was my daughter inside or not. But no one was speaking to me, and I was starting to get nervous. I rechecked the number on the door to make sure it was the right apartment. There was no mistake. This was Rob Trilling's place.

This time I called out, "Rob, are you in there?"

The brown hair appeared at the door again. This time I could see a little of the young woman's face. It wasn't Juliana. She said, "Rob not here." Her accent was thick, but I could understand her.

"When will he be back?"

"I say Rob not here." Her voice had risen in volume. I couldn't tell if she was angry or frustrated that I wasn't listening to her.

I said, "Look, I really need to talk to Rob."

There was a long silence. I reached for the door and grabbed its edge so she couldn't close it easily. Then I felt a sharp pain shoot through my hand. I jerked it away from the door. I had a gash across my index and middle fingers. Blood started to seep between my fingers and down the back of my hand.

I mumbled, "What the…"

A four-inch blade popped out of the opening in the door. The hand tightly gripped the knife, pointing it right in front of my face. I could see her knuckles turn white from the pressure.

This time, speaking slowly and concentrating on each word, the woman said, "I say Rob not here. Go away. Go away right now."

"I'm Mike Ben…"

The door slammed shut and the dead bolt twisted into position.

I went outside, wiping the blood from my hand with a paper bag I'd found in the hall. It didn't look like the wound needed stitches. But I didn't intend to put my hand on that door again.

As I walked toward my car, a heavyset man with the thickest mustache I'd ever seen looked over at me. He was cleaning out some buckets with a hose. I guessed he was the super Wu had spoken to. I went over to talk to him, and he confirmed that he'd run the building for nearly sixteen years.

I explained that I was Trilling's partner at the NYPD.

"I love having a cop in the building. Especially one like Rob. Very levelheaded, that one."

I didn't need Dennis Wu to tell me the super's nationality. I could tell by the super's accent he was Armenian. He could've been a commercial for hardworking Armenians in the US. He probably wore size 45 work pants to fit his belly. But he was friendly, and I decided to not waste the opportunity to talk to him. I said, "The girl in his apartment didn't sound like she spoke much English."

"She has not been there long. I've never spoken to her. I seen her walk out one day and that was it. They're a little loud now and then. Sounds like a soccer team from the apartment underneath. But I said something, and Rob told me they would try to keep it down."

I looked up and noticed several cameras around the building. "Looks like you have a pretty good security system."

The super smiled. He had a gold crown on one tooth. "No one can come or go without my system recording it. Haven't had anything stolen in three years. That's got to be some kind of record here in New York."

It didn't take any effort at all to convince him to show me his security system. The system was everything the super had said. Four cameras on the building periphery, two cameras in the lobby, and one in each hallway and stairwell. Very impressive.

I said, "Can I test it out?"

"What do you mean?"

"Let me pick a day and I'll count how many times I see Trilling."

The super was intrigued to have a law enforcement professional evaluate his system. He took a moment to show me how it worked on a simple Windows operating system.

Of course, I immediately went to the night Gus Querva was shot. The super stood over my shoulder.

I scrolled through the video taken by the cameras in the lobby until I saw Trilling enter.

The super pointed and said, "There, there — you see him?"

I nodded. The time stamp said 6:05 p.m. He would've just been coming from the office. Then I fast-forwarded through the lobby cameras. And I kept fast-forwarding, looking to see when he appeared again. I didn't see him until 7:05 the next morning.

The super said, "You can't really tell much from that."

"Let me see if I can find him on the other cameras." And that's what I did. I raced through the cameras in the stairwell and in the hallway by Trilling's apartment. He never came out of his apartment.

I turned to the super and said, "How long do you keep these videos?"

"All saved on the cloud. They always keep them for at least one year."

I convinced him to let me burn a copy of the single day onto a DVD. I explained that it could be a good training tool about what to look for on surveillance videos.

The super slapped me on the back as I was leaving. He said, "You seem like you would be a good partner to Rob. He's a good boy. I worry about the way people treat police. I worry about Rob."

All I could say was "I worry about him too."

CHAPTER 88

IT WAS STILL midmorning when I left Trilling's apartment. The phone rang and I saw it was Harry Grissom. I didn't know what bad news was waiting for me, so I hesitated to answer. That's a terrible place for your mind to be, especially if you're a cop working on a major case.

Harry didn't even bother with the greeting. All he said was "I just got an official notice of suspension on Trilling."

"Shit. I guess it means they intend to go after Trilling hard."

"It says that personnel interviewed him yesterday. Did the admin and read him his work rights. That sort of shit."

"What time yesterday? I was with him in the morning and Wu couldn't find him later."

There was a pause and I knew Harry was studying the document on his computer screen. Finally Harry said, "Looks like it started at 10:15, until 11:05."

"What time did the antifa guy get shot?"

"God damn, I must be getting old. Shooting happened at 10:50. Get over to personnel and figure this out."

"On my way."

It felt like only a few minutes later I was walking through the doors of the NYPD personnel department at One Police Plaza. I heard someone call from the other room and found Sharone Baxter-Tate sitting behind a wide, cluttered desk.

She had a brilliant smile and ushered me to the seat in front of her desk. I explained that I wanted to talk to her about Rob Trilling.

"Seems like a nice young man. Sorry to see he was suspended. I never see the reason. I just have to inform them of their rights and what they can and can't do while suspended. I'm guessing he had some kind of a personal issue. Maybe he drank too much?"

"No, nothing like that."

"Moonlighting without permission?"

"Nope." I really hadn't come here to answer her questions. Before she could ask another, I said, "I just want to verify when Trilling was here and how you keep track of the time when you're interviewing someone."

Sharone said, "I talked to him in the morning."

"Can you be more specific?"

She reached into her desk and pulled out a worker's rights form. "See, there is a space for the start and ending times of the interviews. I look at that clock right behind you and write down whatever it says. Yesterday I started the interview with Officer Trilling at exactly 10:15 and ended at 11:05. I didn't round up or round down. He was right on time for his meeting, and I noticed we finished our chat at 11:05."

I checked the digital clock on the wall against the time on my phone. They matched. I looked at Sharone and said, "And you were here with him the entire time?"

"I'm required to read the documents aloud so no one can claim they didn't understand what was going on. It almost always takes forty-five to fifty minutes."

I was already up and out of my chair, heading for the door, as I thanked Sharone Baxter-Tate. "I'll get back to you and explain everything one day soon. Please keep all that original paperwork secure."

I didn't hear her response as I hustled out the door.

CHAPTER 89

I'D GATHERED A fair amount of evidence that pointed to Rob Trilling *not* being the Longshot Killer. I still wasn't sure what to do with the information. In the back of my mind, I was worried command staff might relieve me and put someone else in to investigate the sniper. They would have a fair argument. I had now prioritized actively looking to exonerate Rob Trilling over the rest of the case. That's not exactly what homicide detectives do.

Walter Jackson called me while I was still at One Police Plaza. "The report on the casing found in Trilling's car came in and I'm emailing it to you now."

I opened the email on my phone and quickly read the report while Walter was still on the line. The report said there was no usable DNA or fingerprints on the casing. Not even a partial print.

"Who wipes a bullet down before they put it in a rifle?" I

thought about it and said to Walter, "Unless the casing was planted." I paused, trying to wrap my head around the possibility that someone might have tried to frame Rob Trilling for the sniper murders.

Walter asked, "Who would do something like that? *Why* would they do it?"

"Good questions. I have no answers." The frustrating part was that I knew I had all the information in my head to figure this out. I just needed to organize it and then worry about articulating it.

I thought about it for a few moments, then said, "One key question for me is, where did someone plant the empty casing in Trilling's car? It would've had to be in the FBI parking lot or possibly even the NYPD parking lot near One Police Plaza. If we could figure out where it happened, it might lead us to the more important question of *who* planted the casing." I added, "Maybe someone was trying to take the heat off themselves. That means we might have to consider another suspect who works in law enforcement."

"That means your original theory could still be true. The killer could be a straight arrow who doesn't like the fact that criminals are not being punished."

"And it has to be someone with access to police files and the inner workings of a criminal investigation."

Then it hit me. How could I have been so focused on one suspect? There was another suspect. Another sniper. Also a cop. I recalled speaking with the former NYPD sniper now on desk duty: Joe Tavarez.

CHAPTER 90

I DIDN'T SHARE my epiphany with Walter Jackson on the phone. I trusted Walter completely. But I didn't want to put him in an awkward position. If I ended up accusing a different person after first suggesting it was Rob Trilling, the fallout could be harsh. Especially if I was wrong. Command staff could move me to some distant precinct to write traffic tickets until I retired. I didn't want Walter to catch any of the blowback, so I didn't tell him what I was doing.

This was going to be a difficult concept to sell. After accusing one cop, I was now saying I was wrong. And I would be accusing a different cop. But I wasn't sure if there was any alternative.

In fact, if I wasn't careful, I could end up ruining the reputations of three different cops on this case: Rob Trilling, Joe Tavarez, and me. I slipped back into personnel to speak with Sharone Baxter-Tate again. It took me about five minutes to verify that Joe

Tavarez had been off duty during each of the five sniper murders. That in itself didn't mean anything. And I recalled talking to his wife, Cindy, some days ago, to verify his alibi for one of the nights in question. She had backed him up, with details about what they'd had for dinner too.

Then I texted Sergeant Jeff Mabus, the ESU supervisor I'd talked to about Trilling. He was on his way to One Police Plaza and agreed to meet me in the back parking lot at the exact same spot where we had spoken last time.

Today, Mabus was dressed more like an NYPD officer. He wore a blue, long-sleeved T-shirt with an NYPD insignia on the chest. He still looked impressive physically.

We both leaned against an unmarked Chevy Tahoe the ESU team used to move around the city unnoticed.

After a quick greeting, I wasted no time. "How well do you know Joe Tavarez?"

"I know him pretty well since we were on the team together for about three years. Very stable and reasonable guy. Why? Are you going to pile on him like everyone else? He saved a young woman's life by making an incredibly difficult shot and hitting an armed man before the perp could kill the victim. Now he's being punished, rotting away as some kind of analyst for doing the right thing—exactly what he was supposed to do as a sniper on the special-ops team."

"I'm not disputing that. I'm just trying to piece together some information. What kind of rifle did he use when he made the shot?"

Now Mabus gave me an odd look. "It was a Remington 700, the SPS Tactical. Why?"

"Because I am trying to figure a few things out, and you're the guy with the knowledge to help me. Was Tavarez angry he was relieved of active duty?"

Mabus considered this question. Finally he said, "Who wouldn't be? You train for one job, do it right, and still get crucified for it. And it's not just Tavarez. Any police sniper who takes a shot is treated about the same way."

I wasn't sure what to say. Now wasn't the time to get into political discussions, and Mabus had a point. "Can police snipers do anything to change that policy?"

Mabus shrugged. "You know the saying: There are two things cops hate. The way things have always been done, and change."

It was an old saying but absolutely true. I made a few more notes, then asked a question I knew the answer to. "What caliber does that Remington 700 take?"

"Either .300 or .308."

That last one matched the casing found in Trilling's FBI car.

CHAPTER 91

HARRY GRISSOM WAS meeting with another homicide detective when I got back to the office. I wanted to burst in and start telling him everything I'd figured out, but I restrained myself. I went back to my desk and started looking again through all the reports, trying to find something I had missed. Key during a good investigation is keeping an open mind. It's a lesson I had to relearn almost every time I started to look at a mysterious death.

As soon as Harry was free, I burst into his office. I laid out exactly what had happened and who I had talked to.

Harry considered everything as he stroked his long gunfighter's mustache. Then he looked up at me and said, "Joe Tavarez could've had access to FBI investigations through his wife. That would explain Adam Glossner and Gus Querva, who were not under investigation by the NYPD."

"So you don't think I'm crazy?"

"That remains to be seen. But you've laid out a logical argument on this investigation. Even with Tavarez's wife alibiing him for that one night. Was she just protecting him? As a responsible supervisor, I can't ignore it all. These findings are going to throw Dennis Wu into a tizzy."

Harry gave me a little smile. I wasn't sure if it was because he liked the idea of aggravating the Internal Affairs sergeant or his use of the word "tizzy."

Harry said, "How do we make the case on Tavarez? He's got to be pretty smart the way he threw the blame onto Trilling. And his wife could be actively helping him in his crusade. We have no physical evidence or witnesses. We don't even have anything that can put Tavarez in the area of the shootings."

"I can try and get all of that through interviews and investigation. It might take some time."

"I don't see command staff giving us much time. They won't railroad Trilling on the killings if we convince them Tavarez is our man, but they won't want to wait either."

I said, "What if we set a trap?"

"What kind of trap?"

"I'm not sure. I just thought of it this second. But I think we'd need Trilling to help us with this trap. It makes sense to use a sniper to catch a sniper."

"What if it's not Tavarez?"

"If we set up a trap right, it won't matter. He just won't show up. No one is hurt and we can decide where to go from there. Do you think you can get Trilling back on duty?"

Harry was already picking up the phone. I knew that meant yes.

I had a new list of priorities. After getting Trilling back, I intended to focus completely on Tavarez. It was like starting the entire case over again.

CHAPTER 92

IT DIDN'T TAKE long for Harry Grissom's clout to be obvious. The first sign that he'd stirred the pot at headquarters was Internal Affairs sergeant Dennis Wu storming into the office and throwing daggers at me with his eyes. A few minutes later, Inspector Lisa Udell arrived in full uniform like she'd been called away from some sort of public ceremony. There were two points on Lisa Udell that no one could argue. She looked impressive in her dress blues. If you were in the right, she'd back you every time.

The two visitors huddled with Harry in his office. Walter Jackson joined me at my desk. We supported each other like two siblings waiting out an argument between their parents.

Walter said, "There's a strong set of personalities crammed into that office."

"At least they're actually communicating." Then some voices were raised. It turned into a series of shouts.

I said, "That's not Harry yelling."

"How can you tell?"

"Because Harry doesn't shout."

Walter looked at me and said, "I guess you're right. Given your ability to stir people up, I would've heard a lot of shouts over the years."

I just shrugged. Walter was right. I could stir people up.

The office door opened. Harry leaned out and motioned me into the office like they were on a coffee break.

As I stepped inside, Inspector Udell said, "Hello, Bennett."

I smiled and said, "Inspector. Nice to see you." I glanced over at Dennis Wu.

He said, "Is it nice to see me too?"

"Of course. It's always a pleasure to deal with a representative from Internal Affairs." I was surprised that earned a smile from Wu.

Harry said, "We've been discussing the Rob Trilling situation. Inspector Udell says we can reinstate him."

The inspector chimed in. "Should be easy. No one even realized he'd been suspended. There's no official notice yet."

I couldn't help myself. I looked at Dennis Wu.

He shook his head and said, "Sounds like another Bennett screwup to me."

Inspector Udell turned to face Wu. "Screwup? Are you some kind of moron? Bennett followed the evidence that was available. He did what he thought was right. He investigated, then corrected a mistake." The inspector turned toward me. "Drove to Albany on a hunch. You can't teach that in the academy." She paused, then looked back at Wu. "Besides, as I understand it, you were at Trilling's apartment when he was sitting in personnel right inside One Police Plaza." The inspector shook her head in disbelief.

Dennis Wu said, "Fine, he's fucking Columbo." He stared at me. "What's your plan?"

"I need to talk to Trilling first. Make sure he'll still work with me. I wouldn't blame him if he told me to hit the road."

Wu said, "Is that an option? Because I don't want to work with you."

Inspector Udell said, "That can be arranged."

Wu said, "You need IA on this. You know it. We gotta keep this quiet until this caper is over."

Inspector Udell nodded. Then she looked at me and said, "What are you waiting for? Get your ass moving."

CHAPTER 93

I FOUND MYSELF back at Rob Trilling's apartment building, feeling a little uncomfortable about the awkward conversation I was about to have. It can be tough to look someone in the eye and tell them you really believed they were a killer. And the way Trilling held his feelings inside didn't put me any more at ease.

I stood in front of his building and rang the buzzer for Trilling's apartment. I looked at the two Band-Aids on my fingers. I wondered if the girl with the knife and the long brown hair was home. The one I'd thought was Juliana at first. I'd say it was none of my business, except my daughter *is* my business. That was an issue I might bring up later. For now, I was on an apology tour.

Trilling's voice came through the intercom and I asked if I could come upstairs.

Trilling paused, then said, "The apartment's a mess. I'll meet you out front in a minute."

I walked over and waited by my car. A couple of minutes later, Trilling strolled out in jeans, a jacket, and cowboy boots.

I said, "I've never seen you wear boots before."

"Is that why you're here? To talk about my fashion choices?"

I got right to the point. "No, I'm here to tell you you're no longer a suspect in the Longshot Killer case. And you're no longer suspended."

Finally, after almost a full minute, Trilling said, "What happened? Have you found the real sniper?"

"I think so." I explained everything about how I thought Joe Tavarez could be the sniper, including my theory that someone had planted the .308 casing in Trilling's car. I even went into my trip to Albany.

Trilling never interrupted me. When I finished, he said, "Darcy Farnan confirmed the trip?"

"Not exactly. She wouldn't say anything officially without your consent. But I can guarantee you she's on your side and wants things to work out."

Trilling looked off into space. When he was done thinking, he turned to me and said, "Darcy's the best." He paused, then added, "You drove all the way to Albany?"

"Yep."

Trilling smiled. "That's smart. And I appreciate it."

"You're cleared to come back. If you want to work on our squad again."

Trilling just looked at me. He didn't say a word. I was starting to get used to that. I decided I could do the same thing. Then he just nodded and said, "When can I start?"

"Right now, if you're up to it."

A woman with short, dark hair walked past us. She gave us a quick look. Something about her seemed familiar to me.

Trilling interrupted my train of thought. "What's the plan for Tavarez?"

"The best I've got right now is that we send a memo or report through the analysts' room. We make sure it's forwarded to the FBI as well. In it, we'll talk about an unnamed cop who's cooperating so he can skate on a whole slew of charges. Then we'll see if Tavarez bites."

"Sounds risky."

I said, "I like the plan sounding risky rather than sounding crazy."

"No, it's crazy too."

CHAPTER 94

I MADE IT home in time for dinner. I needed a respite from the craziness of this investigation. Rob Trilling and I had discussed the case. His initial anger had given way to understanding. I think his outlook could've best been described as "logical." He understood duty and honor. That meant he understood I had been duty bound to investigate the possibility that he could have been the sniper.

I'd considered asking him to come home with me for dinner again. I knew Juliana would've been thrilled. But I didn't know what the story was with the woman at Trilling's apartment, and it wasn't something I wanted to get into with him just yet. He and I both needed to focus on our incredibly dangerous plan to trap the sniper.

It was so nice to listen to the chatter around the table. Trent leaned in from the far end of the table to say to me, "I have some puns for your friend at work."

"Walter?"

"Is that Mr. Jackson? The great big guy?"

"That's him. I'm not sure I want to start the precedent of *me* telling *him* puns. But I'd definitely like to hear yours. Whatcha got?" I smiled at my son, who looked about to burst with excitement.

Trent said, "Hear about the butter rumor? Don't spread it." He got a couple of chuckles from the older kids, and Mary Catherine gave him a mercy laugh. The lack of a big reaction didn't dissuade him. "I've got another." He looked around the table to make sure he had everyone's attention. A true showman. "I had a photographic memory. But I didn't develop it." That one got a better response.

Chrissy and Shawna jumped in with some basic riddles. Shawna's was the best, asking, "Why did the rooster cross the road?" She didn't wait for any guesses. "To prove he wasn't a chicken."

We all had to giggle at that one. I never knew my kids were so talented with jokes. I never really felt this way waiting for a pun to come from Walter Jackson. Then Jane cleared her throat and waited until everyone was looking at her. She glanced over at my grandfather, who nodded his encouragement.

Jane said, "I know I've been sort of secretive lately and hiding out at the library a lot. I've been getting tutoring and doing research for a speech I've been asked to deliver at Columbia because of my performance in Debate Club. It started last month and just sort of snowballed from there. I was jealous of Trent when he spoke at the mayor's office, and it spurred me to work harder and do well. The speech is going to be this Friday night. I hope everyone can make it."

My second oldest daughter is not prone to showing off, but she was clearly quite satisfied with her announcement. She sat with a smile on her face as she glanced around the table. Then, with perfect delivery, she said, "You may all applaud now."

Mary Catherine was quick to say, "Sounds like we have a great Friday night plan. Dinner, then we hear Jane rock Columbia." She focused on Jane. "What are you talking about?"

Jane just smiled. "I was told I could talk about anything, so I'll just tell you it has to do with our family. I'll let you guys wonder about it until Friday. There has to be some mystery in our lives."

The laughter and celebration were almost enough to take my mind off the sniper case.

CHAPTER 95

IT WAS AMAZING how much we accomplished with everyone working together. This hodgepodge team of homicide investigators, Internal Affairs investigators, analysts, and even an inspector had created a fake cop with a history and a court schedule.

I hated to admit it, but Dennis Wu had designed a realistic scenario in the fake memo. On the surface, the memo was only meant to warn law enforcement of unusual activity near one of the NYPD off-site buildings in lower Manhattan. The memo had just enough information to tease Joseph Tavarez and make him act. It basically said that a corrupt officer who was cooperating to avoid indictment would be meeting at the off-site building around 2 p.m. The extra cops were supposed to transport the bad cop to a hearing at 4 p.m.

We'd made sure the memo came through Joe Tavarez's office

around 5 the previous evening. We wanted to also be sure that Tavarez saw the memo that night because his schedule had him listed as off duty today until 4 p.m.

Rob Trilling was trying to catch up on as much as he could and peppered me with questions. We were now set up in an NYPD surveillance vehicle that no one would notice. A beat-up hatchback. From it, we could see the off-site building where the fake cop was supposed to enter and leave. We could also see some of the surrounding buildings.

Trilling said, "How many people do we have out here?"

"For a big case, this is an absolute skeleton crew. Terri Hernandez and a couple of the detectives from our squad are on the perimeter. We have a special team led by Jeff Mabus of four ESU members for the takedown. I think Dennis Wu is lurking somewhere. We're all on the same secure radio channel."

Trilling said, "Are we trying to limit the possibility of a leak by only using a few people?"

"You're starting to catch on. This is nothing like fugitive cases or patrol, is it?"

"I never would've been able to put this together."

"After today you will."

Trilling said, "Where's the lieutenant on this surveillance?"

"He's inside our trap building. He's going to move the curtains and turn some lights on and off to make sure the sniper sees someone in the building. We purposely didn't put a surveillance team on Tavarez so he wouldn't get hinky."

"Get what?"

I grinned. "It's a word old-school cops use to mean suspicious. One of the problems with surveillance is if you're following someone with some experience, they often spot the tail."

"Words are a little like fashion. Their popularity rises and falls with different generations."

"That's pretty smart. Did your grandfather teach you that?"

"Modern Theories of Society, Columbia University." He gave me a decent, smug smile, then cocked his head and said, "I'm curious. Do you also call marijuana 'Mary Jane'?"

I laughed out loud at that one. Trilling sounded like one of my sons when they broke my balls. It was also possibly the first joke I'd ever heard him crack.

I said, "I'll try to work on my vocabulary. I'll admit I cringe when I hear older people try to use street slang. I guess that's why I use out-of-date terms."

Maybe he *was* becoming a New Yorker.

CHAPTER 96

THE SURVEILLANCE STARTED to drag on. I'd been on dozens of stakeouts like this. Even ones where the suspect acted hinky. I'll admit, I might not have been worried, but I could feel my nerves. There was a lot that could go wrong with this plan. Even though I wasn't in command, everyone knew it was my idea. The whole thing was my case. And I'd already made one major error on it. Thank God I'd been able to figure it out and correct it.

Trilling said, "If Lieutenant Grissom is inside our fake office, where are the ESU guys?"

"In an unmarked Chevy Tahoe a few blocks away. We're the main team watching the fake office."

Trilling sat up in his seat quickly. He moved, trying to see a building across the street. "I got something."

I looked toward the older apartment building. "What do you see?"

"It's tough from this angle, but I think a man walked into that building via the front door, carrying a case of some kind. I didn't get a good look."

I put it out over the radio and said we'd keep everyone updated. It's a good idea that everyone knows what others are seeing during a surveillance.

Harry came on the radio. "Everyone stays in place until we hear something more definite from Mike."

I hit the Transmit button when he was finished. "It's the building to the south and west of you. Trilling thinks he saw a male walk through the front door with a case of some kind. We don't have a perfect angle from here." My heart was starting to beat faster.

Now Terri Hernandez came on the frequency. "I'm looking right at the building now. I can see in the lobby through the front door. There's no one visible from here."

Trilling said, "Should I get out and walk past the building? Or maybe try to get inside?"

"Let's give it a minute. I want you out of sight. As long as Harry is staying away from the windows, the sniper doesn't have a target. I'm sure the ESU guys are getting ready and can move anywhere we tell them to go." It was easy to advocate patience but much harder to practice it. My first instinct was also to get out of the car and go to the building myself. But if Tavarez had scoped out the area and was watching from somewhere else, we'd blow the whole surveillance.

Trilling twisted in his seat. He almost shouted, "Look, on the second floor! Looks like a community balcony."

I followed his line of sight and saw that the narrow balcony had some plants. Then I saw something move. I only got a glimpse, but it did look like a man with a rifle. And from the front of the balcony, he was aiming directly down on our fake office.

Just as I grabbed the radio from the console of the surveillance car, someone rapped on the driver's-side window. It was enough to make me jump. When I turned, I almost said, *What the hell,* out loud.

Leaning down, looking into the car, was our suspect, Joseph Tavarez.

CHAPTER 97

I STARED AT Joe Tavarez with my mouth open. I had to blink my eyes a couple times, wondering if I was dreaming. *What the hell?* It really was Joe Tavarez standing on the driver's side of our car.

I turned quickly to Rob Trilling. "Keep watching the balcony. See if you can confirm what the man has with him. It may not be a rifle."

Tavarez signaled for me to lower my window.

I held up my hand and reached for the handheld radio we'd been using on surveillance. "Hold, hold." I gave it a moment for everyone to focus on their radios. Then I said, "Terri, can you confirm what the man on the balcony is holding?"

Terri Hernandez came on the radio. "Stand by."

Joe Tavarez crouched down so his head was even with mine. I finally said, "Tavarez, what the hell are you doing here?"

"I came to help. Not as a sniper, just as a cop."

I could only continue staring at him in disbelief. A thousand thoughts rushed through my brain.

Tavarez said, "I saw the memo. Then I saw the Emergency Service memo about detailing some ESU members to this operation. I figured out exactly what you were up to. When I saw you sitting in the car, I knew I was right. I know what you're doing."

"Right about what?"

"You're trying to catch the sniper."

The radio crackled and I held up a hand to Tavarez again.

Terri Hernandez came on the air. "I have a male in a dark hoodie. He's crouched low and some plants are blocking his face. He's definitely looking toward our off-site building."

"But you don't see a rifle?"

"Not at the moment. I saw what I was pretty sure was a rifle a few moments ago."

"Keep a sharp eye. Everyone else, hold your positions until we verify a few things."

I turned my head to face Tavarez outside the driver's-side window. "I still don't understand what you're doing here, Joe."

"You think the sniper is someone in law enforcement, don't you? I knew this would need to be kept quiet and you couldn't use many cops. I'm not officially on duty until 4 p.m. Consider me just an extra set of eyes."

Now, from my right side, Trilling said, "I see him clearly at the near end of the balcony. He's scanning the area."

I barked at Tavarez, "Get down!" I didn't want him to give away our position.

After a moment, Trilling said, "Now he's changed positions and I can't see him."

Tavarez came level with the window again. He said without prompting, "You don't understand what it's like to be sidelined."

Trilling chimed in, "I do."

I said, "I can appreciate that, Joe, but you didn't think this through."

Terri Hernandez came on the radio. "I see him. Suspect is holding a scoped rifle. No question."

Just as I held the radio up to acknowledge Terri Hernandez, our windshield in the surveillance vehicle shattered. My brain registered the sound of the gunshot at about the same time that glass sprayed into the car.

I ducked low in the seat as the rest of the windshield dropped onto the dashboard.

Trilling bailed out of the car instantly. It took me a moment, then I yanked the latch to the door, but it didn't open easily. I realized that Tavarez was huddled against the car and I had to bark, "Joe, move away from my door!"

Tavarez scrambled to the rear wheel.

I tumbled out of the car onto the asphalt, then scuttled back to the protection of the vehicle. My hand hit something wet in the road. Blood. I looked up and saw the bullet had struck Tavarez in the ear. I blurted out, "Joe, you're hit."

"No shit. It's just my ear. I'm okay." He reached up and touched his ear gingerly. "God damn, that was too close."

I started to call out on the radio when I realized I'd left it in the car. Before I could open the door and reach for the radio, another shot rang out.

I did what every cop under fire does: I crouched down for cover and wished I had more.

CHAPTER 98

I WASN'T THE only one trying to find shelter behind the surveillance vehicle. Joe Tavarez and Rob Trilling were both huddling near the rear of the vehicle. I noticed Trilling had stayed calm and kept surveying the street for a safe path to get to the building where the sniper sat.

After another shot, I risked opening the driver's door to reach in and snatch the radio off the seat. I heard radio traffic, someone already asking what had happened.

I shouted into the radio, "Shots fired, shots fired! Shooter is on the balcony!"

Jeff Mabus, in charge of the ESU team, came on the air. "We're moving as a group into the lobby. Too dangerous to split up."

Terri Hernandez said, "I can cover the front door."

Trilling called to me from his position at the rear of our car. "I'll cover the back."

I saw him low-crawl from the car until he was covered by another building. Then he started to run.

I glanced over at Joe Tavarez, who had his Glock pistol trained on the roof. His ear poured blood onto his shoulder, but he held his position.

I said, "Joe, we gotta stop the bleeding from your ear."

"It can wait. We can stop this asshole right now if we keep our cool."

I said, "Joe, that's someone who read the memo. Someone in the analysts' room or maybe the FBI. Do you have any ideas who it could be?"

Tavarez peered up at the balcony like he might recognize the man with the rifle. Then he snapped his fingers, leaning back slightly as he turned to me. "Son of a bitch."

I said, "What is it, Joe? Who's up there?"

Another shot rang out. It was from a different position on the roof. The bullet ripped through the car's side window. It hit Joe Tavarez in the center of his back and exited through his chest.

Tavarez toppled onto the asphalt with a thud. Blood immediately spread across the street.

I quickly reached out and grabbed him by the arm to drag him back behind the car. I checked his pulse. It seemed futile, but it felt like he might still have a heartbeat.

I grabbed the radio and called out, "Officer down, officer down! We need medical help!"

Harry Grissom came on the radio. "How bad is Trilling?"

"He's not the officer down."

"Who else is there with you?"

I didn't want to confuse things. I just said, "Harry, stand by." I heard sirens. Help was coming. I saw a woman and two kids step out of a building across the street. I screamed, "Police! Get back inside!" The woman gathered up the children and stared at me and Tavarez lying on the ground. I shouted again, "Get back inside!" The woman turned quickly, fumbled with the door handle, then shooed the kids inside and followed them.

I felt again for a pulse on Joe Tavarez's throat. Nothing. He was definitely dead. I stayed low just in case the sniper was still up there, looking for a new target. When I peeked over the rear panel of the car, I saw no movement on the balcony or the roof. The radio was quiet.

After a minute, I saw Harry scurrying along the street toward me. He stayed low behind parked cars. I heard him on another radio channel, directing arriving cops, setting up a perimeter and generally keeping things running.

Harry slid in next to me and looked over at Tavarez's body. Harry said, "That's Joe Tavarez."

"I know."

"Then who the hell has been shooting?"

"No idea."

Harry checked Tavarez again for any signs of life. When he was done, he just shook his head. Then he said, "Where's Trilling?"

"Covering the back door of the shooter's building."

Jeff Mabus came on the radio. "The balcony is clear at the end of the second-floor hallway. No one on the roof either. No sign of the shooter anywhere."

Terri Hernandez said, "He didn't come out the front."

I had to use my cell phone to call Trilling. We had shared the radio in the car. As the phone rang, I realized he could be in danger. Each ring made my heart pound harder. I mumbled, "Answer. Answer."

Then he did. Thank God. Trilling said, "I haven't seen any-one in the rear of the building."

"Keep your eyes open. He's on the move. Watch for Mabus and his guys."

"Roger that."

I looked over at Harry, who summed up the situation. "That did not go well at all."

"You should've been a poet."

CHAPTER 99

I SAT ON the curb, a few feet from Joe Tavarez's body. I watched the paramedics slowly pull a tarp over him. Even the wide tarp couldn't cover the giant pool of blood on the asphalt. Rob Trilling plopped down on the curb next to me. I didn't feel like talking. Trilling made the perfect companion.

We sat in silence as Harry Grissom spoke with the four-person ESU team.

I was in shock. Seriously. The only thing I could do was think about how Joe Tavarez gave his whole adult life to service, only to be benched and then killed for trying to help. Sometimes this job didn't make any sense at all to me.

Trilling put a reassuring hand on my shoulder. I just wanted to go home. I wanted to spend time with my family. But I knew that wouldn't be in the cards for me today. There was still way too much to do.

A shiny new Dodge Charger rolled to a stop across the street. Trilling said, "Someone from command staff?"

I watched for a moment, then said, "Worse. It's Dennis Wu."

The Internal Affairs sergeant was the only one at the scene dressed in a suit and tie. He looked at all the flashing lights from the emergency vehicles and shook his head. As Wu walked past me, he said, "Looks like you're oh for two, Bennett. Excellent job, as always."

I felt Trilling start to rise in anger. I grabbed his arm and pulled him back to the curb. I said quietly, "Wu's right. Let it go."

After a few more minutes, Harry Grissom came over and leaned against the car we'd been driving. "I guess we can write off Joe Tavarez as a suspect."

I knew it was Harry's way of easing me back into reality.

He said, "We have to figure out who else, exactly, saw that memo back at headquarters. It might take some time." Harry let out a sigh, then said, "Why don't you and Trilling make notification to Cindy Tavarez, Joe's wife. I know you'll be sensitive to the moment, but maybe she'll know something. Anything. Maybe she mentioned the memo to someone."

I nodded. Harry was doing me a favor by getting me away from the scene and Dennis Wu.

Harry gave us his car since our surveillance vehicle was shot to pieces. I turned down Trilling's offer to drive. The FBI office wasn't too far from here. I took one more look at the body covered by a tarp. I wondered what Joe Tavarez had been about to tell me just before he got shot.

I said a prayer for him.

CHAPTER 100

I PULLED HARRY'S car into someone's reserved spot in front of the FBI. Rob Trilling and I were inside the building a few seconds later. The expression on the receptionist's face when I identified myself made me pause.

The young woman said, "You're here about Cindy Tavarez, right?"

"How'd you know that?"

She held up a long, slender finger as she spoke to someone on the phone. We only had to wait a minute to see who the receptionist had called: Assistant Special Agent in Charge Robert Lincoln.

Lincoln didn't bother to greet us at all. Not even a nod. He walked right up to me and said, "We've already informed Cindy about her husband. One of the NYPD officers on a task force told me about the incident and I didn't think we should withhold that from Cindy." Then he folded his arms across his chest and stared at me like I was going to refute his reasoning.

I said, "I appreciate your thoughtfulness. We'd like to ask Cindy a couple of important questions. We don't feel like it can wait."

"Why?"

I hesitated, the natural instinct of any cop to not share details of a case before it's finished. "It appears that someone from either the NYPD or the FBI is the Longshot Killer. Or at the very least fed him information. We need to know if Cindy mentioned to anyone today's covert operation we had going on. I think this is an important issue for both of us."

Lincoln took a long moment to consider the situation. I couldn't get a read on his facial expression. After a full twenty seconds, Lincoln made a decision. He looked at Trilling and me and said, "This way."

We followed him up the stairwell and through a maze of hallways until we were in the analysts' common room. Cindy Tavarez sat on a long brown couch with two women, one on either side of her. She held a soaking-wet paper towel and used it to wipe the tears from her eyes.

We hung back until Cindy looked up at us and burst into a new set of sobs. Her two friends, who had been comforting her, moved from the couch so I could sit down. I sat quietly while Cindy first asked me a few questions. I told her everything I knew. When I thought she was calm enough for me to continue, I hit her with my big question.

"Who saw the memo about the NYPD operation to take an indicted cop to court?"

Cindy sniffled. "We all did. It was one of the more interesting memos to come through the office in a long time. We all looked at it and speculated about what was going on. When I talked with Joe about it last night, he told me his theory that it wasn't what it looked like. He'd seen some other memo about using four Emergency Service members in plain clothes. He thought it was some kind of operation to catch the sniper." Cindy blew her nose into the wet paper towel.

I couldn't help but glance around the room as she spoke, wondering who else could be a suspect. No one jumped out at me.

CHAPTER 101

WE WAITED WHILE Cindy Tavarez composed herself on the couch. Another analyst, an older woman named Rochelle Lynch, joined us. I got the impression that Rochelle was a senior analyst. She also had a clear head. I gave the two of them a moment to discuss the issue and to look through a printed-out roster of analysts.

I noticed that ASAC Robert Lincoln hadn't gone anywhere. He stood back and let us conduct the interview, but he clearly wanted to be in the loop. That made me nervous as ever with the FBI.

I felt jittery, like I had to do something. Anything. That happens in homicide cases when things take weird turns and you're not sure how to proceed. Joe Tavarez showing up at a trap we'd set intending to catch him definitely qualified as a weird turn. I wanted to figure out who the Longshot Killer was and stop him right this minute.

Rob Trilling started to make notes next to the names Cindy and Rochelle were going through. All the analysts had been with the FBI for years. A couple of the younger ones weren't in the office yesterday. When they came to the name Darnell Nash, both women paused.

I said, "That's the guy who served with Joe in the Army, right?" Before Cindy even nodded, everything clicked into place. I remembered Joe telling me that Darnell may not have been a sniper in the service but that he could shoot really well.

I blurted out, "Is Nash here?"

Rochelle Lynch answered. "He's in the building. I noticed he came in a couple of hours early, but that's not unusual. Sometimes analysts take care of personal business and make up for it with extra time."

I sprang up from the couch and looked at Lincoln. "Can you call Nash, get him to come here without scaring him?"

Lincoln started to speak, then something outside caught his eye. He did a double take, said, "Too late. He's definitely scared." He pointed out the window.

I stepped forward and saw Darnell Nash getting into a white Ford Focus, then backing out of the parking spot.

I spun and almost yelled to Trilling, "Nash is trying to run! Let's see if we can chase him down."

Lincoln kept a calm tone as he said, "You'll never catch him if you parked out front. My car is the second from the door. Follow me."

We didn't hesitate to fall in behind the FBI assistant special agent in charge.

CHAPTER 102

I'D ALWAYS ASSUMED Robert Lincoln was a little older than me, but you couldn't tell by the way he moved. He raced through the maze of halls and had to wait for us to catch up when he bolted down a flight of stairs.

We burst out into the same lot where I'd seen Darnell Nash jumping into a Ford Focus. I followed Lincoln to a brand-new Chevy Tahoe. I hopped into the front passenger seat and Rob Trilling slid into the back seat.

As he started the SUV, Lincoln said, "The only reason Nash even has a car in this lot is because he's handicapped. He's missing the lower portion of a leg. Besides, I doubt he wanted to walk around Manhattan with a rifle."

I said, "The one time I talked to him, he told me he'd stepped on an IED."

Lincoln said, "That's more than I know about him. Aside from meeting him on his first day and saying hello in the hallway, I've never really interacted with Nash. I can't tell you if I think he's good for the shootings or not. But he's certainly not helping himself."

I had to grudgingly admit I was impressed at how Lincoln remained calm even as he peeled out of his parking spot, darted through the lot, then spurted out onto the street. Amazingly, he soon managed to get Nash's Ford Focus within sight.

I could tell by the way Nash was driving that he wasn't trying to evade us. He didn't even know we were behind him. That was a testament to Robert Lincoln's ability and experience. He had to have been some kind of great street agent years ago to be this smooth behind the wheel. Maybe I'd misjudged the guy.

I saw the Focus turn and said, "Did you see him turn right?"

Lincoln kept an even, calm voice as he replied, "I see him. I see him. And I'm going to pull an old Baltimore police trick." A block before where we'd seen Nash turn, Lincoln took a right down a narrow side street. The move paid off when at the next block Lincoln paused and we saw Nash drive right past us.

Lincoln said, "He may not know anyone's following him, but he's being careful. That kind of round-the-block turn is one of the oldest counter-surveillance tricks in the book." He let one more car pass and fell in behind the Focus again.

Lincoln stayed cool as he said, "Nash just signaled to turn left." He glanced over his shoulder and slid into the left lane. Then he suddenly jammed on his brakes and muttered, "Dammit. Busted."

Nash had purposely stopped instead of turning to see if any cars were following him. Not a bad move for a guy who wasn't a full-time drug dealer. Now we were stuck and he'd clearly seen us.

Darnell Nash punched the gas and squirted around the corner. By the time Lincoln brought the Tahoe around, we could see the Focus making a crazy U-turn and heading toward the East River.

Lincoln leaned down and flipped a switch that activated the hidden blue lights at the top of his windshield. His siren started to blare from under the hood. We made the U-turn as easily as Nash. Confused drivers tried to move out of our way, but we were stuck in heavy traffic.

Once we were moving east, Lincoln called back to Trilling, "There's a lockbox directly behind your seat. The combination is 2-5-8-1. I assume you know how to operate an AR-15."

I caught the quick smile slipping across Trilling's face. Now we were playing a game that he understood.

CHAPTER 103

I ABSOLUTELY HATE high-speed chases. I'm not crazy about the FBI either. Now I found myself in a high-speed chase with an FBI agent.

I don't like the feeling of being a passenger during a car chase. Despite what people see on police shows, high-speed chases are relatively rare but wildly dangerous. It seems like someone always gets hurt: either the suspect fleeing, the cops chasing, or some innocent bystander.

Darnell Nash took a left turn and then another right. Lincoln got on the radio and started calling for help.

After a few moments, Lincoln said, "He's headed toward the Battery Tunnel."

I had to brace myself as Lincoln took a right turn a little sharply. For a moment, I thought we might be tipping over. If it

weren't for the heavy traffic, we would've caught the underpow-
ered little Ford easily. I had no idea where Nash was headed.

We came out of the tunnel on the other side of the river with a
sprawling construction site to our right. It looked like a giant
bomb had hit South Brooklyn. Half of the site was filled with
cranes and machines working in a pit far below street level as
construction workers laid the foundation for a huge new
building.

I heard Trilling ask from the back seat, "Where'd he go?"

Lincoln slowed the Tahoe and cut off its lights and siren.
Heavy traffic continued, but I didn't see any sign of the Ford
Focus in the lanes up ahead.

Trilling asked, "What's that over there?" He pointed between
the two front seats. I followed the line of sight from his finger to
what I now realized was the Ford Focus. All I could see was a little of the trunk and roof, but it looked like it was parked on the
far side of the construction site.

Lincoln said, "He tried to avoid lane closures and cut through
the site. Looks like he got stuck." As Lincoln exited the highway
and turned onto a street running alongside the site, he got on his
car's radio and again called for any FBI agent in the area to come
over and help.

I looked across the construction landscape and realized there
was no way to drive across there easily. But we might make it on
foot with fewer delays.

Lincoln pulled over and we all jumped out of the Tahoe. No
one needed to tell us to take cover immediately. Based on some of
Darnell Nash's previous shots, there was no question he could hit
one of us from across this hectic construction zone.

Trilling held the AR-15, which had a short scope on it. He

checked the magazine and made sure the rifle was charged. On either side of Trilling, Lincoln and I crouched behind a mound of construction debris. A broken plastic pipe stuck me in the ribs.

Lincoln said, "I'm afraid we're trapped here until more help arrives. I wouldn't recommend trying to move from the safety of this cover."

Trilling was looking through the scope at the far side of the construction site. He said, "I see him at the base of the pylon on the left side of the site. It doesn't look like any of the construction workers have even noticed him."

Lincoln asked, "What's he doing? He should be trying to get away."

"Just standing there. I think he's seen the Tahoe and he's looking for us on the site."

I said, "He knows we're not going to take a shot at him for just standing there. We can't say the same thing. We can't just sit here. He may decide to shoot one of the construction workers instead."

Trilling, still looking through the scope of the rifle, said, "I'm open to ideas."

I said, "Good, because I have a plan."

CHAPTER 104

ROBERT LINCOLN, Rob Trilling, and I crowded together behind construction debris. I peeked around the edge of the pile and across the site. The site had workers spread out as well as working in groups. Not an ideal situation.

I said, "I'll cut around to our right and try to stay out of Nash's sight all the way across the construction zone. You should be able to see me most of the way. When I get to the far side, I'll see how hard it'll be to charge him."

Once I started explaining my plan out loud, I realized it had some serious flaws. The biggest one was the risk that I might be shot in the head.

Lincoln said, "You won't even make it that far. That's exactly what he's waiting for us to do."

"I don't see any other choice. I'm concerned that he's going to get agitated in a minute and just shoot a construction worker."

Lincoln said, "I'm going to make a fake run to the left. I'll draw his attention. That's when you go." Before I could even respond, he sprang to his feet and started jogging toward the left side of the site.

I was seriously reassessing the FBI ASAC. My initial impression that Lincoln was an administrative geek could not have been more wrong. This guy had balls the size of Trenton.

Trilling scrambled back to his position where he could see Nash. He looked through the scope for a second, then called out, "Nash has got his rifle up! Take cover. Take cover."

Lincoln reacted quickly. He ducked down and jumped to his left. Just as he landed behind a heavy concrete block, I heard the report of Nash's rifle. My head snapped to the left, and I could see dirt and dust kicked up by the bullet just a few inches from where Lincoln was crouching.

That was my signal. I sprang up and started racing to my right with my body bent in half, trying to keep whatever I could between me and Nash.

I saw some of the construction workers on the east side of the site start to panic. Lincoln was on the run again and shouting for the workers to take cover.

I followed suit and started yelling the same thing on my west side of the construction site. Most of the workers just stared at me as I scurried past with my head low. They hadn't heard the rifle shot over the sound of the heavy machinery.

Nash fired again. I wasn't sure where the bullet was aimed. But the construction workers on my side of the site heard it this time. They all scrambled, desperate to find cover.

I sprinted onto an original stretch of sidewalk that skirted this half of the giant lot, giving up some cover for speed. When I was about a third of the way around the construction site, I saw a woman lying on the sidewalk behind some kind of metal container, holding a toddler in her arms. I slid in next to her like a base runner trying to beat a play at home plate.

She was crying as she held a little girl close to her chest.

My badge was hanging around my neck, so she realized I was a cop. I asked, "Are you hurt?"

She shook her head. Her black hair flew in every direction as a gust of wind hit our position.

I said, "You'll be safe here. Just stay right in this position. I've got to run to the far end of the site."

As I tucked my legs under me to get a running start, the young woman reached out and grabbed my arm. "Please don't leave us alone." Her voice was shaky.

I gently moved her hand. "Trust me. You stay right here and this will all be over in a couple of minutes."

"Do you promise?"

"Swear to God."

I did a quick peek over the top of the container. I didn't see anything except running construction workers. I stuck my head up a second time to get a better look. It was about then that Robert Lincoln jumped up on the other side of the site and waved his arms.

I couldn't take my eyes off him. Then another shot rang out from the far end of the construction site. Lincoln went down. It looked like he'd been hit. I shook my head, wondering what had just happened. But he'd bought me two seconds to scramble up and start running again.

I made it another thirty yards down the sidewalk. Now I could look to my left and see the area where Nash was hiding. I saw the flash from the barrel of his rifle. But he was shooting downrange.

Then I heard another rifle shot. It had a different sound. I looked over my shoulder in time to see Trilling fire the AR-15 a second time. Whatever he was doing to make Darnell Nash keep his head down was working. I decided to grab a lot of real estate with an all-out sprint.

By now, most of the workers were either off-site or hiding in safe positions. That might make my job a little easier.

I stopped behind a post a little wider than a telephone pole. It looked like the post was used to guide the big trucks as they backed into the site. As I took a second big gulp of air, a bullet struck the post just above my head.

Instinctively, I dropped to the ground. Not that it did me any good. The next shot hit the ground only an inch from my right leg. Dirt and debris flew up onto my chest and face.

I didn't need a third shot to tell me this wasn't the place to take a break. I did a burpee back onto my feet like an Olympic athlete and continued to run hard to the end of the construction site.

Now it was Trilling's turn to fire again.

CHAPTER 105

I'D MADE IT all the way to the far corner of the construction site when Rob Trilling fired again twice. Not quite a double tap but two shots in quick succession. I saw them both impact a pile of rubble in front of Darnell Nash.

I could only see Nash intermittently. Occasionally his head popped up or he moved back enough that I could see him behind the pile of debris. He was a little farther from me than what I'd originally thought. And it was all open space between us. As soon as I started moving in Nash's direction, all it would take would be a casual turn of his head and I'd be in deep shit.

Trilling took another shot, which made Nash duck down and cover his head. I realized it was time.

I couldn't afford to hesitate. I just started running hard. And I mean *hard*. My long legs covered a lot of ground, but it didn't mean I wasn't terrified the whole time. I wondered whether I could cover the distance before I took a .308 round in the face.

As I got closer, I could see around the beam that had blocked my view before. Nash had his rifle up, resting on a wooden truss. He was focusing through the rifle's scope and didn't notice me racing toward him until the last second.

For the record, the last second is always the most important one in a situation like this.

As soon as Nash noticed me, he turned to point his rifle, but I was already leaping off my feet and sailing through the air. My shoulder knocked the barrel of the rifle before he could point it at me. I hit him with the full force of my body weight. We slammed backward into a fifty-five-gallon drum filled with something liquid. We hit the sealed barrel hard enough to make the liquid slosh inside.

Now we were in a close-quarters scrum. It felt like we were in a pit even though we were just on the shale-and-gravel ground. Somehow the rifle ended up between us, pointing almost straight up in the air. It was wedged between a couple of boards, and we both reached for it at about the same time.

Nash got his hand around the trigger guard, so I wrapped my arm around his. I'd rather have him locked against the rifle than punching me in the face. As we wrestled, the rifle went off. It was shocking to hear the sound of the high-powered rifle so close to my head.

I raised myself off the ground into a squat. Now I had my hand around the barrel of the gun and ripped it from Nash's grasp. I let the momentum carry me and tossed the rifle twenty feet away.

Then I squared off against Nash.

CHAPTER 106

I WASN'T PARTICULARLY happy about fighting a younger man, a former Marine who looked like he'd stayed in pretty good shape despite his titanium leg. The way Darnell Nash had his body turned told me he understood the basics of a fistfight.

But I had experience. I'd been in actual street fights. People had tried to stab me, hit me with pipes, slash me with broken bottles, and once someone even tried to choke me with a garden hose. Nash had learned to shoot in the military and worked a desk job at the FBI.

We circled each other for a moment. I'd gotten the rifle out of Nash's hands. That was the most important thing. Now it was more of a waiting game until someone came to help.

Then I realized the mistake I'd made. Nash had maneuvered so that he was now between me and his rifle. I couldn't waste any time. I reached for my Glock, locked in the holster on my right hip.

Before I even had the pistol fully clear of the holster, Nash lunged toward me and slapped it away. Somehow I initially managed to hold on to the gun. Then his punch to my solar plexus knocked me for a loop and I let the pistol drop out of my hand.

It hit several empty fifty-five-gallon drums and disappeared between them. When I looked up, Nash was smiling. He knew he had the advantage now.

I ducked a wild right hand and immediately threw a low kick, hoping to take out his knee.

Nash lifted his leg, so I struck his lower leg, his prosthesis made of titanium. The shock that went through my system was incredible. It was like someone had hit me with a TASER on the foot. I limped back a few feet and decided to take another tack. I said in a loud voice, "Is this what you want to do? Fight a cop doing his job?"

That brought Nash up short. He just stared at me for a moment. Then he shook his head. "You're right. I don't want to fight you. I just want to get away. Considering all the help I've given the NYPD the last few months, I think you might let me go."

"You've misread the situation. And me. You're wrong. Nobody appreciates what you've done the last few months."

"The cops and courts aren't doing anything to help people. Killers are let out on bond. No one cares when poor people have their money stolen by fraudsters. I still think you'll let me walk. I'll even leave my rifle over there." Nash turned his back to me.

He'd made a decent point. It's tough to be a cop. I got it. I still only let Nash take two steps before I tackled him. When I tried to yank his wrist behind his back so I could cuff him, Nash did a little spin move on the ground and we ended up face-to-face again. Then he bit me on the hand.

Before I could react to the bite, he headbutted me. My nose started to pour blood. Then Nash squirmed out of my grip. He took two steps toward the rifle on the ground, but I was able to reach out, grab his ankle, and yank him back toward me.

He was strong and I was a little woozy. I needed help but couldn't reach my phone. We grappled like wrestlers until somehow I found my arms around Nash with my hands locked behind his head in a modified full nelson.

Once Nash had stopped struggling in the powerful hold, I looked up and saw FBI ASAC Robert Lincoln step around the pile of debris where Nash had hidden. Lincoln had a nasty gash on his head and blood had soaked into his white shirt. He turned away and I heard him say in a calm voice, "I've got eyes on Bennett. He's got Nash."

As Lincoln took control of Nash and cuffed him, I sat on a toolbox to catch my breath.

A few seconds later, Rob Trilling stepped around the same pile of debris, cradling the AR-15 Lincoln had given him. He took in the scene with Nash lying face down on the shale-rock ground and me sitting a few feet away. Trilling looked at me and said with a deadpan delivery, "See? I told you I wasn't the shooter."

CHAPTER 107

AS SOON AS we took Darnell Nash into custody, I wondered when politics might jump up and slap me in the face. I was surprised that Robert Lincoln didn't object when I announced we needed to take Nash to One Police Plaza to be interviewed. In fact, the FBI ASAC asked if he could come along.

The NYPD headquarters houses some operational units as well as most of the administrative offices. It's not set up for prisoners or interviews, but I figured this would qualify as a special circumstance. It wasn't hard to slip in through a back door with the prisoner and commandeer an empty office.

Rob Trilling made sure Nash was comfortable. He grabbed him a bottle of water and a package of crackers with peanut butter. Usually officers try to be aware of prisoners' needs. It can come back to haunt a detective later if the prisoner complains about being mistreated and giving a confession under duress. In this case, I thought it was one military veteran looking after another, no matter what the circumstances.

Lincoln took a seat in the corner while Trilling and I sat in sturdy metal chairs across a table from Nash. Lincoln had been very good about accepting the fact that the NYPD was the lead on this case. The fact that the suspect was an FBI employee didn't even come up. This guy was surprising me at every turn today.

We got some background and read Nash his Miranda rights. He didn't try to deny anything. I wasn't a psychotherapist. I didn't want to get into the reasons why he did what he did.

After a few minutes, I asked, "Are there other victims we're not aware of?"

Nash didn't answer immediately. Then he shook his head.

"So Marie Ballard was your first victim?"

He nodded.

"And the antifa activist your last one?"

That made Nash laugh. "There's no way I'd ever consider that scumbag a victim. He tried to murder two cops by burning them. Have you seen his rap sheet? Domestic violence, arson, theft. I'm sure his parents are proud."

Nash looked directly at Trilling. "Sorry I shifted the blame to you by planting that casing in your car. I knew why you'd been called back to the NYPD. I also realized your background would make you a tempting suspect. I hated doing it to a fellow vet. I apologize."

Trilling didn't say anything. He gave Nash a little nod.

Nash said, "I was so tired of not contributing. After the Marines, everything seemed sort of pointless. This gave me a sense of accomplishment. I know you all think I'm a nut and you can't believe I'd do something like this, but you'll see I was right.

When we start letting people get away with crimes so easily, society goes to hell."

Nash said, "I didn't realize that was Joe Tavarez earlier today. Joe was like a brother to me. I saw movement by the car and realized I'd stepped into a trap. I was just trying to get away. I knew if I shot someone, it'd throw the whole operation into chaos, and I could slip away. It hasn't hit me yet that I shot my best friend." He looked down and shook his head. "I'll never be able to look Cindy in the eye again. Hell, the list of things I'll never do again is really long."

He turned and glanced at Robert Lincoln behind him in the corner. Then he looked back at both of us. "Any chance you could leave me alone in here for a while? It'll save the taxpayers a lot of money and me a lot of embarrassment."

I shook my head. After all the time I'd spent on this case and all the heartache I'd gone through, I couldn't believe I actually felt kinda sorry for this guy. He was rational enough to know he'd ruined his life along with so many others.

I felt a little sad being in on the interview. I wished we could save a veteran like this. Smart, educated, and dedicated. Maybe a little too dedicated. It is times like this when I wish I had more answers.

CHAPTER 108

INTERVIEWING AND ARRESTING Darnell Nash, and everything that went with it, took us into the evening. When I got home, Mary Catherine and the kids had already huddled around the TV. They looked like a group of fans watching a sporting event, but they were actually watching a live NYPD news conference about the sniper investigation.

No one even glanced away from the TV when I stepped into the apartment. Contrary to the scoldings I'd gotten as a kid—that I would ruin my eyes by sitting too close to a TV— my grandfather was positioned about three feet from the screen. The kids were grouped around him in rows, with Mary Catherine at the center of the back row. Naturally she got to sit in the recliner with everyone else either leaning on it or sitting on the floor.

I made my way across the living room, then slipped through

the kitchen to come into the living room behind the crowd. I eased up to the rear of the group without anyone noticing me.

On the screen, the NYPD public information officer provided background on the case from a podium in front of a US flag, a New York City flag, and a blue, green, and white NYPD flag. Behind the PIO was the usual NYPD brass. I saw a few faces who'd actually been involved in the case. Inspector Lisa Udell again looked impressive, standing next to the police commissioner. A little farther back, I noticed Harry Grissom wearing a fairly sharp suit and looking less grizzled than usual.

Ricky, sitting next to my grandfather, said, "Where's Dad? It was his case. Why isn't he at the news conference?"

That's when I said in a good, clear voice, "Because I'd rather be here with you guys." It was true. Harry had asked me if I felt up to attending the news conference. I had politely declined, citing the fact that I had been in a gun battle today.

The kids sprang off the floor and swarmed me like piranha around a bloody cow leg. Or whatever happens down in the Amazon. Mary Catherine was particularly agile, coming out of the chair and spinning around to hug me. I wondered if there was any event in life that would ever equal the feeling I have when my whole family embraces me.

I waved off questions about why I was home so we could watch the end of the news conference. Most everyone went back to their original places in front of the TV. Except for my grandfather, Seamus. He stood next to me and wrapped a bony arm around my shoulders and gave me a squeeze. He said in a low voice, "This city needs to thank God it has someone like you around."

A murmur of excitement rippled through the kids as Harry Grissom stepped to the microphone and gave a quick recap of the actual arrest. He left out a lot of detail, which I was glad to avoid discussing with my family. Most cops never want to let their kids know the kind of danger they face every day.

Harry opened up questions from the media. There looked to be about twenty reporters and seven or eight cameramen all wedged into an area in front of the podium. I smiled when the first person Harry called on turned out to be none other than Lois Frang of the *Brooklyn Democrat*. Suddenly I realized why Harry looked so dapper and cleaned up. He had a new girlfriend. I'm sure he'd never use that phrase or even admit it, but it was clear the way he was gazing at Lois from the podium that she was more than just a reporter for a little-known newspaper in Brooklyn.

Lois asked, "This seems like quite a complex case. Did any one tip or piece of info break the case open?"

Harry straightened at the podium and leaned toward the microphone. "We found multiple pieces of evidence that allowed us to assemble information leading to the arrest of Darnell Nash. I'd like to acknowledge not only NYPD personnel but also FBI personnel, who helped us narrow the focus of our investigation."

That was the most politically correct statement I had ever heard Harry Grissom make. But it was true. The damn FBI had saved my bacon today. And I wouldn't be forgetting it anytime soon.

CHAPTER 109

AFTER THE NEWS conference, we all settled down to a modest feast of sloppy joes and a Greek salad. I could tell by the awkward pairing of cuisines that our resident chef, Ricky, had not prepared the meal. He was a little bit of a nut when it came to the dining experience. He always insisted that every side dish complement the main dish. But when you regularly feed thirteen hungry people for dinner on an NYPD detective's salary, cheap meals like sloppy joes are essential.

Brian hurried into the kitchen. A few seconds later he walked out holding up a bottle of champagne. Not the ritziest and not the nastiest of champagnes. He had a broad grin on his face as he said, "Dad solving this case means we can finally pop the cork."

It was Korbel, and it sounded like a fine idea to me, so I gave him a little nod.

Brian was prepared, with a dishrag around the collar of the

bottle. He pointed the bottle at an angle and worked the cork slowly. It still made the good popping sound. Brian managed to catch the cork in his hand and avoid spilling any of the champagne.

My grandfather stood up and took plastic champagne flutes from a bag sitting on the dining room table. That's when I knew the entire incident had been preplanned. The place got boisterous fast. The kids all politicked for some champagne. We settled on letting anyone over the age of twelve have a sip and anyone over sixteen a small glass.

I held two plastic glasses, each filled halfway. I turned to Mary Catherine and offered her one, but she held up her hand. I knew it had to do with her fertility treatment. So I gave it to my grandfather, who gladly threw it down with gusto.

Now I could focus on my sloppy joe dinner. I couldn't believe how much better I felt listening to the chatter around the table. It made me wonder what it'd be like to be around the house full-time. Retirement was just around the corner if I wanted it to be.

It didn't help that Seamus sat next to me. About midway through dinner he said, "You doing okay, boyo?"

"I am now."

"We haven't seen much of you lately."

"It was a big case."

"Technically, every homicide is a big case. Don't try and tell me that a family in the Bronx is any less grief-stricken than a family in Tribeca when a family member is murdered."

"You know I don't feel anything like that. I don't think I'd even talk to someone who thought that was true. This investigation was complicated. That's what made it a big case."

"You've got a big family too. They need you more than the police department does."

I nodded without responding. This was a recurring theme. What I think a lot of people have to deal with in life: finding the right balance.

After dinner—and a dessert of pound cake made by Chrissy and Shawna, with serious oversight by Juliana—we played a few hands of Go Fish using three decks of cards.

About an hour later, as soon as we were able to name Bridget the Go Fish champion, Mary Catherine gave me a subtle signal that it was bedtime.

CHAPTER 110

IT HAD BEEN a remarkably long and stressful day. I knew Mary Catherine was constantly tired from her treatments, and wrapping up a big case was always draining. We said our good nights to the wild mob that is our family, then headed to our bedroom.

The sheets and the pillow under my head felt like heaven. I could still hear the kids talking in the hallway and around their bedrooms. The boys had a habit of shouting to one another from the bathroom to their bedroom. Still, there was something comforting and normal about the noise.

Mary Catherine snuggled up close to me in bed. She said in a soft voice, "I don't know what's better, a family get-together or being so close to you in bed."

"Definitely bed. None of those annoying kids around."

She let out a gentle laugh and draped an arm across my chest.

Mary Catherine said, "Also, I'm not loud or whiny, and I change my underwear every day."

I snorted at the shot at Trent, Eddie, and Ricky, whose hygiene practices were still evolving. Much like any adolescent boy's. "I'm glad you have a goal, like changing your underwear every day. I think you're doing great at it."

Mary Catherine gave me a little bite on the shoulder.

Then I turned so I could look her in the eye and said, "How are you doing? I'm sorry I've been a little scarce. Seamus reminded me at dinner."

"He's a good conscience. And he's been a huge help. All the kids adore him, and he's still the only one who's heard Jane's complete speech."

I asked, "And what does he think of it?"

"You know your grandfather. He never lets out a hint. It must be all the practice he's had keeping confessions to himself."

I smiled at the idea that one had to *practice* to keep quiet.

Mary Catherine propped herself up on her elbow. "I have a secret I've been keeping for a couple of days."

"Oh, yeah?"

"Yeah." She twisted in bed and grabbed something out of her nightstand. She turned and held out her hand.

Just as I was about to ask, *What's this?* I took a closer look and saw the pink plus sign in the middle of the white plastic handle. It took only a moment to click in my brain exactly what I was looking at. My eyes shifted from the pregnancy test to my wife's beautiful face.

All I said was "Really?"

Mary Catherine nodded vigorously. She said, "I still have to confirm it with the doctor next week. That's why I haven't said anything to anyone else yet."

I tried to grasp this news. I didn't even go into the future implications, like being the oldest father at graduation. Or teaching a kid to drive when my eyesight was failing. Looking at Mary Catherine, I realized how happy she was. Maybe it was partially because she didn't have to go back for any more fertility treatments. But it was much more than that. There was actual joy on her face. And the idea of a new baby rumbling around the house made me ecstatic.

Mary Catherine looked at me. Finally frustration overcame her, and she said, "Well? What do you think?"

"Hallelujah!"

"And you'll keep it a secret?"

"From the kids?"

"Anybody."

"This is big news. I might blurt it out."

She smiled. "You Bennetts just love telling good news."

"And kissing beautiful women." I planted a kiss on Mary Catherine's lips.

Her smile was contagious. So were her giggles. Then we laughed and hugged and I had to say a quick prayer of thanks.

CHAPTER 111

WHEN I WOKE up the next morning, it felt like a new age had dawned. We were having a baby. I wanted to gently shake Mary Catherine awake and shout that we were having a baby.

We were having a baby, my nightmare case was over, and Jane was speaking at Columbia University. I wanted to pinch myself. Just to make sure I wasn't dreaming.

As I flipped pancakes, Fiona shuffled into the kitchen wearing big pink bunny-shaped slippers that Seamus had bought her. She looked at me and said, "What are you smiling about?"

I turned and kissed her on the forehead. "You'd be smiling too if you had kids like mine."

Fiona screwed her face up and said, "You're weird."

"But happy." I put a little singsong in my voice.

Fiona shook her head and shuffled out of the kitchen.

I took the kids to school. We even made it on time. I gave a quick wave to Sister Sheilah. Oddly, for all of my ups and downs with Holy Name's senior nun, whom I had known since my own first day of kindergarten, I badly wanted to tell her about Mary Catherine's pregnancy. But I restrained myself.

Forty minutes later, I strolled into the Manhattan North Homicide office still in a phenomenally good mood.

Rob Trilling was at his desk. He looked up and right away said, "What put that smile on your face today?"

"Just the way things are rolling." We chatted for a few minutes, then I went over some notes from the case with him.

Trilling looked at me and said, "Robert Lincoln called me from the FBI. He said I could come back on the fugitive task force whenever I wanted."

"You don't like it here? I understand if you don't like the way the sniper investigation unfolded."

Trilling shook his head. "I already told you. I understand what it's like to do your duty no matter what. You did what you had to do. That's not the issue." He had an agitated expression on his face that I couldn't interpret. Finally he said, "I have a problem I need your help with."

Coming from Rob Trilling, that made me nervous. When a guy like Trilling says he has a problem, the chances are it's fairly serious. It could be anything. I nodded and said, "All right, what's bothering you?"

"I need to show you in person. Can you take a quick ride with me?"

I nodded and followed Trilling out of the office. It was a new adventure.

CHAPTER 112

I QUICKLY REALIZED that we were headed toward Rob Trilling's apartment, but I didn't ask any more questions about the "problem." If he wanted to show me something, I'd see it first before I made any comments.

Instead, as we drove, I came clean to him about my earlier visit to his apartment and speaking with the building's super. I also told him about going through the security tapes, looking for when he left the building during one of the shootings.

At a stoplight, Trilling turned to look at me and said, "You snuck into my apartment building and tried to get George to rat me out?"

I instantly felt like a shithead. I hated that Trilling interpreted it that way. I started to say, *I just wanted to verify that you were* not *the sniper.*

That's when Trilling started to laugh. Maybe the first time I'd heard him really laugh out loud. He said, "Relax. I appreciate how you went about the case. I'm just messing with you."

Now I was shocked speechless. I heard Rob Trilling laugh *and* he pranked me, all in the same day? Unbelievable.

When we arrived at the building and walked up the stairs to his second-floor apartment, Trilling turned to me and said, "I'm a little surprised you haven't figured out my problem already, if you looked through those security videos."

He opened the door to his apartment and ushered me inside. I heard low murmurs and conversation as the door opened, but it all stopped the instant I stepped into the darkened apartment.

A TV mounted on the wall was playing some kind of kids' program that spelled out simple words like "cat" and "run."

Five women all turned and stared at me at the same time. One was in the kitchen, two were watching the TV show, and the other two appeared to be doing yoga. They were all in their twenties with dark hair and features. I recognized one of the women. She'd walked past us while Trilling and I were outside the building speaking by his car.

I looked at Trilling and he understood my question instantly.

"They're the women from the heroin operation in the Bronx. I went to their immigration hearing after we busted that William Hackford asshole who shot at us. They were going to send them to some sort of facility unless someone agreed to take responsibility and sponsor them."

"And that someone was you?"

Trilling just shrugged.

"I hope you understand that with ten kids still at home, I can't take any of them."

"That's not what I was asking. We're actually getting along all right. The girls know to be careful when they leave, and George, the super, thinks it's just one girl living here. They all look similar enough that he thinks they're all the same person. They're on a walking routine so each of them gets out of the house for at least an hour a day and they keep the place absolutely spotless."

"So this is why you were so vague about your alibi. And why you never wanted me coming inside."

Trilling nodded.

"And it was one of these young ladies who told me you weren't home, and when I tried to get more information, she cut my fingers with a knife."

Trilling cringed a little. He looked at the woman in the kitchen. "Ayesha told me about that. I figured it was you. She speaks the best English of any of them. But they're all improving every day."

I looked toward the tiny kitchen. The young woman working at the counter waved at me with a paring knife in her hand. She had a big smile. I didn't know if it was a smile of apology or a smile telling me never to come near her again.

Trilling introduced me to the other women, who all had Pakistani names except the youngest. She called herself "Katie." I didn't ask why.

Trilling explained his biggest problem was the cramped living quarters and that he was running out of money buying food for everyone. It took one call to my grandfather to find some agencies willing to help out with the food.

Trilling told me he didn't mind if the women stayed with him a while longer. He felt like their brother taking care of them.

I realized just how happy I was that we were able to figure out the sniper case and keep a conscientious young man like this out of trouble.

CHAPTER 113

FINALLY FRIDAY NIGHT had arrived. Jane's world debut as an orator. It had taken a near-Herculean effort to get everyone ready on time and dressed appropriately. Part of it was because it'd been since Mary Catherine's and my wedding that everyone dressed in their finest clothes, and the kids, especially the youngest ones, seemed to have been using some sort of special growth hormone.

Basically, everyone wore some version of their Sunday church clothes. Ricky's blue blazer from Holy Name had undergone a slight alteration—Mary Catherine had carefully removed the emblem from the front pocket. The blazers were only for special occasions at school, so we weren't worried about putting it back together anytime soon.

Columbia University's main campus is located in the Morningside Heights neighborhood, bordering Harlem above the

Upper West Side. Jane had been with the other speakers at Have-meyer Hall since about five o'clock. I was excited about her speaking in this particular venue because it was the most filmed classroom in the world, showing up in movies like *Spider-Man* and *Ghostbusters*. And on more TV shows than I could count.

The historic hall was four stories of classic stone and brick-work. The classroom's interior had a much more modern feel. The hardwood paneling reminded me of a courtroom, with a gallery super-sized to hold hundreds of people.

We stuck together in the lobby while we waited to catch a glimpse of Jane. People were coming and going in all directions. I kept a close eye on Shawna and Chrissy. Mary Catherine called everyone together like a quarterback in a football huddle. She spoke in a low voice, but there wasn't one kid there who didn't understand exactly what she was saying.

"No video games, no loud talking, and no whining." All the kids nodded. Mary Catherine added, "And have a good time." She looked up at me and Seamus and gave us a wink.

Jane came through with a group of other young people. She stopped for a moment and spoke to her brothers and sisters. She gave Mary Catherine a hug and blew me a kiss from across the crowd. She smiled and gave my grandfather a thumbs-up. He returned it enthusiastically.

As we turned and the first set of kids started to file into the lecture hall, I had to take a deep breath.

My grandfather slapped me on the back and said, "You okay, boyo?"

"Great. Trying to ground myself so I don't look like a fool. I'm just so proud of all these kids."

"Now you know how I felt so many times with you. From

basketball games to the NYPD academy graduation, I know exactly what you mean."

I couldn't believe the compliment my grandfather had just given me. It made the wave of emotion that much more intense.

The twelve of us filled up an entire row with only one empty seat left over at the far end. I heard some of the comments from other people about the size of our family. Nothing I wasn't used to. We were pretty remarkable.

The first three student speakers were from different high schools across the city. Two of them talked about the environment and what we needed to do to save the Earth. One young man from Regis High School talked about the benefits of volunteering in the city and all the opportunities the work can bring.

I still had no clue what topic Jane had chosen for her speech.

My second eldest daughter stepped confidently to the podium. My heart pounded and I felt my face flush. I was both thrilled and terrified—I knew I'd think whatever she said or did was great, whether she was happy or not with her performance.

Jane looked very mature, thanking the university and Sister Mary Margaret, her English and debate instructor. I looked down one row to see Sister Mary Margaret sitting with a couple of the other nuns from Holy Name. She had to wipe a tear from her eye. So did I.

After Jane finished all her introductions and thank-yous, she looked over the podium to the row of seats filled by our family. She pointed us out and introduced us to the crowd, saying, "My immediate family. I have nine brothers and sisters, plus my father, my stepmother, and my great-grandfather. And if you can't tell by looking at us, all ten of us siblings are adopted. Proudly. Purposefully. My father was born here in the city. I have a sister who's Hispanic, a brother and a sister who are Black, and a great-grandfather who was an immigrant from Ireland. I'd say that qualifies us as New Yorkers as much as anything else." That earned a few snickers from the crowd.

"When I was researching this topic, my great-grandfather pointed me to an unfamiliar quote. 'Happiness is having a large, loving family…in another city.'"

That brought a roar of laughter.

Then Jane threw in, "That's from someone named George Burns. A great philosopher, according to my great-grandfather."

That earned laughter from anyone old enough to know that George Burns had been a comedian.

"I don't know if most people have an idea of what adoption is like. But my brothers and sisters and I are closer than most blood relations. We're all from different backgrounds. In fact, I think I was adopted from Scandinavia."

Seamus leaned into me and said, "She's killing. She's as good as Denis Leary."

Jane continued. "Our family is a microcosm of the city. Each of us is different, but in order for things to run smoothly, we all have to work together." She looked directly at me and beamed. "My father made sure each of us understood the importance of democracy. We vote on important issues. I have to admit that my father gets two votes, so he straddles the line between democracy and dictatorship." She had the crowd eating out of her hand.

"It's all the things my siblings and I have in common, not our differences, that are important. Just like the people who live in the city. We have to look past our personal prejudice to try and understand people with different perspectives.

"It's not only the different perspectives from my family that help me, it's also the love and support they give me. The fact that every single one of them is in the audience tonight means so much to me. It also means that I can look out into the audience at any event where I speak and know that when my family is present, I'll always get applause from at least a quarter of the attendees." She paused politely for the chuckling and laughter rippling through the audience.

Jane said, "We yell and argue, then compromise. It's how we keep moving. No one hates someone for their opinion. No one ignores the others. Just like New Yorkers, we're a big, wonderful family.

"As Maya Angelou said, 'I sustain myself with the love of family.'" Jane made it a point to look quickly but directly at our entire row. "In closing, I want to look at my family and say, 'You mean more to me than anything else. Thanks for always supporting me.'"

Mary Catherine used a tissue to wipe her eyes then blow her nose. Next to me, my grandfather did the same, only not nearly as quietly.

The crowd applauded. Loudly. First our entire row stood up, then a number of others followed our example. I couldn't hold it in any longer and I started to cry.

Jane came off the stage and joined the family. She sniffled as she said, "You guys are the best. I couldn't imagine anything better than tonight."

Then I said without thinking, "I can think of one thing." When everyone turned to me, I said, "Mary Catherine is pregnant." I avoided her scowl as I looked at the astonished faces of my family. A cheer rose up. We huddled around Mary Catherine, everyone giving her a hug.

Jane ended up next to me near the end of the line. She looked at me and said, "Really, Dad? You had to tell us tonight? On my night?"

"I'm sorry, sweetheart, it slipped out."

A smile swept across her face. "I know, and I love it. More material for a future paper." She hugged me.

I was having a pretty damn good day.

ACKNOWLEDGMENTS

The authors appreciate the insights Palm Beach County Sheriff's Deputy Mike Hansen and NYPD Lieutenant John Grimpel gave on this book.

ABOUT THE AUTHORS

James Patterson is one of the best-known and biggest-selling writers of all time. Among his creations are some of the world's most popular series, including Alex Cross, the Women's Murder Club, Michael Bennett and the Private novels. He has written many other number one bestsellers including collaborations with President Bill Clinton and Dolly Parton, stand-alone thrillers and non-fiction. James has donated millions in grants to independent bookshops and has been the most borrowed adult author in UK libraries for the past fourteen years in a row. He lives in Florida with his family.

James O. Born is an award-winning crime and science-fiction novelist as well as a career law-enforcement agent. A native Floridian, he still lives in the Sunshine State.

Have You Read Them All?

STEP ON A CRACK
(with Michael Ledwidge)

The most powerful people in the world have gathered for a funeral in New York City. They don't know it's a trap devised by a ruthless mastermind, and it's up to Michael Bennett to save every last hostage.

RUN FOR YOUR LIFE
(with Michael Ledwidge)

The Teacher is giving New York a lesson it will never forget, slaughtering the powerful and the arrogant. Michael Bennett discovers a vital pattern, but has only a few hours to save the city.

WORST CASE
(with Michael Ledwidge)

Children from wealthy families are being abducted. But the captor isn't demanding money. He's quizzing his hostages on the price others pay for their luxurious lives, and one wrong answer is fatal.

TICK TOCK
(with Michael Ledwidge)

New York is in chaos as a rash of horrifying copycat crimes tears through the city. Michael Bennett investigates, but not even he could predict the earth-shattering enormity of this killer's plan.

I, MICHAEL BENNETT
(with Michael Ledwidge)

Bennett arrests infamous South American crime lord Manuel Perrine. From jail, Perrine vows to rain terror down upon New York City – and to get revenge on Michael Bennett.

GONE
(with Michael Ledwidge)

Perrine is back and deadlier than ever. Bennett must make an impossible decision: stay and protect his family, or hunt down the man who is their biggest threat.

BURN
(with Michael Ledwidge)

A group of well-dressed men enter a condemned building. Later, a charred body is found. Michael Bennett is about to enter a secret underground world of terrifying depravity.

ALERT
(with Michael Ledwidge)

Two devastating catastrophes hit New York in quick succession, putting everyone on edge. Bennett is given the near impossible task of hunting down the shadowy terror group responsible.

BULLSEYE
(with Michael Ledwidge)

As the most powerful men on earth gather for a meeting of the UN, Bennett receives shocking intelligence that there will be an assassination attempt on the US president. Are the Russian government behind the plot?

HAUNTED
(with James O. Born)

Michael Bennett is ready for a vacation after a series of crises push him, and his family, to the brink. But when he gets pulled into a shocking case, Bennett is fighting to protect a town, the law, and the family that he loves.

AMBUSH
(with James O. Born)

When an anonymous tip proves to be a trap, Michael Bennett believes he personally is being targetted. And not just him, but his family too.

BLINDSIDE
(with James O. Born)

The mayor of New York has a daughter who's missing. Detective Michael Bennett has a son who's in prison. Can one father help the other?

THE RUSSIAN
(with James O. Born)

As Michael Bennett's wedding day approaches, a killer has a vow of his own to fulfil . . .

SHATTERED
(with James O. Born)

After returning from his honeymoon, Michael Bennett discovers that his former partner is missing. After everything they've been through, he will never give up hope of finding her – he owes her that much.

OBSESSED
(with James O. Born)

Detective Michael Bennett must discover who's murdering young women in New York – before his eldest daughter is targeted.

They run the most in-demand private
investigation agency in New York City.

But who really are the detectives who call
themselves Holmes, Margaret and Poe?

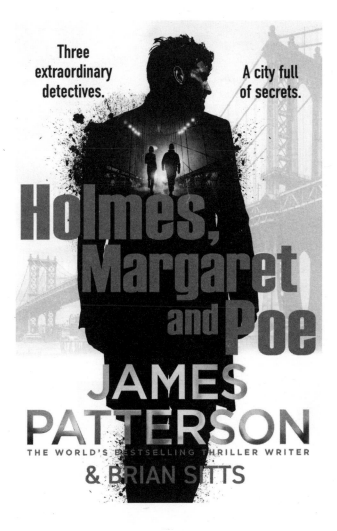

Three
extraordinary
detectives.

A city full
of secrets.

Holmes, Margaret and Poe

JAMES PATTERSON
THE WORLD'S BESTSELLING THRILLER WRITER
& BRIAN SITTS

OUT NOW!

CHAPTER 1

Last year

THE VACANT INDUSTRIAL space that Realtor Gretchen Wik was trying to unload was located in a recently gentrified Brooklyn neighborhood called Bushwick. The area was becoming trendier by the month, but this particular building was cold and dead—and apparently unsellable.

Gretchen had been sitting at her sales table on the first floor since noon, tapping her nails while she stared out through a grime-coated window. In five hours, she had not been visited by a single prospect.

The property consisted of nine thousand square feet on two levels. But it was run-down and needed a lot of work. At this point, Gretchen felt like the worn wood floors and flaking brick walls were mocking her. She checked her watch. In exactly two minutes, her open house would officially be a bust.

Then she heard the front door open.

"Hello?" A voice from the entry hall. Gretchen's pulse perked up. She pushed back her chair and walked briskly toward the door, her three-inch heels clicking on the hardwood. She rounded the corner to the entryway.

"It's *you*!" said a tall, light-skinned Black man in a camel over-coat. For a second, Gretchen was thrown. Then the man pointed at the folding sign in the foyer, the one with Gretchen's face plastered on it.

"Right. Yes," said Gretchen, turning on her best smile. "Positive ID." She held out her hand. "Gretchen Wik, Lexington Realty."

"Brendan," said the visitor, "Holmes." He had large brown eyes and a neatly shaved head. Gretchen did her routine two-second over-view. Coat: expensive, well tailored. Shoes: Alexander McQueen. This guy might be a lookie-loo, but at least he didn't seem like a total waste of time. And right now, he was the only game in town.

"Welcome to your future," said Gretchen. She waved her arm toward the open space. Then she heard the door opening again.

"Sorry, have I missed it?" Another male voice.

This time it was a fit, compact man with wavy, dark hair and the kind of thin moustache that can look either silly or sexy, depending on the owner. On him, Gretchen thought it worked—kind of brood-ing and rakish at the same time. Most important, he was another prospect. The day was looking up.

"You're in luck," she said. "Right under the wire."

"I'm Auguste. Auguste Poe." Soft voice, with a solemn tone. And the slightest wisp of liquor on his breath.

"I'm Gretchen," said the agent. She paused for a second as the names registered. *Wait.* First somebody named *Holmes,* and now *Poe?* What were the odds? Or was this some kind of put-on?

Before Gretchen could ask any questions, both men walked ahead of her into the main space. She caught up and launched into her spiel—the same one she'd been practicing at her lonely table all morning.

"Gentlemen, you're looking at the very best bargain in Bushwick. Late nineteenth century construction, slate roof, terra cotta details, original skylights…"

"Pardon me? Anybody home?" The door again. A female voice this time, with a charming British accent.

Gretchen switched on her greeting smile again, getting even more excited. Two minutes ago, she had zero prospects.

Now, suddenly, she had three.

Also By James Patterson

ALEX CROSS NOVELS

Along Came a Spider • Kiss the Girls • Jack and Jill • Cat and Mouse • Pop Goes the Weasel • Roses are Red • Violets are Blue • Four Blind Mice • The Big Bad Wolf • London Bridges • Mary, Mary • Cross • Double Cross • Cross Country • Alex Cross's Trial (*with Richard DiLallo*) • I, Alex Cross • Cross Fire • Kill Alex Cross • Merry Christmas, Alex Cross • Alex Cross, Run • Cross My Heart • Hope to Die • Cross Justice • Cross the Line • The People vs. Alex Cross • Target: Alex Cross • Criss Cross • Deadly Cross • Fear No Evil • Triple Cross • Alex Cross Must Die

THE WOMEN'S MURDER CLUB SERIES

1st to Die (*with Andrew Gross*) • 2nd Chance (*with Andrew Gross*) • 3rd Degree (*with Andrew Gross*) • 4th of July (*with Maxine Paetro*) • The 5th Horseman (*with Maxine Paetro*) • The 6th Target (*with Maxine Paetro*) • 7th Heaven (*with Maxine Paetro*) • 8th Confession (*with Maxine Paetro*) • 9th Judgement (*with Maxine Paetro*) • 10th Anniversary (*with Maxine Paetro*) • 11th Hour (*with Maxine Paetro*) • 12th of Never (*with Maxine Paetro*) • Unlucky 13 (*with Maxine Paetro*) • 14th Deadly Sin (*with Maxine Paetro*) • 15th Affair (*with Maxine Paetro*) • 16th Seduction (*with Maxine Paetro*) • 17th Suspect (*with Maxine Paetro*) • 18th Abduction (*with Maxine Paetro*) • 19th Christmas (*with Maxine Paetro*) • 20th Victim (*with Maxine Paetro*) • 21st Birthday (*with Maxine Paetro*) • 22 Seconds (*with Maxine Paetro*) • 23rd Midnight (*with Maxine Paetro*)

DETECTIVE MICHAEL BENNETT SERIES

Step on a Crack (*with Michael Ledwidge*) • Run for Your Life (*with Michael Ledwidge*) • Worst Case (*with Michael Ledwidge*) • Tick Tock (*with Michael Ledwidge*) • I, Michael Bennett (*with Michael Ledwidge*) • Gone (*with Michael Ledwidge*) • Burn (*with Michael Ledwidge*) • Alert (*with Michael Ledwidge*) • Bullseye (*with Michael Ledwidge*) • Haunted (*with James O. Born*) • Ambush (*with James O. Born*)

Blindside (*with James O. Born*) • The Russian (*with James O. Born*) • Shattered (*with James O. Born*) • Obsessed (*with James O. Born*) • Crosshairs (*with James O. Born*)

PRIVATE NOVELS

Private (*with Maxine Paetro*) • Private London (*with Mark Pearson*) • Private Games (*with Mark Sullivan*) • Private: No. 1 Suspect (*with Maxine Paetro*) • Private Berlin (*with Mark Sullivan*) • Private Down Under (*with Michael White*) • Private L.A. (*with Mark Sullivan*) • Private India (*with Ashwin Sanghi*) • Private Vegas (*with Maxine Paetro*) • Private Sydney (*with Kathryn Fox*) • Private Paris (*with Mark Sullivan*) • The Games (*with Mark Sullivan*) • Private Delhi (*with Ashwin Sanghi*) • Private Princess (*with Rees Jones*) • Private Moscow (*with Adam Hamdy*) • Private Rogue (*with Adam Hamdy*) • Private Beijing (*with Adam Hamdy*) • Private Rome (*with Adam Hamdy*)

NYPD RED SERIES

NYPD Red (*with Marshall Karp*) • NYPD Red 2 (*with Marshall Karp*) • NYPD Red 3 (*with Marshall Karp*) • NYPD Red 4 (*with Marshall Karp*) • NYPD Red 5 (*with Marshall Karp*) • NYPD Red 6 (*with Marshall Karp*)

DETECTIVE HARRIET BLUE SERIES

Never Never (*with Candice Fox*) • Fifty Fifty (*with Candice Fox*) • Liar Liar (*with Candice Fox*) • Hush Hush (*with Candice Fox*)

INSTINCT SERIES

Instinct (*with Howard Roughan, previously published as Murder Games*) • Killer Instinct (*with Howard Roughan*) • Steal (*with Howard Roughan*)

THE BLACK BOOK SERIES

The Black Book (*with David Ellis*) • The Red Book (*with David Ellis*) • Escape (*with David Ellis*)